The Islamist of Pepynbridge
1

The Islamist of Pepynbridge
by
Peter Morrell
ISBN: 978-0-9933714-4-8

This novel is a work of fiction. Whilst some living where it is set may recognise similarities between Pepynbridge and Medborough and actual places in the East Midlands of England, names and characters of those who actively participate in the narrative, rather than being tangential to it, for example David Cameron, Maajid Nawaz and Qasim al-Raymi, are the product of the author's imagination and any resemblance to actual persons, living or dead, is unintended and entirely coincidental.

Scripture quotations are taken from the New Revised Standard Version Bible, Anglicized Edition, copyright © 1989, 1995 National Council of Churches of Christ in the United States of America. Used by permission. All rights reserved.

The right of Peter Morrell to be identified as the author of this work has been asserted in accordance with the Copyright Designs and Patents Act 1988.

A copy of this book is deposited with the British Library

Published by

i2i Publishing. Manchester.
www.i2ipublishing.co.uk

The religion of the Islamists is not primarily
an attempt to explain the world, or to shew
the place of creation in the course of nature.
It originates in a need for sacrifice and obedience.

Roger Scruton - The Soul of the World

PLAN OF PEPYNBRIDGE

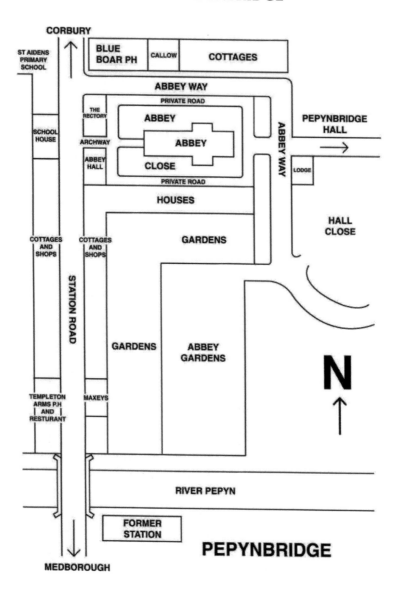

Acknowledgements

Creating *The Islamist of Pepynbridge* has required research into Islam and Islamism as well as into other topics that feature in the novel. I acknowledge the assistance I have received, both from publications in the public domain; and from individuals from whom I sought help in person.

Publications (in chronological order of publication):

S Abul A'La Maudadi, *Jihad in Islam* (Damascus: International Islamic Federation of Student Organisations, 1977)
Sayyid Qutb, *Milestones* (New Delhi: Islamic Book Service, 2001)
Patrick Sookhdeo, *Global Jihad* (McLean, VA, USA: Isaac Publishing, 2007)
Ed Husain, *The Islamist* (London: Penguin Books, 2007)
M. A. Khan, *Islamic Jihad* (New York Bloomington: iUniverse, Inc, 2009)
Scott Atran, *Talking to the Enemy* (London: Allen Lane, 2010)
Maajid Nawaz, *Radical* (London: WH Allen, 2012)

Individuals (in no particular order)

Canon Paul Rose for his overview of my Christian theology; **Stephen Hession** for his advice about sacred music; farmers **Peter Mee** and **Nick Vergette**, for their enlightenment about grain drying and storage; **Tom Wide** for advice over the cover design; **Lionel Ross** of **i2i Publishing** for his support in publishing both this and my previous novel, *The Rector of Pepynbridge*; my daughter, **Harriet** and her husband, **Charlie**, for their support and helpful suggestions; and, as ever, my wife, **Mary**, for her long-suffering patience while I secluded myself in my study for hours on end; and for her constructive comments upon the first draft of *The Islamist of Pepynbridge*

GLOSSARY OF TERMS

In most instances, the meanings of mainly, but not exclusively, Arabic words and phrases used which may be strange to the reader, are given in the text. This Glossary is intended to provide supplementary reference assistance.

Arabian, Indian and Italian

Al-Andalus (Ar)	Moorish Spain
Allah (Ar)	Islamic Word for God
"Allahu Akbar" (Ar)	"God is the greatest"
Alyasa (Ar)	Elisha
Ash-Sharq alAwsat (Ar)	The Middle East
Ayah (Ar)	Verse in the *Qur'an*
Bay'a (Ar)	Commitment
Biryani (Ind)	South Asian rice dish
Brio (It)	Vigour, vivacity
Dhul-Khfl (Ar)	Ezekiel
Garavi Gujerat (Gu)	Weekly news magazine, published in Gujerati and English
Hadith (Ar)	Collection of reports quoting Muhammad
Harām (Ar)	Forbidden
Hizb ut-Tahrir (Ar)	International Islamist political organisation
Imam (Ar)	Mosque worship leader
Injal (Ar)	Gospel
'Isā (Ar)	Jesus
Ishiya (Ar)	Isaiah
Istishhad (Ar)	Martyrdom
Jalfrezi (Ind)	South Asian curry
Jihad (Ar)	Struggle or perseverance
Jihadist (Eng)	Spiritual struggler – sometimes violent
Jinnī (Ar)	Supernatural creature in Islamic theology ("Genie")
Jizya (Ar)	Tax paid by Christians, Jews and Sabians in Muslim communities in return for protection from persecution
Ka'aba (Ar)	Cuboid structure in the Mosque in Mecca. The most sacred site in Islam
Kafir (Ar)	Non- Muslim or non-believer
Kafirun (Ar)	Plural of *Kafir*
Mu'alim fi al-Tariq (Ar)	Milestones, written by Sayyid Qutb
Maryam (Ar)	Mary

Mujadid (Ar)	Warrior engaged in *Jihad*
Murtadd (Ar)	Apostate
Musa (Ar)	Moses
Qibla (Ar)	Sign indicating direction of Mecca
Qur'ān (Ar)	The Holy Book of Islam
Ridda (Ar)	Apostasy
Sabians (Eng)	Sometimes called Nasoræans, Mandæans or Christians of St John, Sabians are a Gnostic sect founded shortly before the birth of Christ and which flourished in the Middle East until the C18.
Sahih al-Bukhari (Ar)	A major *Hadith* of Sunni Islam
Salāt (Ar)	A Muslim prayer
Salawāt (Ar)	Plural of *Salāt*
Shahada (Ar)	'There is no God but *Allah*, and Muhammad is the messenger of *Allah*'
Šahīd (Ar)	Martyr
Šuhadā (Ar)	Plural of *Šahīd*
Shari'a (Ar)	Islam law prescribed by the *Qur'ān* and *Ahadith* (Hadiths)
Sunna (Ar)	The Way. Teachings, deeds and sayings of Muhammad and reports about his companions
Sura (Ar)	Chapter of the *Qur'ān*
Taqīyya (Ar)	Dissimulation
Tagiya (Ar)	Skull Cap
Thawb (Ar)	Tunic
Topi (Ind)	South Asian word for *Tagiya*
Ummah (Ar)	World-wide Muslim community
Wudū (Ar)	Ritual ablutions before *Salāt*

English Addresses and Abbreviations

CCTV - Closed Circuit Television
CPS - Crown Prosecution Service
CTIU - Counter Terrorism Intelligence Unit
GCHQ - Government Communications Headquarters at Cheltenham
IC4 - Police term for South Asian person
Marsham Street - Home Office
MI5 - UK's domestic counter-intelligence and security agency
New Scotland Yard - Headquarters of Metropolitan Police Service
Thames House - Headquarters of MI5
UCAS - Universities and Colleges Admission Service

THE ISLAMIST OF PEPYNBRIDGE
BAY'A
(Commitment)

Friday, 16th January 2015

"We're going to live in Pepynbridge."

The speaker was Aashif Malik, Ash for short, seventeen years old, of above average height, slim build, an air of diffidence and a complexion that announced his South Asian heritage. There were four other young South Asian men gathered in the room that Friday afternoon at Medborough Academy. One of them, Zaeem Zahra, Zed for short, looked older than the others. Short and stocky, with broad, strong features, heavy brow and piercing, almost black eyes, he was eighteen. Aabdar known as Ab, Faazil known as Faz, and Naasir known as Naz, were all seventeen, slim and presented much like Ash. The room was some 5 metres square, with a window looking out onto a courtyard. There was a low table in the middle with six fabric-covered chairs around it. Rolled up prayer mats shared the top of cupboards against one wall with an electric kettle, a carton of milk and a jar of instant coffee. On the other side of the room, above a sink and draining board and secured to the wall with blue tack, was a *qibla*, an A4 print of a black cube, with a golden band around it and an arrow pointing diagonally to the top right hand corner of the sheet, indicating the direction of Mecca. The five were sitting on chairs, with mugs of coffee on the table in front of them.

"We?" enquired Zed.

"Me, my mum and dad, and my sister."

"When?"

"In March, I think. Dad's agreed to buy the house. There's the legal bits to be done. And we've got to sell ours in Medborough before we move. Anyway, Dad said he hoped it would be in early March."

"That'll fit in nicely with the mission," observed Zed. "You haven't said anything at home about a mission, have you?" Ash shook his head.

Whatever the mission was, and Zed had not told them what it was, Ash was supportive. He knew it would advance the cause of Islam in the face of what he had come to despise as the thoroughly corrupt and godless Western culture that surrounded him. Together with the others, Ash felt privileged to be part of the mission, whatever it was.

A month earlier, Ash had approached Zed, whom other Muslim pupils had described as devout, and had asked him what he could do in the fight for Islam. Zed had been cautious, responding slowly, testing Ash out with long conversations about Islam; what it meant to him. Ash had not really known. His Muslim parents were not observant and he and his sister, Jaleela, Leela for short, received no instruction at home about their faith, although he knew that Leela studied it alone in her room, aided by her iPad. Like Leela, Ash had been left to find his own way. He had read the *Qur'ān* in English translation; surfed on his laptop for Islamic, and then jihadist sites; and then he had approached Zed.

Their conversations had not just been about the *Qur'ān*, Islam's Holy Book, and the *hadith*, the teachings and deeds of Muhammad. They had discussed the history of Islam; how it had conquered much of the Western world following the death of Muhammad in 632; the flourishing of its culture and civilisation in what is now Syria and Iraq and in *al-Andalus*, Spain, until the Muslims were expelled from the Iberian peninsula in 1492; the subsequent humiliations endured by Muslims at the hands of Western Crusaders; and later under European colonists in India, in the Middle East and in Africa. Zed had shewn Ash videos of how Muslims had suffered in recent times under American, British and French oppression; and Zed had acclaimed the heroic efforts today of Islamists in Arabia, Syria, Iraq, Somalia, Libya and Nigeria to recover for *Allah* the *ummah*, the world-wide community of Muslims.

After referring to *suras*, verses in the *Qur'ān* supporting the use of force against *kafirun*, unbelievers, Zed had told Ash,

"Sayyid Qutb wrote in *Milestones* **that the** *jihad* **of Islam is to secure complete freedom for every man by releasing him from servitude to other human beings so that he may serve his God, Who is One and Who has no associates."**

Ash knew about Sayyid Qutb; how he had been a leading member of the Muslim Brotherhood in Egypt; a champion of Islamic *jihad*; inspirational in the founding of *al-Qaeda*; convicted of plotting the assassination of Abdel Gamal Nasser; hanged in a Cairo prison in 1966. The original text of *Milestones* had been smuggled out of prison in 1964 and Zed had lent Ash an English translation, published in 2001, which Ash had read.

"So how do we go about it?" Ash had asked; and Zed had introduced Ash to the Islamist theology of martyrdom.

"Martyrdom?"

"Yes! Dying in the service of *Allah* and His Prophet, peace be upon him."

"You mean suicide?"

"No, I don't! I mean martyrdom. *Istishhad*."

"Why?"

"Because suicide is *harām*; forbidden by the *Qur'ān*; *sura* four, *ayah* twenty-nine. But *istishhad* is not. Far from it! It is a duty; *sura* nine, *ayah* five. Instead of examination by interrogating angels or temporary punishment in the fires of hell, the *šahīd*, the martyr, is rewarded by *Allah* with immediate entry to Paradise with all sins forgiven." Which, Zed had supported with passages from the *Qur'ān*. "And you know, Ash, how the *Qur'ān* describes Paradise?"

"I do, Zed. Adorned in silken robes in a garden shaded by trees, laden with fruit; where boys like sprinkled pearls serve you with ginger flavoured water; and where dark-eyed virgins whom neither man nor *jinnī* will have touched before, await in tents. But Zed, I don't know about girls, you know. I'm not sure what I should do with the virgins; or how to do it."

"Ash, your shyness will disappear. *Allah* will shower you with every blessing."

There were many such conversations, which culminated in Ash declaring,

"You know what, Zed? I'm fed up! My parents are hopeless. Dull doesn't begin to describe them. They present everything in shades of grey. I don't need shades of grey. What I want and what I need is black and white; good and bad; signposts to guide me in a proper way; an unambiguous code I can rely upon. In English culture, all is relative; and the *kafirun*, or some of them anyway, are immoral. Girls wear revealing clothes. Men and women get drunk in public. Fornication. Adultery. Gays buggering each other. It's dreadful and I can't believe that they're happy. I and we and they need to have something clean and clear to rule their lives; and the *Qur'ān* does that, doesn't it?"

Zed had nodded and Ash had continued,

"Zed, I want to fight for that. I want to witness to Islam so that people will realise how much it means to me; so that other Muslims will be emboldened by my example, and the *kafirun* humiliated by it. *Allah* gave me my life, so I owe it to him. I want to be a *šahīd*; celebrated across the *ummah*. You understand, don't you, Zed?"

"Of course I do! But, Ash, not all Muslims support *istishhad*. Partial Muslims, like your parents, Ash. They're *kafirun*, impure. They don't support *istishhad*."

"They don't, Zed! I blame them for not raising me as a good Muslim." And Ash had pleaded, "There must be something I can do, Zed?"

Which was what Zed had been waiting for.

"What part of the world do you come from, Ash?"

"From Pakistan. The Punjab. I was born in Lahore."

"So, you're Sunni, then?"

"I am."

"Then you're welcome to join us. We're all Sunni."

Thus it was that in December 2014, just before the Academy had broken up for the Christmas holidays, Ash had been recruited by Zed into *IstishhadUK*.

The members of Zed's *IstishhadUK* cell were pupils at Medborough Academy, a self-governing, publicly-funded secondary school, with an ethnically broad mix of students of both genders. During term-time, Muslim pupils who wished to do so met at Friday lunchtime for prayers in a room provided by the Academy for that purpose. Only a few did. On Fridays, Muslim pupils were allowed to go home in late morning so that the boys could accompany their fathers and brothers to the mosque in Medborough. On 6th January 2015, at the beginning of the spring term, Zed had arranged with Francis Metcalf, the head teacher, that every Friday from the 9th January, he could use the room for prayers and meetings by older Muslim students, but after school when the other pupils had gone home.

On Wednesday, 7th January 2015, two Islamist brothers, Saïd and Chérif Kaouchi, members of *al-Qaeda* in the Arabian Peninsular, AQAP, had shot and killed eleven journalists in the Paris office of the satirical magazine, *Charlie Hebdo*, because some years previously it had published a cartoon of the Prophet. Not only was the depiction of Muhammad *harām*; but the cartoon had ridiculed Muhammad, who was shewn wearing a turban with a bomb in it, which was worse than *harām*. The cartoon had insulted Islam. The Kaouchis had shot dead a policeman in the street as they had escaped, shouting that they had avenged the printing of cartoons of the Prophet, peace be upon him. The following day, Thursday 8th January, another AQAP Islamist, Amedy Coulibaly, had shot dead an unarmed policewoman in Montrouge, a suburb to the south of Paris. Then, at lunchtime on Friday 9th January, Coulibaly had taken a number of shoppers hostage in a Jewish supermarket in Paris. Later that afternoon, the Kaouchi brothers had been killed in a hail of security forces' bullets as they had emerged firing assault rifles from a print works 20 miles north east of Paris where they had taken refuge.

All this the cell knew when it had gathered in the prayer room that same Friday. After performing *wudū* and observing *salāt*, ritual ablution and prayer in accordance with Islamic guidelines, the cell members had rejoiced over the spectacular blow that AQAP had struck for Islam, in the knowledge that the martyrs, Saïd and Chérif Kaouchi, were now arrayed in robes of silk and reclining upon soft couches in Paradise. The news that, after killing four hostages, Amedy Coulibaly had been shot dead by French Special Forces when they stormed the kosher supermarket in Paris had come too late for their meeting.

On 9th January, Zed had spoken about why they were meeting. He had explained that their cell was affiliated to three other jihadist cells. In the United Kingdom, cells were encouraged to form, he told them, but did not have leaders. They had co-ordinators, which is what he, Zed, was. He kept in touch with the co-ordinators of the three other cells and they had agreed on a mission, the nature of which would be disclosed to them later. Zed had emphasised the need for security.

"GCHQ has massive computers that record and decipher emails and mobile phone calls. At no time must any of us contact each other by phone; or send each other emails."

"Not even about something different?" one of the others had asked.

"No! We must leave no electronic trace that would tell the authorities that we are associated."

"But the Academy knows we are!"

"Huh!" observed Zed contemptuously. "I don't suppose they've noticed who meets here on Friday afternoons. And even if they have, they won't care. They're clueless when it comes to things like this; like what we're up to."

"So, how do you keep in touch with the other three co-ordinators?" asked another.

"We meet at important football and cricket matches. We don't sit near each other during the match, but at half-time if it's football, or during the lunch interval if it's cricket, we meet in a café or bar. Before we separate, we agree the place and time of our next meeting. Secure and undetectable so long as the security services don't know that we meet. And if we carry on as we are, they won't."

Zed had explained that the Medborough cell would meet in the prayer room at five o'clock every Friday afternoon during term time. During the holidays, Zed would keep in touch with them by dead drops; hiding places near their homes where he would leave a note, which they should check regularly and, if necessary, use to reply. During the summer holidays, they would undergo training arranged by the four co-ordinators and be told about the mission. All Zed would say was that it would happen towards the end of the year and that it would involve *istishhad*. The targets would be soft and unguarded. It would be much bigger than Paris and, like Paris, would create fear and consternation, not just in Britain, but around the Western world. And it would attract praise and admiration in the *ummah*, the world-wide community of the Islamic faithful. It would be hailed as a blow to free mankind from the oppression of Western democracy; from government according to laws made by human beings that flouted and usurped the authority of *Allah*, the only source of law, *Shar'ia*; a blow bought with their lives and rewarded in Paradise. *Allahu Akbar!* God is the greatest! All of which Ash, flushed with enthusiasm and his critical faculties firmly suppressed, embraced unreservedly.

Zed had insisted that they should regard themselves "...as acting under cover; just as though you've been dropped behind enemy lines; which, in a sense, you have been. You should treat everybody else as potentially hostile. You must arouse no suspicion that you are not part of contemporary Western culture. So, no growing of a beard; no wearing of traditional Muslim dress, no *thawb* or tunic, no *tagiya* or *topi* skull cap. Get yourself a *kafir* girl friend, if you can. Go to pubs and drink alcohol. Eat pork if offered it. Go for cool music. Okay?" The others had nodded.

Ash had said,

"So, I can continue playing cricket, then?" The previous summer aged 16 Ash, a promising all-rounder, had played for the Academy Colts.

"Of course you can," Zed had re-assured him. "In fact, you should. Really good cover!"

What Zed did not tell them was that the four cells in England were operating under instructions from Nasir al-Wuhayshi, the leader of AQAP based in Yemen. That could wait until he knew them better and was sure of their loyalty.

Ash's parents had shewn no interest in their son's enthusiasm for Islam, which had not surprised him. And so it was that, whilst presenting outwardly as just another ordinary seventeen year old English youth of South Asian origin, Ash had inwardly embraced violent Islamism.

Because, at their second meeting on the 16th January, Ash did not know what the mission was going to be, he did not understand why Zed said that his move to Pepynbridge was going to fit in with it.

The five of them finished their coffee, washed up the cups in the sink and left. It was five to six, five minutes before the gates of the Academy would be locked for the night whenever, as was the case today, there were no evening activities or meetings.

From his first floor study, Francis Metcalf, head teacher at Medborough Academy, middle-aged, lean, balding and wearing a sour air of authority, watched the five pass through the Academy's gates. He picked up a telephone from his desk and tapped in a number.

"Yes?"

"Sergeant Hay?"

"Yes?"

"Francis Metcalf here."

"Who?"

"Francis Metcalf, head teacher at Medborough Academy."

"Oh, Yes! Hello! What can I do for you?"

Sergeant Andrew Hay, in his thirties, shaven headed, square jawed and tight lipped, with small blue eyes set in chubby features, was attached to the Eastern Counter Terrorism Intelligence Unit incorporating Special Branches from several East of England county forces. Seconded to Medborough Police, Hay had paid Francis Metcalf a visit several months earlier. The Academy reflected the multicultural demography of the city, with many Muslim pupils on its roll. Sergeant Hay had explained that he had been asked to keep an eye out for any signs of Islamism, Islamic extremism, in Medborough. If the head teacher noticed anything at all out of the ordinary that involved young Muslims, he would be grateful if he could let him know. Francis Metcalf had assured him he would. Now Francis Metcalf told Andrew Hay about Zed's request to use the room set aside for Muslim prayers at a different time from its customary use; and that on the past two Fridays, Zed and four other senior pupils had been using it between five and six o'clock.

"Senior?"

"Yes! They're all aged seventeen except for the one who asked me if he could use the room. He's eighteen and in his last year here."

"Can you let me have their names, dates of birth and home addresses, please Mr Metcalf? Email them to me?"

"Yes, of course! I'll do so now. Your email address?" Hay supplied it.

"Thank you. If I discover anything that you should be aware of, I'll let you know."

"Thanks. 'Bye!"

Ash walked the half a mile or so to his parent's home in Elmgrove Gardens and let himself in. His mother, Saabiriah, known as Sabi, was in the kitchen, preparing the evening meal. In her late thirties, she was a slim, pretty, South Asian woman, short of stature, softly spoken with a gentle, but capable air about her.

"Hi, Mum!"

"Hello, Ash! All well?"

"Yup!"

"So what did you do at Friday prayers today?"

"What we always do, Mum. We pray. We read bits of the *Qur'ān*. Zed teaches us about Islam. Then we drink coffee and chat."

"And so what did Zed teach you today?"

Although Ash resented his mother's curiosity, Zed had told him not to arouse suspicion by refusing to engage. Better to indulge in *taqīyya*, endorsed by the *Qur'ān, sura* 16, *ayah* 106, and sanctioned by a *hadith* in *Sahih al-Bukhari*. *Taqīyya* meant dissimulation; lying to conceal one's true beliefs and motives from opponents. For this purpose his mother, like his father, was an opponent, a *kafir*.

"He was inviting us to look at *sura* five in the *Qur'ān*; and about how we should abstain from alcohol and gambling."

"Quite right, too! I'm pleased you're receiving wise counsel."

"Yes, Mum! Where's Leela?"

"Upstairs in her room, doing her homework. You must have some as well."

"I have. What time's supper?"

"When Dad gets home. He's got a private clinic this evening, so about half past eight."

"Okay. I'll go up to my room and work."

Ash climbed the stairs, sat down at the desk in his bedroom and took some work out of his brief-case. It did not take him long to complete. He was studying for A-Levels in English, Mathematics, Information Technology and Economics. Bright, his homework presented him with no challenge. When he had finished, he heard Leela and his mother chatting downstairs, but decided to stay in his room until his father returned. He began to surf the internet on his laptop, looking for, and when found, absorbing the content of Islamist websites.

Ash had been seven when, in 2004, the Maliks had left Lahore for Britain. His father, Abidulah, Abi for short, had qualified in medicine at the Lahore Medical and Dental College where he had met and married Sabi, a nurse. She had abandoned her profession after giving birth to Ash in 1997. Abi had specialised in psychiatry and, as soon as he had qualified, he had applied for and been granted an unlimited visa to live and work in the United Kingdom. On arrival, he had successfully negotiated the General Medical Council's route to registration in his specialty and in 2010 had secured a consultancy at Medborough General Hospital. The family had moved from London to a modern, detached, four bedroom house in Elmgrove Gardens, Medborough. In 2013, Dr Malik had accepted an invitation to join a group of consultants who, as well as working in Medborough General Hospital, practised two evenings a week out of a private clinic in the city. His income had jumped and he and Sabi had decided to move out of Medborough. They had contracted to buy a house in Abbey Gardens, Pepynbridge, an estate built in the noughties on land previously owned by Alfred Wicken, whose family had lived and farmed in the village for generations. Alfred had been, and still was a mainly arable farmer; but unwisely had diversified into dairy at considerable cost just before the price of milk had plummeted. He had abandoned the project at great loss, which he had recovered by selling ten acres of his land for housing in Pepynbridge.

The result was Hall Close and Abbey Gardens; each comprising what some in the village derogatively termed executive housing; five bedroom houses with small gardens.

Pepynbridge was a settlement of some two thousand souls. It was divided into what, on the one hand, was referred to as 'Old' Pepynbridge; mainly old properties along Station Road and Abbey Way; and, upon the other, Hall Close and Abbey Gardens, stigmatised by long-term residents as 'New' Pepynbridge. Some families in 'Old' Pepynbridge had lived in the village for generations. There had been some recent infilling along Station Road with modern cottages in what had once been gardens. Those newer properties, like those in Hall Close and Abbey Gardens, were largely occupied by professional people, some retired and the remainder who either worked from home, or commuted the fifteen miles into Medborough; or to London, eighty miles south by train. The inevitable tensions and divisions that had arisen upon the influx of newcomers had diminished with time, particularly since the arrival in May 2014 of the rector, the Reverend Herbert Onion, whom everyone called Herbie. Herbert had united nearly everyone in the village around a musical programme designed to help raise the million pounds needed to repair the roof of St Aidan's Abbey, the parish church which dominated Pepynbridge.

In December 2014, Herbert had successfully weathered a trial at Medborough Crown Court on false allegations of sexual abuse by Alfred Wicken's 15 year-old daughter, Sophie. His acquittal had been followed by a flood of sympathy and support for him. In February 2015, he had married Julie Swift, the 35 year-old and previously unmarried head teacher of St Aidan's Church of England Primary School, who by then was expecting their first child.

Abi Malik had researched and discovered that, as well as its agreeable location and surroundings, there was a thriving cricket club in the village that played in Hall Park, behind Pepynbridge Hall. Ash's developing talent as an all-rounder had persuaded Abi that Pepynbridge would be the ideal place, not only for him and Sabi to live until he retired; but also to complete the raising of Ash and Leela.

Through Colin Forbes, another consultant psychiatrist in Medborough, Abi had come to know Richard Maxey, a retired general practitioner who lived in Pepynbridge, was one of two church wardens, and with whom Abi had discussed his proposed move. Richard Maxey had introduced Abi to Jack Driver, a partner in Driver and Sickle, a law firm in Medborough, and the organist at St Aidan's Abbey. Jack Driver had been pleased for his firm to act for Abi on the purchase of the house in Abbey Gardens; and on the sale of the house in Medborough. Contracts for the purchase of the house in Pepynbridge had been signed the day before, Thursday, 15th January, with completion within a few weeks. Abi and Sabi had put the house in Elmgrove Gardens on the market and hoped it would sell in time for them to move to Pepynbridge before the end of March.

Ash heard the front door opening. His father was home. Reluctantly he logged off and went downstairs. He reminded himself, as he always did, that he must give no ground for his parents or Leela to suspect the Islamist path he had chosen to follow. His parents were, he acknowledged, kind, gentle, but boring, with no strong views on religion or politics. Abi was absorbed by his clinical work; and Sabi by her devotion to her home, husband and children. So far as Ash was concerned, conversation at mealtimes was anodyne; about prices: of houses; of white goods; of rice, lentils, bread and the like, none of which were of the slightest interest to him. Any attempt by Ash to move onto more controversial topics was always sidetracked. He had once asked what his parent's views were on Christianity and the Church.

"Christians are good people," Abi had replied. "Lovely buildings; beautiful music; much more interesting than Islam."

"So, what would you say then if I started going to their churches?"

"Wouldn't mind at all, Ash. You might learn something worthwhile if you did. And you'd certainly make some useful contacts for later on in life."

"But the Holy Book is very critical of Christians," he had said, "and of Jews."

"Oh, I know, but you don't want to take everything that's written in the *Qur'ān* at face value. It was written in Arabia a long time ago, and in very different circumstances from today. It has little relevance to life in the West in the twenty-first century."

"But isn't it the word of God?"

"So they say."

"Who are they?"

"Amongst others, the Islamists. Dangerous people, who want to take us back to the pre-medieval world of Muhammad."

"Peace be upon him, Dad?"

"Peace be upon him, if you must, Ash. But my warning to you is: don't take the *Qur'ān* too seriously. Eh, Sabi?"

"I agree. Dangerous!" Ash's mother had said, drawing a line under the topic as they had done before; and as they would do again, reflected Ash. Which, he mused this evening at the table, was probably what had driven him to approach Zed. Now he must keep the contempt he felt for his parents firmly under wraps.

Ash took his place at the table, upon which Sabi had placed plates of chicken *jalfrezi* and rice. Abi Malik sat at the head. In his late forties, tall, generous of girth with a round bald head, chubby cheeks with laughter creases stretching out from his eyes, he enjoyed his work, his family and, as was obvious from the way he attacked the plate before him, his food.

"We've had an offer on this house," he said.

"Acceptable?" said Sabi.

"Four hundred and fifty thousand. We're asking four hundred and seventy-five. I think the offer is enough."

"How much are we paying for the house in Pepynbridge?"

"For Abbey Gardens? Six hundred and fifty thousand."

"Can we afford it?"

"With the money I'm earning from private practice plus my salary from the NHS the answer is; we can. The bank has offered us a mortgage of four hundred thousand. But it would lend us four hundred and seventy-five thousand if we needed it. So, I'm confident we can afford it."

"Good news, then?"

"Indeed. Pepynbridge is a pretty village with a beautiful Abbey church, famous for the quality of its music. And Ash, there's a cricket club." Ash looked up and raised his eyebrows. "They play in the Cambridgeshire League on Saturdays; and in the Rutland League on Sundays."

"Really?" remarked Ash.

Both leagues were well regarded. He should be able to play for the Seconds; perhaps even for the Firsts. Something to look forward to before...his train of thought tailed off.

Across the table, Leela, pretty, short and slim, with long, glossy, black hair and wide-set, large brown eyes set in a triangular face ending in a pointed chin, had remained silent during the conversation. But she had been observing Ash shrewdly. There was something hidden about him, she sensed, but she wasn't sure what it was. She was two years younger and there was no point in asking him. Their relationship was not like that.

◆◆◆◆◆◆◆◆◆◆◆◆◆◆◆◆◆◆◆◆

Tuesday, 20th January 2015

The telephone on Francis Metcalf's desk rang.

"Yes?"

"Sergeant Hay here. We've run checks on the five whose names you gave us. They're all clean."

"Clean?"

"None of them have a police record and there's no intelligence to suggest that they're up to mischief."

"Good!"

"Yes, well, please keep an eye on them, would you for us, and let me know if you see or hear anything suspicious? Okay?"

"Yes, of course, Sergeant!"

Francis Metcalf replaced the receiver. It was an odd country, he thought, where a head teacher was asked to act as the eyes and ears of the security services. But, remembering what had happened in Paris two weeks ago, he accepted that he may indeed have a role to play, albeit unofficially. Later that day after the Academy had closed, he went to the room that Zed and the others were using and looked around it. To his relief he discovered nothing untoward.

◆◆◆◆◆◆◆◆◆◆◆◆◆◆◆◆◆◆◆◆◆◆

Friday, 20th to Monday, 30th March 2015

"We break up next Friday lunch-time," the speaker was Zed, "so no more prayer meetings this term." The five members of the cell were in the prayer room at the Academy. *Salāt* had been observed and now they were sitting, drinking mugs of coffee. "And we return on Tuesday, 14th April. So the holidays will be an opportunity to test our dead drops, yeah?" The other four nodded. "So, by next Friday, each of you will tell me where your drop will be. And by the following Monday, I want each of you to leave a blank sheet of paper in it. Then I want you to check it every now and then to collect anything I may have put there, okay?" They nodded again. A few minutes later, the meeting ended.

Ash took the bus to Pepynbridge. The previous Monday, the Maliks had moved into Abbey Gardens. That weekend, Ash explored the village and, after checking first that there was nobody in Abbey Close, and, once inside, that it was empty, the Abbey. At the Academy on Monday morning he sought out Zed, who motioned to him to go outside. On the playing field, away from inquisitive ears, Ash said,

"Zed, in Pepynbridge Abbey, behind the altar I think it's called, there's a semi-circular building."

"Separate from the Abbey?"

"No, part of it. You get into it through a doorway. In fact, there are two doorways, one either side of the altar." Zed said nothing, but looked at Ash intently. Ash continued, "There are three chapels, they call them, in the semi-circular bit. The middle one is for Mary; you know, the *Maryam* mentioned in the *Qur'ān*?" Zed nodded. "There's a statue in there of her holding a baby; probably *'Īsā*. The statue is quite big and there's a space behind it. It's dusty, so no one cleans it. I'll leave my note there, if that's okay?"

"Sounds good, Ash. I'll have a look at it during the holidays. Don't write anything in your note in case someone discovers it, okay? Just leave a sheet of paper in it. If it's suitable, I'll put a note there saying so, okay?" Ash nodded. "And we'll meet up again the first Friday of next term, okay?" Zed turned and went back into the building without waiting for a reply.

On the last day of term, Friday, 27th March, Francis Metcalf watched his three hundred or so pupils streaming out of the Academy gates at half past twelve and reached for his telephone.

"Sergeant Hay?"

"Yes?"

"Francis Metcalf here from Medborough Academy."

"Yes, Mr Metcalf?"

"I just thought I'd let you know that I've nothing to report about the five Muslim pupils I told you about in January. They're still using the prayer room every Friday afternoon, but I've no idea what they do or say in there." There was a silence at the other end. "Sergeant Hay?"

"Yes, Mr Metcalf, I'm still here." A pause followed; and then, "Mr Metcalf, will you be there this afternoon?"

"I shall be here until about six o'clock."

"If you don't mind, I'll call you back."

"That's fine," and the telephone went dead. An hour later, it rang.

"Yes?"

"Sergeant Hay here, Mr Metcalf. Sorry about that."

"About what?"

"Messing you about?"

"Not at all."

"Just so you know what's going through my mind. I've been in touch with our RIPA Authorising Officer to see whether we might have grounds for putting a listening device in the room. You know, under The Regulation of Investigatory Powers Act? RIPA for short?"

"I wouldn't be very happy about that, Sergeant."

"Of course you wouldn't, Mr Metcalf. And you'd be right. There are no grounds for it at the moment. But..." Hay paused as he looked at the computer screen on his desk "...I'm looking at Section Twenty Eight. If we..." another pause "...or you, suspect anything amiss, we could do that. The same applies to their emails and telephone calls. No grounds at the moment. We'd never get a warrant. But if there were grounds for suspecting anything…" he looked at the screen again "…involving crime or public safety?" His tone was interrogative.

"Of course, Sergeant. I quite understand. If I suspect anything like that, I'll let you know immediately."

"Thank you, Sir." The line went dead.

Francis Metcalf turned to his computer and typed "The Regulation of Investigatory Powers Act" into his search engine, clicked on the legislation.gov.uk website and brought up Section 28, which he printed off. After reading it, he wondered if he should talk to Driver & Sickle, the Academy's solicitors in Medborough. Too soon, he decided; and I hope it doesn't come to that. At six o'clock, he locked the door to his study and drove out through the gates of the Academy, waving as he did so to the caretaker, who was waiting to secure them. Francis Metcalf was looking forward to his Easter break.

The following Monday, 30th March, Ash hid a folded blank sheet of paper behind the statue of the Virgin and Child in the Lady Chapel in St Aidan's Abbey.

◆◆◆◆◆◆◆◆◆◆◆◆◆◆◆◆◆◆◆◆◆

Saturday, 4th April 2015

Shortly after one o'clock on the afternoon of Saturday, 4th April, a dirty, 2006 registered Ford Escort was driven westwards out of Medborough. Zed was alone at the wheel. After Thurnby, the main road dipped down, crossed a junction controlled by lights, passed a sign announcing

'The Nuclear Free City of Leicester' and climbed a slight hill. At the top, Zed turned left into Spencefield Lane and then right into Whitehall Road. He continued down Ethel Road and Chesterfield Road and into St Peter's Road at the heart of the South Asian community. A short way down, Zed turned into a narrow side street, lined with Victorian terrace houses. He parked, locked the car and walked back to St Peter's Road, where he turned left. After a short while, the road became Sparkenhoe Street. Zed turned left into Conduit Street which led to London Road, the A6, and the railway station. By now it was half past two. King Power Stadium, the home of Leicester City Football Club, lay up the London Road to the south, a twenty minute walk away. After a week when March had departed like a lion, high pressure was building and the day was dry and still, but overcast and cool.

Leicester City was playing West Ham. When he arrived at the stadium, Zed bought a ticket for £44 and took his seat in the West Stand, section B3. At half time, he left his seat and the stadium and went to The Foxes' Den, a nearby fast food outlet. It was where he and the other three co-ordinators had been meeting every four weeks since the previous December. There were usually other South Asians in there and the Islamists' presence aroused no interest. Discreet enquiries of the staff had disclosed that the CCTV was regularly wiped. It was safe. Just inside the door, two other men of South Asian appearance were waiting. Zed greeted them and they exchanged small talk about the match. After a few minutes, a fourth man of similar appearance joined them. They ordered soft drinks and Veggie Burgers, which were not *harām*, and sat at a table.

The noise level was high, but they spoke softly to minimise the risk of being overheard.

The other three looked older than Zed, which they were, but not much. Raed had travelled from London; Waahid from York; and Yaaseen from Lincoln. There was nothing distinctive about their appearance; nothing to attract the attention of the curious. Clean-shaven, they wore jeans, blouson jackets and trainers. After exchanging courtesies, Zed said,

"Heard from the Chief?" Zed was referring to Nasir al-Wuhayshi, the leader of AQAP.

"Yes!" replied Raed. "He wants to know how our recruitment is going."

"I've got four, apart from myself."

"That's enough," said Waahid. "Any more and it's too risky. Four's enough, eh?" Raed and Yaaseen grunted their assent. Waahid continued, "I have four as well."

"I should have well before July," said Raed.

"Me too," added Yaaseen.

"Are the main targets the same?" asked Zed.

"Yes!" responded Raed. Only he was in contact with AQAP in Yemen and, with the acquiescence of the others, had assumed the role of leader. "Have you all identified subsidiary targets?" They all said they had; one for each member of their respective cells. In the end, if all went to plan, there would be twenty šuhadā.

"Apart from ourselves," asked Waahid, "how many casualties?"

"Anywhere between two and four hundred. Not all killed, but a lot of them will be; and scores more seriously hurt; lost limbs, blinded, that sort of thing."

"Great!" said Zed. "And about the get-together in July?"

Raed had identified a stretch of woodland "...which happens to be very close to Pepynbridge. It's called Middlehay Wood. I spent quite a bit of time researching where we should meet. Middlehay Wood is reasonably central for us. It's big; about four hundred hectares. When I was there last week, I met a Forestry Commission bloke who told me there'll be no one in there in the summer. In autumn, winter, and spring, people cull deer in there and, sometimes in winter, they shoot birds. But in summer, no one goes there. It used to be a bomb dump in World War Two and there are some empty sheds. We'll use one of those."

"Any public rights of way?" asked Zed.

"Two, but the sheds are well away from them. And we'll not be making any noise. Just recording šahīd videos; looking at šahīd vests and teaching everyone how to arm and detonate them. Yaaseen, you said you know someone who may be able to help with them?"

"Yes, Raed. A friend of mine in Lincoln has a shop selling field sports stuff. I'm interested in firearms and so is he. He can supply almost anything in that line, legit or not. I went to see him and he sells these."

He passed over copies of a print off the website of Katch & Kill of Lincoln featuring what was called a 'Fly Vest'; a gilet or waistcoat, designed to be used by a fisherman with, it was proclaimed, '16 pockets all well positioned and equipped with heavy-duty zips or Velcro'. The price was £29.99.

"Ideal for a šahīd vest," observed Raed. "Right, I want each of you and each member of your cell to order one of these, okay? Separately and on-line. They must bring them on 20th July. I'll have dummy explosives and a detonator and I'll demonstrate how to pack the vest with explosives and detonate them. And each of us will record a video explaining that we are members of *IstishhadUK* and why we have martyred ourselves for the sake of the Prophet, peace be upon him. Behind the person speaking to the camera there'll be a Black Standard, a black flag with the *Shahada* in white on it. Now…" and Raed handed out another sheet of paper to each of the others, "…that's what I want all of you to say when you're being videoed, okay? Make copies and give them to your members, okay?" The others nodded. "If anyone wants to personalise it, so much the better, so long as the meaning isn't altered or diluted. And when we meet, before we start doing any of that, each of us will have a chat with members who are not from our own cell, to make sure they know what they've let themselves in for; and warning them of the consequences of betrayal."

"Death?" enquired Waahid.

"Death," replied Raed. "Gagged and bound; put in my black cab; taken by us at night to a bridge over a big river a long way from here; stripped, throat cut over the parapet and thrown into the river. By the time the body is recovered, it's travelled a fair way downstream with the current and the police have no idea how or where it got there. And then I burn his clothes and have the cab valetted by a close and trusted friend of mine to remove any trace of the *murtadd*; the apostate."

"Cool!" said Zed. The others nodded.

"But your boys need to be told that anyway, if you haven't done so already." It was Raed again. The others confirmed that they had.

"After that, I'll say a bit to fire them up and then tell them about the mission."

"How long will we be there?" asked Zed.

"Just the day, but we'll meet early. I'll confirm the times later. And we'll use as few vehicles as possible, so as not to draw attention to ourselves. But you've all got the date? Monday, the twentieth of July?" They nodded. Raed gave them directions to the wood. "When you arrive at the entrance to it, drive in and almost immediately turn right and drive down the track until you see me, okay?" More nods.

"One more thing. Have any of you noticed being followed? You've all been trained to spot security people, haven't you?"

They confirmed that they had; and that, so far as they could tell, they were not under surveillance.

"Okay then. Next meeting here on the second of May. Leicester at home to Newcastle. Kick-off at three. Okay?" More nods. "Let's go!" he said, adding softly, "*Allahu Akbar!*" Softly, the others replied, "*Allahu Akbar!*" and they left, not acknowledging each other outside The Foxes' Den, but separately walking away to where they had parked their vehicles. They neither knew, nor had the means to discover, how long CCTV recordings at Leicester Railway Station were preserved, so none of them had travelled by train.

◆◆◆◆◆◆◆◆◆◆◆◆◆◆◆◆◆◆◆◆◆◆◆

Easter Sunday, 5th April 2015

St Aidan's Abbey stood in Abbey Close in the middle of Pepynbridge. Once the church of a Benedictine monastery, upon its dissolution, Thomas Cromwell had decreed that the Abbey should be retained intact as the parish church. Abbey Close was bounded on its west by a long, two-storey Tudor building, pierced by an arch leading to Station Road, the principal thoroughfare in Pepynbridge; on its north and east by Abbey Way; and on its south, by a line of Tudor cottages. The Abbey, with two side aisles, flying buttresses and a massive tower over the crossing, defined the village. Inside, the nave and the chancel with their stone-vaulted ceilings were architecturally of a piece. Large traceried windows in the nave and chancel clerestories and in both side aisles let generous light into the Abbey even on a dull day. From the crossing, transepts stretched north and south, each ending in a large Perpendicular window. In the north transept, the Host was reserved in a chapel dedicated to Saint Sebastian. In the south transept, St Aidan's Chapel was used as the choir vestry. To the east of the crossing, the chancel was flanked by intricately carved nineteenth century choir stalls and, above on one side, a pipe organ and console. On the east end wall behind the high altar was an unpainted carved wooden reredos depicting Jesus and the twelve apostles. Above it was a large Perpendicular window. Behind the reredos and reached through two archways on either side of the high altar, a semi-circular ambulatory contained three more chapels beneath an exquisite fan-vaulted ceiling. The chapel in the centre was dedicated to the Blessed Virgin Mary; another was used as the clergy vestry and the third was a museum where the

Abbey's treasures of plate and books, both medieval originals and beautiful facsimiles created by Manuel Moleiro of Barcelona, were displayed in cabinets beneath toughened glass. Pride of place belonged to a folio facsimile codex of the Great Canterbury Psalter, otherwise called the Anglo-Catalan Psalter, resting by itself in a locked showcase. Each week, a fresh page was turned to display dazzling medieval images, adorned with real gold leaf. The original text in multiple columns and part of the illumination had been created at Canterbury between 1170 and 1190. Then for a reason lost in the mists of time the codex had been taken to Barcelona where in about 1340 its illumination had been completed. It had then passed successively through the hands of Margaret of Austria and Mary of Hungary. By 1565, it was housed in the Duke of Burgundy's library in Brussels. In 1796, Napoleon Bonaparte had it removed to Paris where it remains in the Bibliothèque National de France. When the facsimile was published, Manuel Moleiro gifted one copy to Canterbury Cathedral; and another to Toledo Cathedral. The copy at St Aidan's was on permanent loan from a parishioner.

The 5th April was Easter Sunday and by 11.30am Anglican High Mass was well under way, with the Abbey replete with worshippers. Outside the south porch a brazier, empty save for ashes at its bottom, bore witness to the Vigil Service that had taken place the previous evening. Now, as the choir and congregation were singing the offertory hymn, *"Jesus lives, thy terrors now can no more, O death, appal us..."*, at the high altar, the Reverend Herbert Onion, robed in a white chasuble and assisted by two acolytes in hooded white cassock albs, was preparing vessels for Holy Communion.

Herbert Onion was of medium height and slight of stature. His face was slender and pale, with dark brown eyes magnified by large, black-rimmed spectacles, and crowned by a shock of black curls. Beneath a narrow nose, unexpectedly sensuous lips were preparing to pronounce the Liturgy of the Sacrament. A thurifer robed in a white cassock alb was gently swinging a thurible from which small puffs of incense escaped at the peak of each trajectory. After another acolyte had received the collection and proffered it towards Herbert for him to bless and the offertory hymn had ended, the thurifer offered the thurible to Herbert, who took it and censed the altar. He then censed the thurifer and handed the thurible back to him. The thurifer censed Herbert, the other acolytes and then, from the chancel steps, the congregation.

In the front row on the south side of the nave sat Alistair and Augusta Pemberton-Smith, proprietors of Pepynbridge Hall, its adjacent Hall Park and several thousand surrounding acres. They were Roman Catholics, but as Herbert had developed Anglo Catholic liturgy in the Abbey, they had chosen to worship there rather than attend the prosaic Roman masses on offer in Medborough. In the same row sat their four children, ranging in ages from 23 to 13, and Augusta's older half-sister, Alice Burton. Aged 71, Alice, an Anglican and the other churchwarden, had been married to a diplomat. She had spent most of her married life abroad and had been widowed eleven years earlier. Childless, she had surrendered her rights in Pepynbridge Hall in favour of Augusta and lived in the nearby hamlet of

Summerhay in a converted watermill that she and her husband had bought as their English home.

Herbert chanted the opening dialogue of Eucharistic Prayer B, to which the choir and some in the congregation responded. He continued by chanting the Long Preface for Easter Day, at the end of which the choir sang the *Sanctus* from Mozart's Mass in C Major, the *Coronation*. After the Eucharistic Prayer and the Fraction, the choir sang the *Agnus Dei* from the same Mass.

Herbert was a gifted musician who, before he had arrived in Pepynbridge in May the previous year, had been the Director of Music at Clarence College, a private boarding secondary school in Medborough. The previous autumn, he had rehearsed the Abbey choir and, with an outstanding boy treble, Roger Slim, a CD had been recorded to raise funds for the repair of the Abbey roof. Now, as a result of the exposure of the recording on YouTube and Facebook and sales through Amazon and other retailers, not only in the United Kingdom, but also abroad, as well as takings from ticketed concerts in the Abbey, the target was coming within reach. Roger Slim's voice had broken in January, rather sooner than Herbert had hoped, but Herbert was training others to fill the top register vacancy, amongst whom was Sophie Wicken. Today, as nearly everyone who worshipped in the Abbey had grown to expect and to cherish, the choir, meticulously drilled by him, was performing the *Coronation* to perfection.

There remained an entrenched group of traditionalists in Pepynbridge who had not reconciled themselves to Herbert's ministry and liturgy. When Herbert had arrived, strong opposition to his commitment to Anglo Catholic worship had been voiced by a small and vocal number of residents, some of whom still served on the Parochial Church Council. Their families had lived in Pepynbridge for generations and they treasured the Low Church tradition that had prevailed in the village since the Commonwealth. They had earned the sobriquet; 'Puritan Tendency', but, over time, their opposition to Herbert Onion had become muted and now they had become the 'Puritan Remnant'. Earlier that morning, as he had done every Sunday since his induction, Herbert had celebrated Holy Communion in the Abbey for them according to the Book of Common Prayer.

The High Mass ended with a full-throated rendering by everyone of the Easter hymn *'Alleluia, Alleluia, hearts to heaven and voices raise...'*

After the Blessing and recession of clergy and choir, the congregants gathered at the west end of the Abbey, gossiping, drinking coffee and eating slices of simnal cake, baked by Julie Onion. Alastair Pemberton-Smith, Richard Maxey and Herbert Onion were chatting.

"Rector," started Alistair, "that was a wonderful service. Thank you. The music was outstanding. And I liked your sermon."

Herbert had preached on the Resurrection, reviewing the evidence that the tomb had been empty and that there had been no corpse; for if there had been, it would surely have been produced by the Temple or Roman authorities to stop the Jesus sect in its tracks. Hence, Herbert had argued, Christians could be sure of the divinity of Jesus; that he was indeed the Messiah.

"Thank you, Alistair. The choir was excellent. As soon as I can find another treble, I should like to record another CD."

"I agree," said Richard Maxey.

"How much more do we have to raise, Rector?"

"Just under three hundred thousand."

"We're getting there," observed Richard Maxey cheerfully.

"I hear that an Asian doctor has moved into the village."

Alistair was in his fifties, tall and well-built, bearing himself like the soldier he once had been. After eight years in the Blues and Royals, he had joined a bank in the City to which he continued to commute three days a week.

"I think you mean Dr Abi Malik," said Richard Maxey. "I've met him."

"So have I," remarked Herbert. "I called on the Maliks the other day. Dr Malik is a consultant psychiatrist at Medborough General Hospital. His wife, Sabi, was a nurse, but now she cares for her family."

A girl in a choir robe, slim, of medium height, with long fair hair framing a round face with blue eyes, a pert nose, generous lips and wearing a determined expression, joined them.

"I know who you're talking about," she announced. The others looked at her, surprised at her interruption.

"Do you, Sophie?"

"Yes, Herbie, I do! The Maliks. Ash Malik is a pupil at Medborough Academy which is where I am. He's two years above me. I don't know him to talk to, but he's a jolly good cricketer."

"Is he, indeed?" remarked Alistair, interested. He was President of the Pepynbridge Cricket Club. He had won a cricket Blue at Oxford and, after he had come down, had played for Combined Services; and after he had left the Army, for Northamptonshire as an amateur.

"Yes!" broke in Herbert, wanting to deny Sophie Wicken a stage. She was a strong-willed girl who, like her father Alfred, sought to dominate. After the fiasco of Herbert's trial at Medborough Crown Court and her attempted suicide, Sophie had been sectioned and briefly detained in the Pemberton Mental Health Unit in Medborough. While there, her mother, Marigold Wicken, had decided she had endured enough of Alfred's excessive drinking and overbearing and dismissive attitude towards her and Sophie and had left him. Now she lived with Sophie, her only child, in a cottage in Summerhay, rented from Alice Burton.

Herbert had recognised that Sophie's conduct had been the result of her father's emotional rejection of her and, after his acquittal, Herbert had visited her in hospital and forgiven her. During the months that had followed her discharge into the community, Sophie had recovered her self-assurance. She had rejoined the choir and, more recently, as she had done the previous summer, she had begun to press Herbert to allow her to sing soprano solos in the Abbey. Under his careful and sympathetic tuition the quality of her voice had improved to a point where Herbert was contemplating using her. She was not yet outstanding, and might never be, but she was certainly good enough to sing in the company of another soprano or treble, preferably one with a stronger voice, if and when he found one.

"Sophie's right," continued Herbert. "And his mother told me he's possessed of a pleasant tenor voice..."

"I wouldn't know about that," broke in Sophie.

"Sophie," said Richard Maxey, frowning, "please don't interrupt Herbie." She pouted, turned and walked away. "She's a good girl," Maxey continued, "but what happened last December left her insecure and unsure of herself. Her reaction is to behave assertively, as she just has. It's her way of compensating for her public humiliation at the end of the trial. She's still under the care of Colin Forbes. She'll improve with time, the great healer. It was brave of her to rejoin the choir."

"I encouraged her to do so," said Herbert. "She's a strong character, like her father."

"Indeed," rejoined Maxey. "Wretched man! I gather he's taken a new woman into Pepynbridge Farm?"

"He has, Richard! Shirley. A divorcee from Peckham of all places, with three young children. She's doing Alfred's books as Marigold used to."

"And more besides, I'll wager. Was Alfred at the nine o'clock service this morning?"

"Yes, he was, Richard!"

"And this Shirley?"

"No! She never comes. She doesn't mix in the village. And nor do her children. Julie teaches them at school. The local children won't have anything to do with them because they're from London. And behaviourally, they present with problems."

"Colin Forbes, Richard?" queried Alistair, seeking to steer the conversation away from the Wickens and back to Ash Malik and cricket.

"Another consultant psychiatrist at Medborough General Hospital; a colleague of Dr Malik."

"I spent over an hour with the Maliks," rejoined Herbert, "and they're good news; welcome additions to the village. They originate from Pakistan where Abi qualified. The parents aren't observant Muslims and don't object to their children joining the choir. I'm auditioning both of them after choir practice next Wednesday evening." Choir practices took place between six and seven o'clock every Monday and Wednesday evening, except Bank Holidays.

"Were they in church this morning?"

"I didn't see them, Richard."

But Ash had been. He had slipped into the back of the Abbey after the Mass had begun so as not to be noticed and had left during the final hymn.

"And what about the cricket?" persisted Alistair. "The club meets..." he reached into an inside pocket, drew out a small diary and opened it, "...this Thursday evening, the ninth, in the Pavilion at six-thirty. Herbie, when you see Ash after choir practice on Wednesday evening, why don't you ask him to come along?"

"I shall, Alastair."

"Good!"

Herbert broke away to talk to other congregants.

Half an hour later the Abbey was deserted save for a few who were clearing up and taking cups and plates to be washed up in Abbey Hall, the southern half of the long Tudor building that divided Abbey Close from Station

Road. The northern half was the Rectory, towards which Herbert and Julie now walked hand in hand. Julie had conceived when she and Herbert had made love for the first time on 22nd December the previous year, following his acquittal at Medborough Crown Court and an outstandingly successful concert in the Abbey. Their child was expected on 14th September. Julie was the head teacher at St Aidan's Church of England Primary School and would continue in that role during the following summer term. She planned to take the autumn term off before resuming her post after Christmas. Julie had lived in School House in Station Road opposite the Rectory, but following her marriage to Herbert in February, she had moved into the Rectory and School House had been let.

Inside the Rectory, the dining table was laid for two. Tomorrow, Easter Monday would be spent with Julie's parents, Harry and Joy Swift, retired teachers, who lived in Ruislip; but today Herbert and Julie were on their own. Lunch was roast chicken, cooked by Julie before Mass and kept warm in an Aga, installed by the diocese in the nineteen thirties when funds had been plentiful. As she put potatoes and vegetables on to cook, Herbert opened a bottle of burgundy.

"Many there at nine o'clock?" Julie asked.

"Ten."

"Not very good for Easter Sunday."

"No, and one of them was Alice. She and Richard are bricks to keep supporting the BCP services. Peggy Taplow was there..." Peggy was a spinster in her seventies whose family had farmed outside the village since the time of

Cromwell "...and Alfred, of course; and Alfred's father, Reginald, and Norman Callow."

Norman Callow had been the head teacher at Pepynbridge Primary School for forty years before Julie had taken over in 2011. At Herbert's trial, it had been Norman Callow who had intervened to expose Sophie Wicken's allegations against Herbert as fantasies.

"Poor Norman," said Julie, "he's struggling a bit after his stroke."

"Yes, we may have to find him a care home," said Herbert. Norman had been widowed several years previously and had suffered a stroke in January that had left his speech and mobility mildly impaired. "But he made it to church this morning."

"And what about Gordon and Roger Slim? I didn't notice them at the eleven o'clock." Gordon's wife, Sylvia, like Julie was a member of the choir and had been in her usual stall.

"They were there, towards the back of the Abbey. They both came up to the rail to take Communion."

When Roger's voice had broken, he had left the choir.

"And how are you with Roger, Herbie?"

Herbert paused, carefully weighing his reply. Consequent upon a disordered upbringing in care when he had been sexually abused persistently by adult male carers, as an adult himself Herbert had found himself attracted to pubescent boys. It was why he had abandoned his post as Director of Music at Clarence College and, at the suggestion of the diocesan bishop, Julian Ross, taken on the challenge of Pepynbridge. He had needed a girl soprano or boy treble for his musical campaign to raise money for the Abbey roof.

In July the previous year, he had been introduced to Roger Slim, then aged thirteen and possessed of a sublimely beautiful treble voice. Roger had also been possessed of sublimely beautiful androgynous looks by which, to Herbert's dismay, he had been bewitched. As Herbert had always done since leaving the children's home aged 15, he had resisted the temptation to interfere with Roger. After a while, he had disclosed his infatuation to Julie. By then, unbeknown to him, Julie was in love with him and it had been her determination to capture and redeem him that had led to their marriage.

"Fine," replied Herbert. "Anyway, his voice has broken and he must have grown nearly two inches since Christmas. He's a good lad and I think he'll develop a pleasant baritone voice, but I don't have a problem with him any longer."

"Any other boy..." Julie paused, before adding "...or boys?"

"Not at the moment. But Julie, you know as well as I do that my problem isn't going to go away. The disorder is entrenched. The difference is that I can look at a boy now and appreciate his looks, but being married to you makes it even easier to resist the temptation to groom or touch him. It's a simple choice. It's either you; or what I struggled with before, in the knowledge that, if I had succumbed, my life would have been ruined. It's a no-brainer, darling."

Herbert smiled across the kitchen at Julie, re-acquainting himself with her light brown, shoulder-length hair, her triangular, lightly freckled face, grey eyes, straight nose, wide generous mouth, pointed chin and unlined and slender neck. Before last December, Herbert, until then a celibate, had been unable to envisage what lay below her neck; but now he knew and suddenly he wanted her.

Julie smiled back and thought, So far, so good! But stay on your guard, my girl!

Julie carried dishes of chicken and vegetables from the kitchen to the dining room table. They sat down, filled their plates and Herbert said Grace. Julie had foresworn alcohol for the duration of her pregnancy, but because it was Easter Sunday she made an exception and sipped at half a glass of wine. Pudding was apple pie and cream. Having led the Vigil the evening before, which had finished after midnight, and celebrated Book of Common Holy Communion and, afterwards, High Mass that morning, Herbert was exhausted so, when they had finished the apple pie and he had drunk most of the burgundy, they went to bed, made love and slept.

Ash arrived back in Abbey Gardens just after twelve. Over lunch, Abi asked,

"Where have you been, Ash?"

"I went to the Abbey."

"Why?"

"Well, it's Easter Sunday, one of the biggest Christian festivals, and I was interested in how it was celebrated."

"And?"

"It was impressive. Lots of incense. Fine Western music. A good sermon from the vicar."

"I thought he told us when he came here that he was a rector."

"Well, I don't know the difference."

"And what was the sermon all about?"

"It was about the fact that Jesus rose from the dead after he had been crucified. And how it proved that he was the Son of God."

"Well, you know what the *Qur'ān* says about that, don't you?"

"Yes, I certainly do! It says that Jesus, or *'Īsā*, was the last prophet before Muhammad, peace be upon him; and that *'Īsā* wasn't crucified but it was made to appear that he had been."

"Correct. And what else?"

"That it's heresy to speak about *Allah* having a son; or being one of three."

"That's what is written. And, as the observant Muslim you profess to be Ash, what do you think?"

Instantly Ash was on guard. He paused, before saying,

"Dad, I don't know what I think."

Across the table, Leela watched her brother with narrowed eyes. She sensed dissemblance, although her parents gave no sign they did as well. They wanted him and Leela to be integrated into Western culture; which was going to be problematic if either of them embraced Islamic fundamentalism.

"Father Herbert, you remember, suggested that you and Leela go and see him next Wednesday after choir practice to test your voices. Will you go?"

"Yes, Dad, I shall. And everyone calls him Herbie."

There had been an edge to the earlier exchanges between father and son, but at Ash's last response, Abi and Sabi relaxed.

"And what about you, Leela?" asked Sabi.

"Yes, I'll go too, Mum."

"Good. We'd like to see you both integrated into the community," said Abi.

"We'll do our best, won't we Leela?"

"Of course we shall Ash," Leela replied. But she wasn't convinced that her brother was as sincere as he was making out. Nor was she sure of the extent to which she, an observant Muslim, would be willing or able to integrate with Western culture.

It was three o'clock before Alfred Wicken staggered out of the Blue Boar and drove his Land Rover Defender unsteadily the mile along the Pepynbridge to Corbury road to Pepynbridge Farm. In the kitchen, Shirley Moore was quietly furious that he had not returned earlier for the lunch she had cooked for him and her three children, who were watching television in the sitting room. As she heard his vehicle enter the yard, she wondered, not for the first time, what had possessed her to move in with Alfred. She had lived in Peckham all her life. When Colin had left her and their three children, she had put an advertisement on match.com. Alfred had responded and they had met in a hotel in South London. Shirley was a good looking woman, with a kind face and a healthy sexual appetite. She was also a competent book-keeper. Alfred had impressed her with an embellished account of his wealth as a farmer; and his obsession with fathering a son to carry on the farm when he retired. He had seemed to offer Shirley the security she had lost. She had visited Pepynbridge Farm for a weekend on her own for a trial run, after which she and her children had moved in. It was not long before she realised that life in the country was totally foreign, not only to her, but to her three children. She was calculating how and when she should return to Peckham.

Alfred walked in and she was reminded of another reason why she longed to leave. He stumbled across the kitchen and seized her in his arms. Despite her recoiling from the smell of beer, he kissed her wetly on the lips and said,

"How about sex, old girl?"

"Not yet, Alfred. After lunch. The children are hungry."

"Oh, alright then." But it wasn't alright so far as Alfred was concerned. He collected a can of lager from the fridge; and, after he had drunk it, he drank another while he ate lunch. Afterwards, he went upstairs where Shirley had said she'd join him after she had washed up. By the time she entered the bedroom, Alfred was snoring. She went downstairs and said to the children,

"Shall we go for a walk?"

This was greeted with a chorus of dissent and Shirley joined them in front of the television.

At the Rectory, Herbert and Julie woke up shortly before seven o'clock and went downstairs; Julie to the living room to watch television; and Herbert to his study to read his emails before, as he always did, locking the south porch door into Abbey at sunset; which, on that Easter Sunday, would be at twenty to eight.

At half past seven, Ash returned to the Abbey and slipped into the Lady Chapel. Reaching behind the statue, he retrieved an envelope. He opened it and drew out a note that read:

Well done Ash. Good hiding place. No one will see you using the drop unless they are in here too and I

know you'll make sure they're not. Don't leave me another note, but keep checking this drop until the beginning of term. Destroy this. Z

◆◆◆◆◆◆◆◆◆◆◆◆◆◆◆◆◆◆◆◆◆◆

Wednesday, 8th April 2015

Easter Monday at the Swifts in Ruislip had been a success. In February, despite their awareness of Herbert's problem, Harry and Joy Swift had attended Julie and Herbert's wedding in St Aiden's Abbey. It had been well supported by the people of Pepynbridge and Julie's brother, Edward, his wife Susan and their three children had been there as well. The occasion had been happy and relaxed and Harry and Joy had been re-assured by Herbert's demonstrated and unembarrassed devotion towards their daughter. They knew that Julie appreciated the risk of marrying someone with a pædophilic tendency, but were confident that she would be able to take care of herself if things went wrong. Nothing had happened since to shake their confidence and they were content to entertain Herbert in their home. In fact, they liked him and were eagerly anticipating the arrival of their fourth grandchild.

On Wednesday, the first choir rehearsal after Easter was under way in the Abbey. Ascension Day lay ahead, but fell on a Thursday, as it always did. The next major Sunday festival would be Pentecost on 24th May, for which Herbert had chosen a Mass by Haydn. The choir, which had been given copies of the score before Easter, rehearsed it. It went well and, by seven o'clock, Herbert felt that they had done enough for the day.

"Well done, choir," he said. "Enough for now. Until next Sunday?"

There was a forest of smiles and nods. The choir members respected and loved Herbert, who had brought an excellence into their lives that, individually, they had never previously imagined they would encounter at first hand. They filed out of the stalls and Jack Driver came down from the console and joined them. As they left the Abbey, Herbert noticed Ash and Leela Malik sitting at the front of the nave.

"Hello!" he said. Ash and Leela rose to meet him. "Ash?"

"Yes, Sir!" he said, diffidently.

"Ash, please call me Herbie. Everyone does. Have you sung in a choir before?"

"Yes! In the Choral Society at the Academy."

"Anything in particular?"

"Bit of Handel. Bit of Bach. Bit of Mendelssohn; and some modern stuff."

"And you, Leela?" said Herbert, turning towards her. By comparison with her brother, she presented as self-assured.

"I've sung in the Academy Choral Society as well."

"And you can both read music?" They nodded. "Fine! Let's go over to the piano." They walked over to a grand piano in the north transept.

"Ash?"

"Yes, Herbie?"

"Do you know Handel's Messiah?"

"Yes, I do! Actually, I have sung solo 'Comfort ye, my people...' "

"Not really consistent with Islam, is it?"

"Oh, it is, Herbie! Islam reveres many of the Hebrew prophets. For example: Moses, whom we call *Musa*; Ezekiel, whom we call *Dhul-Kifl*; Elisha, called *Alyasa*; and Isaiah whom we call *Ishiya* and who wrote '*Comfort ye, my people...*'; and, of course, Jesus, or '*Īsā*, the prophet before the last one, Muhammad, peace be upon him."

"Yes, of course!" Herbert remembered from theological college. "Silly of me! Now, for some music!" He delved into a space beneath the piano stool and drew out two scores of the *Messiah*. He gave one to Ash and sat at the piano, placing the other on the rest. When they had both found the place, Herbert began to play.

As soon as Ash sang the phrases that open the *Accompagnato*, Herbert realised that he had found a competent, if not outstanding tenor; light, but clear and faultlessly in tune. He allowed Ash to complete it and then said,

"And '*Every valley...*'?" Ash nodded and they continued to its end.

"Ash," said Herbert. "You have a pleasant tenor voice. Thank you for your recital. Would you be willing to join the choir?"

"Yes! I would, please!" responded Ash enthusiastically and Herbert smiled. But her diffident brother's uncharacteristic lack of reserve surprised Leela.

"And what about you Leela? What's your voice?"

"Soprano, Herbie."

"And what would you like to sing?" She hesitated. Her voice was good, but she was wary of choosing something to sing in the presence of someone who, she surmised, knew much more about music than she did.

"Have you ever sung *Laudate Dominum* by Mozart?"

She had. It was a notoriously difficult piece and Herbert had suggested it because it would challenge the voice of a girl of Leela's age. If she said she had not sung it, he would not invite her to do so. But she knew that she could sing it and sing it well; and the fact that it been suggested by Herbert gave her the confidence to reply,

"Yes, I have!"

"Well, then, let's give it a try." Herbert rummaged under the piano stool and handed her the sheet music.

When Roger Slim had been auditioned by Herbert the previous July and on every occasion afterwards when Herbert had heard Roger sing before his voice had broken, Herbert had recognised how fortunate he had been to have encountered such top register talent and purity. As soon as Leela began, he realised that he was encountering both afresh. Leela's soprano soared above the arches and echoed from the vaulted roof. Her voice was not like a boy's treble. It was postmenarcheal; a young adult soprano, but with no vibrato or cracking and invested with an honesty and lack of sophistication which was precisely what Herbert was looking for. Herbert sang the *Gloria* chorus and was pleased that Ash joined in. Towards the end of the *Gloria*, Leela's ethereal "Amens" emerged like a stream of silver, pure and polished. When Herbert had played the concluding chords, he closed his eyes and privately thanked God.

"Wonderful!" he said, opening his eyes and looking at her. "Thank you, Leela. I hope that you'll join the choir as well?"

"It depends," said Leela.

"Upon what?"

"Upon whether I shall be expected to participate in worship. I'll sing in your choir, Herbie, but I must remain true to my Muslim faith. You understand that, don't you?"

"Of course I do," responded Herbert. "But I thought that devout Muslims disapproved of music."

"Some Islamic scholars do, Herbie. Others don't, especially regarding women. Provided music is not used by a woman in a sinful context, some scholars say it's okay."

"But doesn't Islam regard Christianity as a sinful context, Leela?"

"Herbie, the *Qur'ān* teaches Muslims to be tolerant towards Christians. I can't recall off-hand the *sura* and the *ayah*, but it does. I live in England and attend a non-Muslim school, so I accept that a degree of adaptation to the prevailing culture is okay. It depends how far it goes."

"Alright, Leela. If you join the choir, you may stay silent whenever we pray. And I certainly wouldn't expect you to come up to the rail to be blessed when communion is distributed."

"Alright, then. I'll see how I get along."

"Excellent! The next choir practice is next Monday, here in the Abbey at six. See you both then?" Ash and Leela nodded. Then Herbert remembered.

"Oh, and Ash?"

"Yes, Herbie?"

"Mr Pemberton-Smith is President of Pepynbridge Cricket Club. He's heard that you play cricket and would like you to attend the pre-season meeting in the Pavilion tomorrow evening."

"That's great, Herbie. I'll be there. Time?"

"Six-thirty. And you know where the Pavilion is?"

"In Hall Park?"

"Correct."

Ash and Leela turned and made their way down the nave towards the south porch. As they did so, they passed Julie Onion sitting near the back. She smiled at them. They returned her smile and left. Julie rose as Herbert followed them down the nave.

"I didn't know you'd stayed behind," he said.

"I was interested. She's got a lovely voice, hasn't she?"

"She certainly has. And he's not so bad."

"I agree, but probably not yet ready for a solo in the Abbey."

"Oh, I don't know about that. We'll have to see what Jack thinks." Herbert was referring to Jack Driver. "Back home?" Julie nodded and they made their way out of the south porch. It was dark. Herbert locked the door behind them and they walked the short distance across Abbey Close to the Rectory. Inside when they were sitting, eating supper, Julie said,

"I wasn't surprised at Leela's reservations about joining the choir. But I was at Ash's reaction. He didn't hesitate."

Herbert thought back and remembered. "That's true," he said. "It struck me as odd. Perhaps he's not religious."

"Oh, but he is, Herbie! He reeled off the Arabic names of the prophets without hesitation."

"Mmm. Yes, it's strange. I'll have another word with their parents about them joining the choir. Just to make sure that they don't have any reservations about it. After all, liturgy at St Aiden's is theologically and quintessentially Christian; and culturally and quintessentially Western. I can ask them about Ash's and Leela's attitude towards Islam. I'll find out if they're at home tomorrow evening."

When supper was over, Herbert telephoned the Maliks. Yes, they would be at home tomorrow evening and would be pleased to see him. Then Herbert called Joshua Cohen, his friend from the days when they had studied together at the Guildhall School of Music and Drama. Joshua was an artist manager and it had been he who had marketed the recording that Herbert had made with the choir and Roger Slim the previous September; and which had raised so much money for the Abbey.

"Yes?"

"Herbie here, Josh."

"Herbie, old son! How's things?"

"Good! Very good! And you?"

"Oh yeah. Fine! Busy, you know. Rushing here and there. New York last week. Berlin tomorrow. Making a dollar or two. So, what's new?"

"Another voice."

"Another one? Blimey! Where d'ya find 'em."

"They just seem to turn up. God's will."

"Yeah, yeah, my old fruit. Don't give me that guff. I know you're a vicar and all that but..." he tailed off, before resuming with, "Tell me about him, Herbie?"

"It's a she."

"A she!"

"Yes! But a girl with a cathedral voice if you know what I mean."

"Of course, I do. Another recording then?"

"I think so. Are you game?"

"Sure! When?"

"September, like last year?"

"Any chance of making it earlier? Better for the Christmas trade."

Herbert thought for a moment.

"I could sort it by the end of July?"

"Perfect, old son! Perfect!

"Do you need to hear her, Josh?"

"No, after the last one, I trust you. Keep me posted, okay?"

"Sure!"

"Shalom!"

"Shalom and thanks Josh."

"No trouble. Keep smiling!" The telephone went dead.

Herbert looked at his watch. It was seven thirty. Nearly another twenty minutes to sunset.

◆◆◆◆◆◆◆◆◆◆◆◆◆◆◆◆◆◆◆◆◆

Thursday, 9th and, briefly, Saturday, 11th April 2015

By Thursday evening, the anti-cyclone that had begun to build on Easter Day was dominant. Warm sunshine was teasing bright green leaves from hawthorn, snowy blossom from blackthorn and flower-candles from horse chestnuts. In the fields, winter wheat was thrusting up half an inch a day and hints of yellow flowers were discernable in the oil-seed rape. Soon the countryside would be suffused with their cloying scent and allergen misery, but just now, together with everything else, they were a welcome harbinger of summer.

That evening Herbert called on the Maliks. Ash had gone to the meeting in the cricket pavilion and Leela was upstairs, doing her homework. Abi, Sabi and Herbert sat in the sitting room. As they had done when Herbert had first called on them, they affirmed that they were not observant Muslims. What about the children? They were silent for a while. Then Sabi said,

"You know, I think that they're both interested in religion. After all, what young person isn't when they're growing up? We were all searching for meaning in our lives in those days, weren't we?"

She turned to her husband.

"We were, although we didn't know each other when we were that young. Ash attends a prayer meeting at school every Friday evening and there's someone called Zed who leads it. They pray and then, so Ash tells us, Zed teaches them about the *Qur'ān* and the *hadith*, but he never says much about what he's learnt."

That's probably where he's learnt about the Hebrew prophets, thought Herbert. I wonder how much more he knows? And given his apparent commitment to Islam, like Julie I am surprised that he agreed so readily to join the choir. But I won't discuss that with Abi and Sabi. I'll see what transpires as time passes.

"And Leela?" he asked

"She reads Islamic books and visits Islamic websites," replied Sabi.

"She doesn't attend the prayer meetings at the Academy?"

"No!" said Sabi, and smiled. "Boys only!"

"Oh, really? Well, I auditioned them both yesterday evening. Leela has an exquisite soprano voice and she would be a great addition to the choir. Ash has a pleasant tenor voice. It's not as outstanding as Leela's, but it's more than good enough for us. They have both agreed to join the choir as I expect they've told you. I just wanted to double-check that you have no objection to them doing so."

"Not at all," replied Abi.

"And what about taking part in worship, whether directly or indirectly?"

"Up to them, eh Sabi?"

"I agree."

After chatting about Pepynbridge, Herbert left, pleased that it had gone well. As he walked back to the Rectory, he again privately thanked God for providing the Abbey with two such voices; one of which was as good as, if not better than, Roger Slim's. Funny about Ash and his interest in Islam. If he didn't last, thought Herbert, it wouldn't be a disaster. In his study, he sat at his desk, with his back to the window that overlooked Abbey Close. He glanced up at the Abbey reflected in the looking glass above the doorway opposite his desk. It was still light and he looked at his watch. Not locking-up time just yet.

To the east of Pepynbridge lay its eponymous Hall. Built in the late sixteenth century by Francis Templeton, a courtier of Queen Elizabeth, it was reached past a lodge and gates from Abbey Way opposite the east end of St Aidan's along a long gravelled drive, bordered by an avenue of lime trees, now breaking into leaf. At the Hall, the drive broadened to embrace a fifty metre wide stone-built front, interrupted by two mullioned bay windows that reached to its eves. An imposing wooden door in the middle led into a hall, two storeys high. Doors led off into reception rooms and a wide staircase climbed to a balcony along the back and sides of the hall. At the back, a gallery ran the length of the ground floor. Paintings dating from the seventeenth and eighteenth centuries lined its walls, including an El Greco collected by Francis Templeton's son, William, who had succeeded his father as a courtier, but to King James I.

William Pemberton, Alice and Augusta's father, had married twice but died without a son. When the Roman Catholic Alastair Smith had married Augusta, he had linked his surname with hers; hence Templeton–Smith; and the Anglican Augusta had gone over to Rome. With four children, subject only to the impact of inheritance tax or its replacement, on the death of the survivor of them, the future of Pepynbridge Hall and Estate appeared secure. Beyond a ha-ha at the back of the Hall was the broad sweep of Hall Park, with a cricket square and a pavilion, where, while Herbert was talking to the Maliks, the Pepynbridge Cricket Club members were gathered, Ash amongst them.

The fixture list had been settled in January and now the talk was of forthcoming matches, teams and catering. As Alistair was addressing the meeting, he spotted Ash. Earlier that week, Abi had sent Alistair a cheque for £75, the annual membership subscription.

"This evening," said Alistair, "I should like to welcome our new member, Ash Malik. Ash, could you stand up for a moment?"

Ash did so and the others present appraised him, noting his above average height, slimness and athletic build. However, where another might have smiled, through shyness Ash's features remained impassive.

"Thank you, Ash," Alistair resumed, and Ash sat back down. Alistair turned to Oliver Standard, the club's professional coach. "Oliver, would you have a moment next Saturday to try Ash out in the nets?"

"Of course!"

"Okay, Ash?"

"Yes, Sir."

"Shall we say ten o'clock?" Ash nodded.

"Fine by me," was Oliver's response, adding. "Ash, may we have a word after the meeting?" Again Ash nodded.

Like Alistair Templeton-Smith, Oliver Standard had played for Northamptonshire, but as a club professional. He had set up a coaching school in Medborough, where his pupils included boys and girls, although none from the Academy, so he had not met Ash. However, he had heard on the grapevine that Ash was a promising all-rounder. As well as looking after his coaching business in Medborough, whenever weather permitted Oliver Standard spent evenings during the winter and early spring coaching Pepynbridge players in nets under lights next to the pavilion. During the playing season he attended First XI matches at home and away. As the opening matches would not take place until the week-end of 18th and 19th April, his offer to undertake some extra coaching on the coming Saturday had been welcomed by the committee.

When the meeting finished, the members adjourned to the bar, leaving Oliver and Ash alone in the committee room.

"Tell me about your cricket, Ash?"

"I lived in Lahore until I was seven. Out there, everyone's crazy about cricket. Kids start playing almost as soon as they can walk."

"On grass?"

"Heavens, No! In the street. And the street is often dirt, not tarmac. Anyway, that's where I started playing. I can't remember how old I was. Very young. When we came to England, I went to a primary school in London, where my dad had a job. He's a doctor. He got another job in Medborough and when we moved, I started at Medborough Academy."

"How old were you then?"

"I was eleven. We moved to Medborough in two thousand and nine. And in two thousand and ten, I started playing cricket at school."

"I think that last year you played for the Colts. Am I right?" Ash looked surprised. "Don't be surprised, Ash! Medborough's not such a big place and the cricket community is pretty close-knit. Do you think you'll be selected this year for the Academy Firsts?"

"I hope so."

"When does the team play."

"On Saturdays."

"So you could play for Pepynbridge on Sundays?"

"I could, but…" Ash hesitated.

"But what, Ash?"

"Well, I've agreed to sing in the Abbey choir on Sundays."

"And so what time are services on Sundays?"

"Eleven o'clock."

"And over by when?"

"Twelve, I should think."

"No problem! On Sundays, Pepynbridge plays in the Rutland League and matches don't start until half past one. Plenty of time for you to get to the pavilion here. And when we play away, the bus leaves from here at twelve thirty; so just time for you to catch it. What were your batting and bowling averages last season?"

"My batting average was twenty-nine. My bowling figures were twenty-four for twelve."

"Respectable," was Oliver's cautious response. Privately he was impressed. They were exceptional for a sixteen year-old, which is what Ash had been last summer. "Ash, when's your birthday?"

"The twenty-fifth of October, Sir. I'll be eighteen this year."

"Call me Ollie, Ash! Every one does. Okay?"

"Okay Ollie." And for the first time during their conversation, Ash's impassive features were broken by a shy smile.

Oliver placed a friendly hand on Ash's shoulder.

"See you here on Saturday at ten. Track suit will do. Bring your bat and pads! 'Bye!"

"'Bye, Ollie!"

Ash left the pavilion and Oliver joined Alistair at the bar. Alistair ordered Oliver a pint of bitter and turned to him.

"Well?"

"Promising, I'd say. I'd heard on the grapevine that he's developing into a useful all-rounder. His averages last season, both batting and bowling, were excellent. We'll see on Saturday. Any objection to my including him in the Firsts next Sunday if I think he should be? We're playing Corbury at home." Corbury was a town ten miles west of Pepynbridge.

"Not at all, Ollie! You be the judge of that." The bar emptied and they left.

Two days later, after an hour in the nets with Ash, Oliver told him that he would be playing for Pepynbridge Firsts on the following Saturday, the 19th April.

On the way back from the nets, Ash slipped into the Abbey and the Lady Chapel. There was nothing but dust behind the statue.

◆◆◆◆◆◆◆◆◆◆◆◆◆◆◆◆◆◆◆◆◆◆

Monday, 13th April 2015

Whenever the choir rehearsed or performed, the sopranos and trebles sat in the choir stalls on one side of the chancel and the alto, tenor and bass voices on the other. So it was that, at choir practice on Monday evening, Ash was sitting opposite Sophie and Leela. They were to rehearse music for the following Sunday; and pieces from the Haydn Mass that Herbert had chosen for Pentecost. Before the rehearsal, Herbert announced that he intended to record another CD of sacred music during the week of 27th to 30th July. He asked choir members to let him know as soon as possible whether they would be available.

"And now…" he continued, pointing to Ash and Leela in turn, "…let me introduce you to Ash and Leela Malik who have recently moved into Abbey Gardens with their parents. Ash, as you can see, is with the tenors…" Ash smiled shyly, "…and Leela is our new soprano." Leela looked up but remained expressionless. Herbert continued, "As you will discover, Leela has an exceptional voice…" Oh well, thought Sophie, bang goes my chance of singing solos; but Herbert continued, "…which means that, with Sophie, whose voice has greatly improved…" he paused and smiled at her, "Well done, Sophie!" and Sophie smiled back, "...we now have two soprano soloists." Sophie's smile broadened.

Leela was sitting next to Sophie in the choir stalls. Although they were in the same year at the Academy, they had barely talked to each other. Leela had been living in Medborough and there had seemed little point. The Maliks had moved to Pepynbridge on 16th March and between then and the end of the spring term on 27th March, Sophie had noticed both Leela and Ash on the bus to and from Medborough, which she caught every week-day at the top of the lane that led to Summerhay from the Pepynbridge to Medborough road. Now that Leela lived in Pepynbridge, had joined the choir and, like me, is a soprano, thought Sophie, it would be a good idea to get to know her. Apart from Sophie, there were no young people in Summerhay. The other cottages in the hamlet, all owned by Alice Burton, were occupied by pensioners. Just as once she had yearned for her father's affection, so now Sophie longed for friendship.

However, as the rehearsal proceeded, Sophie's attention was drawn to Ash opposite her. Sophie was in Year 10 and Ash was in Year 12 and they had never come across each other. Now, for the first time, she had an opportunity to study him. She took in his finely-drawn features, the large, deep brown eyes set beneath a broad forehead, the aquiline nose, the understated way he framed his lips as he sang, and the athleticism betrayed by broad shoulders which, she noticed when he stood, narrowed down to a slender waist. Since her infatuation with Herbie had ended so badly, triggered as it had been by her observations of him during services in the Abbey, Sophie was conscious of the danger of judging attractive males simply by appearance or status. She had, she hoped, learnt that lesson. But as well as being seriously fit, Ash was obviously musical; and, so she had heard, he could play a good game of cricket. She imagined him, not clad in jeans and a grey sweater as he was this evening, but in a white sports shirt and white cricket trousers; and she became aware of familiar, but potentially hazardous erotic stirrings within her; stirrings which she quickly suppressed, switching her gaze from Ash to the sheet music on the shelf in front of her. She had missed her cue and hoped that Herbie had not noticed.

But Herbert had and, knowing Sophie well, had divined her feelings. Well, he thought, she could do a lot worse than Ash. Indeed I'm encouraged that, after her infatuation with me, she's shewing an interest in someone her own age; and, what's more, someone who would not be the father-lover substitute that, in her fantasising, I was last year.

When the rehearsal finished, Sophie contrived to leave the Abbey before Ash. Her bicycle lay propped up inside the south porch. She stopped beside it and, as Ash passed, she turned towards him.

"Hi!" she said.

Ash stopped and looked at her. He had recognised her from school but, like Sophie, had only observed her properly for the first time across the chancel this evening. He had remembered Zed's suggestion that he should get himself a *kafir* girl friend. Sophie was pretty and, unlike him, she exuded self-assurance. But he had dismissed the notion of approaching her, not knowing how to initiate an encounter. Now it had been taken out of his hands, he was grateful. As he looked into her wide blue eyes, he thought, I'd quite like to get to know this girl. She'll do!

"Hi!" he replied.

"Are you going my way?"

"I live in Abbey Gardens."

"Well, you're not then. I've got to cycle to Summerhay."

"Where's that?"

"Oh, about two miles away. Outside Pepynbridge. You go down Station Road, over the river Pepyn at the bottom of the village, up the hill and, at the top...you know where the bus stops to pick me up in the mornings?" Ash nodded. "...you turn left and go downhill to the river. Our cottage is just past The Mill, where Mrs Burton lives."

"Sounds nice."

"It is. We moved there in December when Mum left Dad."

"Oh, I'm sorry."

"Don't be. Dad's a..." Sophie paused and decided not to say shit. Instead, "Dad's not very nice. He's a bully. And he's a drunk. And I'm glad we no longer live with him." Ash looked shocked and Sophie decided leave it there. They were joined by Leela.

"Are we going home, Ash?"

"Yes, Leela." He looked intently into Sophie's eyes and said, "See you again soon, I hope."

"Of course you will, silly! On Wednesday at choir practice. See you!"

But Sophie had recognised his clumsiness for what it was; an overture; and not unwelcome, either. She turned and wheeled her bicycle towards the archway that led out of Abbey Close into Station Road.

"She's nice," said Leela. "She's in the same year as me at school. I think I should get to know her, don't you?"

"Why not?" Ash replied, reflecting that if Leela and Sophie become friends, it'll make it easier for Mum and Dad if Sophie and I started seeing each other. And, as an afterthought, if we do, Zed'll be pleased when I tell him. Term is due to start tomorrow, so no need to check the drop in the Abbey. He and Leela walked home.

◆◆◆◆◆◆◆◆◆◆◆◆◆◆◆◆◆◆◆◆◆

Sunday, 19th April 2015

The rest of the week passed predictably and uneventfully. At choir practice on Wednesday, Ash and Sophie had exchanged discreet smiles across the chancel. On Friday, Ash had gathered with the other members of the *IstishhadUK* cell in the prayer room, but apart from Zed reiterating ground already covered, there had been no further discussion about why they were there and the meeting had ended before six o'clock.

At Mass on Sunday, the choir performed well in the Abbey and, whilst Ash condemned the theology that underpinned it, he discovered that he enjoyed the ritual and the singing. Afterwards, he went home, changed into his whites and walked down the drive and around Pepynbridge Hall to the pavilion at the edge of Hall Park cricket ground.

Grey skies had given way to fitful sunshine, but a north-easterly breeze was keeping the afternoon cool. A line of deckchairs stretched along the front and to each side of the pavilion. For a village match, there was a respectable crowd of spectators, some wrapped in blankets against the chill. Amongst them were Abi Malik, anxious to support his son; Leela; Sophie; Herbert and Julie; and Alistair Pemberton-Smith and Richard Maxey, who shared a keen interest in cricket and were intrigued to see how the Club's new recruit made out. It was the first match of the season and Corbury was an unknown quantity. Pepynbridge won the toss and elected to bat. Oliver Standard had put Ash sixth in the batting order as, despite Ash's competent display in the nets, Oliver was unsure how he would perform competitively. By the time Ash walked to the crease, Pepynbridge were 71 for 4 and struggling against good medium pace bowling.

Ash played himself in cautiously, scoring an odd single until he had the measure of the bowlers he was facing. In his third over, he struck a loose ball for four; and then another boundary off the next delivery. In the following over, after his batting partner scored a single off the first ball, Ash faced again. He let the first delivery pass him wide of his off-stump. The next one was on his stumps and Ash stroked it to the leg boundary. Off the last ball of the over, he hit a cover drive for four. Corbury's captain decided to change tactics in the face of this assault and called on an off-spinner. As soon as Ash faced him and had read his spin, he set to work. After he had hit two more fours, the bowler lobbed a full toss. Ash struck it true and it flew over the roof of the pavilion.

"He's good, Alistair," remarked Richard Maxey. Abi Malik overheard him and smiled.

"Yes, I believe he is," responded Alistair cautiously. When Pepynbridge yielded its final wicket for 234 runs, of which the unbeaten Ash had scored 120, Alistair's caution had dissipated. "Yes, Richard," he said. "I agree with you. He is good."

There followed a break for tea and Sophie watched Leela and Dr Malik enter the pavilion. She followed them. There were plates of sandwiches and cup-cakes on a long narrow table behind which two helpers were serving tea and coffee. Small round tables with chairs were scattered around the room, at one of which were sitting Abi, Ash and Leela. Sophie took a cup of tea over to them.

"Mind if I join you?"

"Of course not," replied Abi, turning towards Ash and raising his eyebrows quizzically.

"Dad, this is Sophie..." he paused and frowned.

"Wicken," supplied Sophie.

"Sophie Wicken. She sings with us in the choir."

"How do you do, Sophie!"

"Good!" replied Sophie. "Ash," she continued, "you were great!"

"Thank you, Sophie. It was fun."

"I bet it was!" Sophie's riposte was brisk and warm and drew a smile from Ash. Then rising from his chair, he said,

"Excuse me. I must go and see Ollie, the Club coach."

Sophie turned to Leela.

"Hi, Leela!" she said.

Leela looked at her expressionlessly.

"Hello!"

"We're in the same year at the Academy, aren't we?" Leela nodded. "But not in the same set." Leela shook her head. "Well, I just thought that now you're living in Pepynbridge we might get to know one another? I live in

Summerhay, so why don't you come over one day? Have you got a bike?"

Leela was wary of bold overtures. It was not that she was shy like her brother. Far from it, but she was cautious by nature; slow to respond to strangers, which is how she regarded Sophie Wicken.

"Leela doesn't have a bicycle," broke in Abi. "We should think about buying her one now we're living in the country. But my wife or I could run her over. Would you like me to do that, Leela?"

Well, thought Leela, no harm in it. Sophie seems nice enough, if a bit forward. Something of a shew-off, I expect, but it would be rude to refuse. She smiled.

"Yes, alright. Thank you Sophie. That's kind of you."

"Who else lives at your house?"

"Just my mum, Doctor Malik. Mum and Dad are separated. Dad's a farmer. He lives at Pepynbridge Farm out on the Corbury Road, about a mile outside the village. But I don't see him very often. We've fallen out."

"I'm sorry to hear that, Sophie."

"Oh, it doesn't matter at all. I'm much happier just living with Mum. But I'm short of local friends and it would be nice if Leela and I could see something of each other."

"When would be convenient then, Sophie?"

"I'll ask Mum. Hold on!"

Sophie rose and walked towards the door, pulling a mobile from a pocket. She spoke briefly into it out of earshot of the Maliks and then returned.

"Would next Saturday be alright? Mum says, come to tea. And I'll shew you the river. It's very pretty there."

"Thank you Sophie," said Leela, adopting a formal tone. "Dad! Would you or Mum be able to give me a lift?"

"I'm sure we could. Sophie, can you leave me a contact number where we can reach you if something crops up?"

Sophie provided Abi with her mobile number.

Just then, Pepynbridge walked out to field. Over the winter, the groundsman had kept the square hard and spare of grass and it had begun to deteriorate during Pepynbridge's innings. Inside the pavilion, after conferring with Pepynbridge's captain, Oliver Standard had said to Ash,

"Fancy opening the bowling, Ash?"

Ash bowled off and leg breaks, using wrist and finger actions that were difficult for batsmen to read. He had noted the state of the pitch before he had left the square and knew it would assist him if he were asked to bowl. It did. Pepynbridge won the match by 57 runs and Ash's bowling figures were 5 for 47; an average of 9.4.

"If he continues to play as he has today, Ollie," Alistair Pemberton-Smith said afterwards to Oliver Standard in the bar, "I shall give my friends at Northants a call."

"You may well find yourself doing that. But let's see how he is by the end of June, eh?"

"I agree."

Friday, 24th April 2015

In the prayer room, the members of the *IstishhadUK* cell were sitting around the table, chatting over mugs of coffee.

Zed asked Ash how he was embedding himself in Pepynbridge.

"I've joined the local church choir," said Ash. "We rehearse twice a week and then sing at the main service on Sunday mornings. Last Sunday, I played my first game of cricket for Pepynbridge Firsts and it went pretty well. No one, I'm pretty sure, has any idea that I'm an Islamist."

"Got a girl friend, yet?"

"Not yet! But there's a girl in the choir who's interested in me and so I'm hopeful we'll get together soon."

"Don't get too fond of her!" Zed warned.

Ash felt a twinge of guilt and, after a barely perceptible pause, he replied,

"Of course not, Zed! No chance! I know where my loyalty lies. To *IstishhadUK* and to Islam. I won't let anything get in the way of that."

Zed, suspecting what had lain behind the pause, said with just a hint of menace,

"Better not Ash! Better not!"

Ash glanced at Zed warily and shrugged mentally. He understood what lay behind Zed's tone but was confident that he could maintain an emotional distance from Sophie, nice though she seemed. However, he hoped that, whatever the mission, he could arrange for her not to be hurt, or worse.

"Well," continued Zed, "we'll continue to meet every Friday from now on, except for Friday, the twenty-ninth of May, when we're on half term. On the twentieth of July, we're all going to meet in Middlehay Wood. Know where that is?"

Ash had never been to Middlehay Wood, but he said that he knew that it was between Pepynbridge and Corbury, about two miles off the main road. The others did not know it.

"Well, it may not matter. We'll see. I expect I'll be able to give you three a lift. You got a car, Ash?"

"I can probably borrow my mum's. If not, I can cycle there. It's not that far."

"Good. So all of you keep that day free, okay? The twentieth of July. We'll be there all day, doing some training. More about that later. In the meantime, there're two things I want you to do."

He handed out copy web sheets from Katch & Kill.

"I want each of you to order one of these Fly Vests. Do it on-line. Have you all got a debit card or a top-up credit card?" They confirmed they had. "Good! Bring your Fly Vest with you on the twentieth of July. And the other thing. You know the DVD recordings that we often see after a *mujahid* has been martyred? He's sitting on a mat with a black flag behind him with the *Shahada* in white on it?" They nodded. "Okay. Each of us will make a video like that when we meet in July." He handed round copies he had made of the sheet that Raed had given him. "That's what we want you to say, okay? If you want to put personal stuff in it, that's okay, but don't alter the message and clear any changes with me before you make the recording. That's all for now. There's not much more to discuss until we meet in Middlehay Wood, but we'll carry on as we are so as not to arouse anyone's suspicions. Okay?" The others nodded. "Anyway," Zed went on, "as good Muslims, we're bound to meet for Friday prayers but it's better not to get too involved in a local mosque in case we let something out by mistake. Keep up your cover and, whatever you do, say nothing about *IstihhadUK* to anybody, not even to a devout Muslim. Okay?"

He stared at each in turn, so that each felt compelled to respond with a positive, "Yes!"

That night Herbert and Julie were lying side by side in bed in the Rectory when Julie said,

"Herbie?"

"Yes?"

"It may have been my imagination, but I thought I felt the tiniest movement just then."

"Did you! Well, that's exciting. How far along are we?"

"Nearly twenty weeks, the way it's calculated."

"How is it calculated?"

"We first made love on the twenty-second of December, but time starts from the beginning of my last period, which was two weeks before that."

"Oh!"

"I'm due to go in for another ultrascan next week."

"Another one? Is that because they're worried?"

"Not at all, Herbie! After the first one in March, they said that, so far as they could tell, everything was fine."

"And the next one?"

"They can tell an awful lot more, including the gender."

"Do you want to know that?"

"Not really."

"Nor do I. Are you given a choice?"

"You are."

"Well, I should say not, then."

They lay in companionable silence for a while and then Julie said,

"I felt it again! Movement! Fantastic! A new life, Herbie!"

"Made in the image of God! A miracle!"

"Yes, Herbie! A miracle! Aren't we lucky?"

"So far, so good. It's in God's hands, Julie!"

"Yes, of course! But I'll keep my fingers crossed all the same. Just in case!"

Herbert smiled into the darkness.

SUNNA
(The Way)

Saturday, 25th April 2015

Sophie was standing outside the cottage in Summerhay when, at half past three, Abi Malik drove up and Leela got out of the car. He arranged to collect her at six and left. Sophie took Leela inside and introduced her to her mother. Marigold warmed to Leela and was happy that Sophie had decided to befriend her. She had always impressed upon Sophie the importance of making the most of her circumstances and the daughter of a consultant clinician certainly met that imperative, even if she was coloured. Not that Alfred would approve, she thought, recalling his prejudice against foreigners in general; and 'wogs' in particular, as he termed them. But what her bigoted **husband might think didn't bother her one bit.**

Sophie and Leela went outside. The spring sun was warm. A gentle south-westerly breeze ruffled the surface of the River Pepyn, which slowed as it neared The Mill. Trees on both sides of the river were just breaking into leaf. On the south bank, skeletal shadows lay across the roughly mown grass between trunks and the stream. The south-facing cottages on the north bank of the river were reached over a bridge by The Mill where Alice Burton lived. There was a lawn between the cottages and the river bank. Sophie **and Leela were standing in** front of Marigold's cottage, squinting against the sunshine. To their left, the lawn continued for a hundred metres until it met a wood. A path, along which the girls now strolled, led through the wood close by the riverbank. Sophie said nothing, giving

Leela time to adjust to her company. They continued until they arrived at a grassy glade, the size of a tennis court. Set back from the riverbank and against the trees was a wooden gazebo with solid sides and back. Its open front faced south towards the river. The floor was covered with coconut matting and there were canvas chairs on which Sophie and Leela sat.

"Sophie," said Leela. "This is lovely!"

"Yes, it is, isn't it? It belongs to Mrs Burton. All the land round here does. She owns the cottages as well and Mum rents ours from her. Mrs Burton has two full-time gardeners and one of them looks after the river banks. He keeps the grass mown. Over there," she said, pointing towards the river, "is a bathing place. That's what this place is called; The Bathing Place. The river is lovely and clear. Come and see!" They walked across the grass to the bank where there was wooden decking and steps down into the clear water. "Look, Leela, you can see the gravelly bottom," Sophie said. And then she caught Leela's forearm and pointed. "Look!" she said softly. "Can you see the fish over there?"

"Yes," breathed Leela. "Is it a trout?"

"No, I don't think so. Probably a rudd or something." As they watched, the fish rose to the surface and sucked at it, making a little ring on the water. "He's feeding on hatching flies," explained Sophie.

Leela was entranced. She had never been anywhere like this; or seen anything like the feeding fish, whatever sort it was.

"This is lovely, Sophie. Thank you for bringing me here. Do you go swimming here?"

"I never have. Not yet. Mum and I only moved here in January, after Mum left Dad. I was in hospital then in Medborough…"

"Why?" interrupted Leela.

"Oh, it doesn't matter. I wasn't in for long. Mum was renting a flat in Medborough, but we're country people and in January Mrs Burton offered to let the cottage to Mum and we moved in. Anyway, you wouldn't swim now. Water's too cold. But later on if there's a hot summer you would. Would you like that, Leela?"

"Oh yes, I would," breathed Leela and a friendship was born. Sophie decided not to ask Leela about Ash just then. She didn't want her to think that her reason for befriending her was her brother. Anyway, thought Sophie, that's not the only reason. I really like you, Leela.

Dr Malik collected Leela at six o'clock and, when she arrived home, she said nothing about The Bathing Place. For the moment, it was their secret; Sophie's and hers.

◆◆◆◆◆◆◆◆◆◆◆◆◆◆◆◆◆◆◆◆◆◆

Saturday, 2nd May 2015

Raed, Zed, Waahid, and Yaaseen were sitting in The Foxes' Den in Leicester, discussing the training day planned for 20th July. Raed was doing the talking.

"We'll meet at nine o'clock, okay? Have you discovered where Middlehay Wood is? You have? Good! I shall get there early to set up the shed. The plan will be to tell the others about the mission; to instruct them how to prepare the šahīd vests; and to record the videos. Before we do any of that, as I said last time we met, we shall need to check out each of them; to root out any doubtfuls. Don't want to let any doubtfuls into the secret of our mission, eh? Any of you got any doubtfuls? No? Good! Oh, and we'll observe *salāt* at the beginning of the day; again at lunchtime; and then once again just before we leave. Tell them to bring prayer mats with them as well."

"What about lunch?"

"I'll bring enough sandwiches and bottles of water for everybody."

They arranged to meet next at Grace Road cricket ground, Milligan Road, Leicester, on 7th June, when Leicester County Cricket Club were scheduled to play Surrey, and then they went their separate ways.

♦♦♦♦♦♦♦♦♦♦♦♦♦♦♦♦♦♦♦♦♦♦♦

Friday, 8th May 2015

Just before seven in the evening, Alfred Wicken, his father, Reginald, and Norman Callow were sitting at their usual table in the corner of the bar of the Blue Boar, part-drunk pints of beer before them. The result of the General Election had been announced. David Cameron had been confirmed as Prime Minister.

"Bloody shame!" said Alfred.

"What is, Alfred?" mumbled Norman, struggling to shape words through partly paralysed lips.

"That Nigel Farage losing down south. Bloody good man!"

Norman shook his head.

"Don't agree. I'm glad the Conservatives won here."

Norman Callow was referring to the constituency of Pepynbridge Forest. In medieval times, it had been a Royal hunting forest. Now it was a stretch of rural East Midlands, just shy of the maximum permitted 5,000 square miles and comprising Corbury, with a population of around 10,000, several smaller towns, some fifty villages, the largest of which was Pepynbridge, and isolated farms and hamlets like Summerhay.

"What's his name?"

Callow reached into a pocket, drew out a folded newspaper, glanced at it and replied,

"Waters. Ralph Waters."

"Never heard of him!"

"Well, Alfred, I don't suppose you voted for him."

"Bloody right, I didn't! I voted UKIP."

"So did I," added Reginald. "Who is this…" he paused, struggling.

"Ralph Waters? He's a barrister. He's said that if he wins, which he has done, he's going to come and live in Pepynbridge."

"Another bloody lawyer in the village," broke in Alfred. "One's too many! That Gordon Slim's nothing but trouble. Poking his nose into things since he arrived here last year. They always want to take over, these incomers." It was a theme the others had heard before and Reginald deftly moved the conversation on.

"Been a good spring, Alfred."

"Yeah, not bad. April was dry, but we're having the rain now. Crops are looking well…"

In Hall Close, Gordon, Sylvia and Roger Slim were eating supper around the kitchen table. Tall and good-looking, Gordon was a successful barrister, practising in London where he had a flat, but working from home whenever he could. His wife, Sylvia, equally tall and good looking, lived full-time in Hall Close where they had moved from London the year before. Their son, Roger, who had inherited Sylvia's looks, attended Corbury School, a fee-paying secondary school as a day boy. There was no bus service, so Sylvia did the twice daily twenty mile round journey to ferry Roger there and back. In her spare moments, she was writing an historical novel on a laptop at the kitchen table about John Russell, a courtier of King Henry VIII with Northamptonshire connections.

"We have a new MP," observed Sylvia. The septuagenarian member for the safe Conservative seat had retired from the House of Commons at the end of the previous Parliament.

"Yes! Ralph Waters," replied Gordon. "I voted for him."

"So did I. Know anything about him, Gordon?"

"He's a highly successful commercial silk in his fifties and a member of my Inn. Gossip has it that his briefs are generally marked with six figures. There's also talk in the Temple that he's made a lot of money from property deals."

"Dad?"

"Yes, Roger?"

"What are your briefs marked?"

"Nothing like as much as his, Roger. But I work in a less lucrative field. Common Law. Road accidents. Old ladies falling down in supermarkets. That kind of thing. Waters practises in the Commercial Court in London, acting for major commercial players. International disputes. Big money."

"Do you know him?" asked Sylvia.

"By sight, but not to speak to. Short; slight; I would even say delicate; silver-haired, with fine hands and a very precise manner of speaking."

"Someone in the village shop said that he was going to come and live in Pepynbridge."

"Yes, at weekends. Alastair's going to let him Coronation Cottage on the Estate."

"Married?"

"No! Gay. And he's got a partner. A retired French rugby union player called, if I remember rightly, Pascal Legrand. He's in his thirties. Big chap and very fit. Ralph has set him up with a personal fitness centre in Gray's Inn Road. It's doing well, I've heard."

"And is this Legrand going to come and live here too?"

"I would think so. At weekends anyway."

"And how's that going to go down in the village? With people like Alfred Wicken?"

"Not well, I would imagine. Especially as Legrand's a black African."

Sylvia drew in her breath sharply. An image of Herbert Onion floated across her mind.

"Pepynbridge does seem to attract odd-balls," she said.

"It's all a challenge, darling. All a challenge."

"I wonder if Alfred Wicken knows."

"No idea, but when he does, expect fireworks."

"Do you know when they're moving in?"

"Yes, I do. Alistair and I were discussing it the other day. Coronation Cottage has been empty for several years and needs renovation. It should be ready by early November."

"In time for Bonfire Night," cut in Roger, mischievously, "and fireworks."

All three laughed gently.

♦♦♦♦♦♦♦♦♦♦♦♦♦♦♦♦♦♦♦♦♦♦

Monday, 25th May 2015

For Ash, May passed uneventfully. He attended choir practices and Sunday services. On Saturday and Sunday afternoons, he played cricket for the Academy and Pepynbridge Firsts, both at home and away, and continued to shine. He attended the *IstishhadUK* meetings every Friday afternoon with Zed and the others. Meanwhile, the friendship between Sophie and Leela developed and deepened. They sat next to each other on the bus to and from Medborough and spent most Saturdays together; either at Summerhay or at the Maliks' home in Abbey Gardens.

Monday, 25th May, had been cloudy and cool. By the evening the sun made a tentative appearance, breaking through the overcast. After choir practice, Sophie said to Leela and Ash,

"Why don't we go to the Blue Boar pub?" Leela registered concern. "Oh, don't worry, Leela," said Sophie. "We won't go inside. There's a garden with tables outside and we can drink out there. And don't worry! I don't mean alcohol. They sell lovely fruit juices."

They walked through the archway between the Rectory and Abbey Hall onto Station Road and turned right towards the Blue Boar. They found a free table in the garden and Sophie asked what the others would like to drink. Then she went inside. As she approached the bar, she caught sight of her father, Alfred, sitting at a table in the corner of the room with her grandfather, Reginald Wicken, and Norman Callow.

"Hello, Sophie!" Alfred said. "Don't see much of you these days. What's your problem?"

"Hello, Dad! I don't have a problem. I just don't choose to come and see you and you know why." Alfred grunted and took a pull at his pint of beer.

"Still dancing, are you?"

Sophie went to ballet classes in Medborough once a week, but she knew that her father was not referring to that, but to the night last July when she had danced naked alone on the lawn at Pepynbridge Farm, fantasising that Herbert Onion was dancing with her and that afterwards they had made love in her parents' bed. That had led to Herbert's trial and Norman Callow's intervention which had resulted not only in Herbert's acquittal, but in Sophie's attempted suicide and subsequent admission to the Pemberton Mental Health Unit.

Bastard! thought Sophie. The cause of it all, Maisie, my therapist has told me, has been your uncaring and bullying attitude to me all my life because I wasn't born a boy to help you run the farm and take it over from you when I grow up. And you simply can't let it go, can you? Here I am, still under the care of a psychiatrist for what happened last year and you think it's funny and clever to tease me about it. Bastard! She had been prepared by Maisie for an encounter like this. She turned her back and ordered three soft drinks at the bar.

"Bloody slag!" Alfred's voice was raised for the whole bar to hear.

"Alfred!" called the landlord from behind the bar. "Any more like that and you're barred! Understood?" There was no reply and Sophie did not turn to gauge her father's reaction. She paid for the drinks and, without looking in his direction, took them outside on a tray. In the garden, she said nothing of the encounter inside.

Subtly over the next three quarters of an hour, Sophie wove ties between herself and Ash. Leela realised what Sophie was up to, but welcomed it. She had grown fond of Sophie and thought that if she and Ash got together, it would be no bad thing, provided they respected Islamic proprieties. Proprieties that forbade an unmarried girl from being in the company of a man without a chaperone unless he was a close member of her family, which Ash was not. It would be alright if, like this evening, I'm with them, she thought, but I'm worried that, if their friendship deepens, they might not want me around.

Sophie went inside once more to buy soft drinks and spared her father no glance. Now, it was nearly eight o'clock and the sun was casting long shadows across the lawn. Sophie was sitting facing the door that led from the pub through the garden to the car park where she had noticed Alfred's Land Rover Defender. Ash and Leela were sitting opposite her, so they did not see Alfred emerge on his way to his vehicle. When he saw Sophie, he stopped and his eyes narrowed. The Maliks had become a familiar sight in the village and he recognised Ash and Leela from their backs. Sophie needed no telling of the thoughts now coursing through his mind. "Bloody wogs!" she could almost hear him saying. But he didn't, although he knew what Sophie was thinking as well as she did. Instead, his face reddening with anger, he made his way to his vehicle. As he drove past, he glared at them and made a V sign with his right hand. The others saw it as well as Sophie.

"Who's that?" asked Ash.

"My dad."

"So, what was that all about?"

"I've told you before that my dad's not very nice. As well as all his other faults, he's a racist. I'm sorry about that."

"Oh, don't worry. We're used to it, I'm afraid. Aren't we Leela?" Leela nodded. "Anyway, it's time for us to go home. Supper's at eight and it's that already. Sophie, I've really enjoyed this time together. We must do it again, okay?"

"Yes, we must!" replied Sophie.

They left the garden together. Ash and Leela turned up Abbey Way towards Abbey Gardens. Sophie called Marigold on her mobile, said she would be home by half past, retrieved her bicycle from the south porch of the Abbey and set off for Summerhay. As she went she reflected that, apart from her father's boorish behaviour which had hardly seemed to trouble Ash and Leela, it had been a successful evening. The more time she spent with Ash, the more she liked him. Sessions with Maisie were in Medborough on Thursdays. Sophie decided that she should tell Maisie about Ash. She had been warned not to enter any romantic relationship without discussing it first with Maisie. But she felt confident that there would not be a problem; confidence that would be born out on the following Thursday.

◆◆◆◆◆◆◆◆◆◆◆◆◆◆◆◆◆◆◆◆◆◆◆

Thursday, 28th May 2015

The Academy had broken up for half term at midday on Friday, 22nd May, so there had been no meeting of the *IstishhadUK* cell that afternoon. On the previous Friday, as the cell would not meet again until 5th June, Zed had asked that dead drops should be checked during half term. Ash avoided checking behind the statue of the Virgin Mary immediately before or after choir practice for fear of attracting unwelcome attention. However, on Thursday afternoon he slipped, he believed unseen, into the Abbey. He felt behind the statue, but there was nothing there. He stepped through one of the doorways into the sanctuary and started to walk down the chancel.

"Hello, Ash!"

The voice was familiar. Ash stopped. At the eastern end of both upper rows of choir stalls, there was a single stall for clergy with wings that partly concealed its occupant. From the clergy stall to Ash's left Herbert Onion stood up and stepped down into the chancel.

"Er, hello, Herbie!"

"Ash, I'm intrigued as to why you keep coming into the Abbey on your own."

"Keep coming in, Herbie?"

"Yes! From my study window in the Rectory I saw you come in here on your own twice in March and twice in April. When I saw you come in again this afternoon, I thought I'd discover why." Shit! thought Ash. I hadn't anticipated that. Of course, thinking about it now, it's obvious that, when Herbie's in his study, he'll want to keep an eye on the Abbey when it's unlocked and insecure. Mentally, he kicked himself. So, how should I respond? Unsure, he waited.

"I just wondered," continued Herbert, "whether you were coming in to meditate or even, dare I say it, to pray. I noticed that you've just come from the direction of the Lady Chapel, which is the chapel behind the altar we keep for quiet prayer. And of course," he added, throwing Ash a lifeline, "I know that Mary, or *Maryam* as she is called in the *Qur'ān*, is revered by Muslims as well as Christians."

Ash grabbed it.

"Yes! That's right, Herbie! How clever of you! I've been coming in here to pray."

"Well, in that case, Ash, don't you think we ought to have a chat?"

Thoughts crowded Ash's mind. It would be rude to refuse. And if, having lied about coming into the Abbey to pray, he did refuse; it might invite unwelcome questions requiring awkward answers. Better, he thought, to play along and see what happens.

"What, now?"

"No time like the present, Ash." Herbert looked at his watch. "It's four o'clock. I've nothing on for the rest of the afternoon. Come to the Rectory, eh?" Two minutes later, they entered Herbert's study. Ash, who had not been there before, looked with interest at the book-lined walls.

"You have quite a library, Herbie," he said.

"Yes, well, I've collected a lot over the years. This…" he said, waving at shelves that filled the whole of one wall, "…is all my musical stuff. And this…" he waved at the opposite wall, "…is all Christian history, theology and liturgy. And then, on either side of the door behind you is a mixture of secular history and biography, although as you can see there…" he pointed to a shelf in the stack to one side of the door, "…those are books on Islam."

As well as a translation of the *Qur'ān*, Ash noted works by Tom Holland, Scott Atran, Patrick Sookhdeo, Maajid Nawaz and Ed Husain. He reflected that Herbie might know as much, if not more, about Islam than he did and warned himself to be on his guard. Ash also noticed a looking glass above the door opposite a large knee-hole desk in front of a window looking onto Abbey Close. Herbie's chair was between the desk and the window, facing the looking glass. So that's how Herbie keeps his eye on the Abbey!

"Coffee, Ash?"

"Yes, please!"

"Milk and sugar?"

"Just milk, please."

Herbert called from the doorway to Julie to make them two mugs of coffee. Then, he closed the door.

"Please sit, down, Ash!"

Herbert indicated one of two wing armchairs in front and to each side of the desk. Ash sat in it and Herbert in the other.

"Could you be interested in Christianity?"

"What, to convert to it?"

"Not necessarily. Just to learn something about it. After all, I know from your parents that you attend a weekly prayer meeting at the Academy, so plainly you're religious. Am I right?"

"Yes, Herbie, you are. But I'm a Muslim."

"Of course you are. I know that. But if you're interested in one faith, it's not a bad idea to measure it up against others, just in case another one would suit you better."

That, thought Ash angrily, is just what I object to about Western culture. The idea that you can pick and choose your religion to suit yourself, as though faiths were displayed for sale on a supermarket shelf. That's heresy. But, I must take care to conceal the strength and nature of my commitment to Islam. So, he said,

"Herbie, that sounds reasonable. After all, I'm only young and..." he added with an irony, necessarily lost on Herbert, "...with luck, I've got a long life before me."

"Quite!"

There was a light knock on the door and, at Herbert's bidding, Julie entered with two mugs of coffee, which she placed on the desk and left, closing the door behind her.

"Okay!" said Ash. "So, what about Christianity, then?"

Herbert rose from the wing armchair and settled behind the desk.

"Let's start with the Bible; what the *Qur'ān* calls The Book. Now, if you don't mind and provided it won't confuse you, I'm going to use English, rather than Arabic, names. So, Jesus instead of *'Īsā*; Gospel instead of *Injal*; Moses instead of *Musa* and so on. Are you alright with that?"

"Yes!"

"Good! Now have you ever read anything from the Bible, Ash?"

"Only at RE lessons at school. Not much, anyway."

"Alright then. The Christian Bible is divided into two parts. The Old Testament or Hebrew Bible and the New Testament. The Hebrew Bible is accepted as authentic by Islam, although Islam insists that its interpretation has been corrupted by the Jews. The prominent, but not the only feature of the Hebrew Bible are the first five books; Genesis, Exodus, Leviticus, Numbers and Deuteronomy. They contain instructions about how to lead one's life down to the tiniest detail. It's called Mosaic Law. Jews and some Christians believe that this was handed down to Moses by God. For them, it is therefore immutable. It cannot be changed and must be obeyed to the letter."

"Like the *Qur'ān*?"

"Exactly! Like the *Qur'ān*. The most general instructions are what are termed the Ten Commandments, which are found in both Chapter Twenty of Exodus and Chapter Five of Deuteronomy. But the Hebrew Bible contains two more commandments that Christians believe are the most important and override all the others. From Deuteronomy, Chapter Six..." Herbert reached for a copy of the Bible on the desk, opened it and read out, " 'Hear, O Israel: The Lord is our God, the Lord alone. You shall love the Lord your God with all your heart, and with all your soul, and with all your might.' And from Leviticus, Chapter Nineteen..." he turned back a few pages, " 'You shall love your neighbour as yourself.' Another feature of the Hebrew Bible is the writings of prophets, many of whom, as you said the other day Ash, are revered by Islam. The Hebrew

Bible also records the history of the Jews, reputedly from some fifteen hundred years before the birth of Jesus until shortly before he was born. With me so far, Ash?"

"Yes, I am. And what you've just said is familiar from my Islamic studies. But Herbie?"

"Yes?"

"Not all Jews stick by the rules in the Hebrew Bible, do they?"

"Not all, by any means," replied Herbert.

During the five years he had spent studying music at both the Junior and Senior Guildhall School of Music and Drama, he had made a number of Jewish friends, including Joshua Cohen, with whom Herbert had engaged in deep discussions about Judaism.

"Judaism," he continued, "is divided into different traditions. Progressive or Reformed Jews regard Mosaic Law as guidelines to be respected, rather than obeyed, which permits them to integrate with and participate in Western culture."

"So they believe in democracy?"

"Indeed, and they participate in it at all levels. A number of Progressive Jews sit in Parliament. On the other hand, there are other strands of Judaism, like Haredi and Hassidic Judaism, often referred to collectively as Orthodox, not a description they welcome…"

"Why not?"

"I don't know, but apparently they don't. Anyway, whilst many from those traditions play active roles in the public square, some at least hold to the view that the law expressed in the Pentateuch, or the Torah as they call it, the first five books of the Hebrew Bible, commands their obedience. As a result, socially their integration with non-Jews, or Gentiles, is correspondingly constrained."

"Like Islamists?"

"Yes, Ash, like Islamists. And like some Christian sects as well. We'll come back to Islamism in a moment. But first let's consider the New Testament. It contains the four Gospels, which narrate the life, teaching, death and resurrection of Jesus, whom Christians regard as the Messiah. Now there is no need for you to remind me that Islam does not accept that Jesus was divine, the Son of God, God in human form. Islam teaches that Jesus was a prophet like the other prophets; and the last one before Muhammad."

"Peace be upon him."

"Yes, well, without meaning any disrespect, it's important to understand that Christians and Jews do not recognise Muhammad as a prophet."

"I know that, but it's impossible for a Muslim to accept that he wasn't, Herbie."

"Ash, I appreciate that. But this afternoon, we're engaged on an academic journey of discovery, not an exercise in piety. We'll get on better that way. But, Ash?"

"Yes, Herbie?"

"I stress that you're free to accept or reject anything I say if you feel uncomfortable with it."

"Okay, then. What next?"

"Jesus endorsed Mosaic Law in general, but he rated the two commandments I've just mentioned, which Christians call the Two Great Commandments, to love God and to love your neighbour, above the rest of Mosaic Law. Jesus made the point, by his conduct as much as by what he said that the rest of Mosaic Law, for example about observing the Sabbath, was subordinate to the Two Great Commandments. And Jesus emphasised that in what we call the Sermon on the Mount in Matthew's Gospel, when he said this." Herbert did not need to refer to the passage. " 'In everything do to others as you would have them do to you.' We call it The Golden Rule. With the exception of a book called Revelation, which some Christians call The Apocalypse, the rest of the New Testament consists of letters written by apostles of Jesus to his followers after his resurrection and ascension into heaven. The most prolific letter-writer was Paul, a convert from Judaism. His argument is that Christians do not have to observe Mosaic Law as found in the Hebrew Bible, so long as they observe the Two Great Commandments. Paul insists that Jesus liberated men and women from the constraints of Mosaic Law. And here we come to the nub of Christianity. Christians believe that God indwells every human being; and that every human being has the choice as to whether or not to allow God to act through him or her. Hence, every human being is an autonomous or self-governing entity. It is for each Christian to decide whether what he or she does is consistent with The Golden Rule."

"And there are no rules as to how to interpret that?"

"No! Because every human being is different; and the variety of human behaviour is infinite. How Christians should behave depends upon the unique circumstances that we face whenever we have to decide upon our ethical response."

"Difficult!"

"Indeed! Or, as I prefer to put it Ash, challenging! The Two Great Commandments are simply stated, but can be fiendishly difficult to put into practice. And over the ages, human beings have sought to avoid making difficult ethical choices by embracing a series of rules or, if you prefer, an ideology that claims to meet every eventuality. The trouble is, no ideology can do that and rigid adherence to one can lead to terrible evil."

Ash was intelligent enough to discern where Herbert was leading.

"So does that explain the evil of, say, Fascism?"

"It does!"

"And Communism?"

"Yes!"

"And Islam?"

"That depends, Ash."

"Upon what?"

"Upon how Muslims view their faith."

"What do you mean, Herbie?"

"Well, Ash, just as many Jews regard Mosaic Law as guidelines to be respected, rather than strictly obeyed, so there are many Muslims, who do not live their lives in strict accordance with *Shari'a*; the law laid down in *Qur'ān*. Like your parents, for example?"

That's one of my problems, reflected Ash, they're *kafirun*. But what he said was,

"That's true, Herbie."

Herbert continued,

"And there are Muslims who sit in Parliament and serve in Government. But Muslims who believe that Islam should determine political and social, as well as personal life, hold that *Shari'a* should govern how societies are run; and that how societies are run cannot be decided by humans. Governance by God, theocracy; rather than governance by people, democracy. It's called Islamism or Political Islam."

Ash nodded and said,

"So what's the difference between Islamism and Orthodox Judaism?"

"The difference, Ash, is that the aim of Islamism is to establish a caliphate stretching from Pakistan to Southern Spain and *Shari'a* throughout the world. Orthodox Judaism harbours no such imperial ambition."

Herbert remembered the many conversations he had had with Joshua Cohen and added,

"Jews care for humanity, Ash. They would like everyone to acknowledge the existence of the one God, but do not regard themselves as entrusted with a mission to convert non-believers. They simply wish to be left alone to practise their faith in peace."

"So Islamism is like Fascism and Communism?"

"That, Ash, is for you to judge."

"But what do you think, Herbie?"

"As I've already said, I think that rigid adherence to a fixed ideology, however well-meaning and well-crafted, inevitably results in evil, as we witnessed last January in Paris; and before that in America on nine eleven and in London on seven seven."

Ash felt Herbert's dark brown pupils, disconcertingly magnified by his over-large, black-rimmed spectacles, boring into his own, challenging him. If I walk out now, he thought, it would send a signal to Herbie upon which, given the current concern about Islamism following Paris and the campaign by Islamic State in Iraq and Syria, he may well feel bound to act. So, I have to stay and engage.

The significance of Ash's ruminative pause was not lost on Herbert. There's a struggle going on there, he thought, and given his age, I'm not surprised. The question is: how far in is he? And was he really going into the Abbey, as he said he was, to pray? There's a conundrum here. My hope is to convert him to Christianity, but, at the same time, I should be alert to something more sinister that might lie deep in this clever young man; a young man who, it seems to me, is serious about Islam, but nevertheless was surprisingly readier than his sister to accept my invitation to join the choir. I'm going to persist with him, but not today.

"Ash, that's probably enough for the moment. Have you any questions on what I've said so far?"

"No, I don't think so. What you've said has taken me by surprise and I'd like to think about it."

"That's fine. Will you come again?"

"Yes, I'll come again. When?"

"How about in a fortnight's time? Thursday, the eleventh of June at six o'clock?"

"Yes, alright."

"And…" Herbert reached over to a slim, pocket-sized volume on his desk, "…this is a copy of the New Testament and the Psalms. I suggest that before we next meet, you read Matthew's Gospel. It was written by a Jew for Jews, so the way in which the author strives to demonstrate that the coming of Jesus Christ fulfilled prophesies in the Hebrew Bible may resonate with someone familiar with the Qur'ān."

I am, reflected Ash, entangled like a fish in a net. To maintain my cover, I have no alternative but to agree. Zed, you'll be proud of me!

"Of course, Herbie! Thank you." Ash took the slim volume and left.

In the looking glass Herbert watched Ash walk past the Abbey, curiosity coloured with unease, although he couldn't quite put his finger on anything concrete. He did not want to believe that this pleasant young man, with a sweet tenor voice and a good brain, was mixed up in Islamic extremism, but he could not rule it out.

◆◆◆◆◆◆◆◆◆◆◆◆◆◆◆◆◆◆◆◆◆

Saturday, 30th May 2015

Sophie's mobile rang, rousing her from sleep. It was half past eight on Saturday morning and she had watched television till past midnight. The ringing persisted. She rolled over and gathered her mobile from her bedside table.

"Yeah?"

"Hi! It's Ash!"

"Oh! Hi Ash!"

"You still in bed?"

"Yeah. Late night."

"Out?"

"Nah! Out in Summerhay? You've got to be joking."

"Listen! It's half term. There's no Academy cricket match today. Mum's lending me her car. Why don't we go out for the day?"

"Where?"

"Anywhere you like?"

"I didn't know you drove."

"Yeah! Passed my test last December."

"When's your birthday?"

"Twenty-fifth of October. When's yours?"

"I shall be sixteen on the twenty-seventh of July. What time do you want to go out?"

"Any time."

"Is Leela coming too?"

There was a pause before Ash replied,

"I haven't asked her."

"Don't you think you should?"

"But, Sophie, this is England, not Pakistan. Boys and girls go out together here unchaperoned. Why should we be any different?"

"Okay, then. Be here by ten! Okay?"

"Yeah! Cool!"

Sophie showered and looked out of the window. It was overcast and, she guessed, fresh. She dressed in jeans, a fine cashmere sweater and denim jacket. Downstairs, Marigold was in the tiny kitchen. Of medium height and slim, with dark hair pulled back into a bun that accentuated her angular features, she looked older than thirty two; the legacy of coping for years with a demanding, bullying and drunkard of a husband.

"Breakfast?"

"Thanks Mum. Mum, I'm going out for the day with Ash."

"Ash?"

"Yeah. Leela's brother. You know, the Pakistani boy who plays cricket and sings in the Abbey choir?"

Marigold stopped what she was doing and gazed out of the kitchen window at the small patch of untidy lawn that was all they had for a garden. Then she said,

"Dad won't like it."

"Don't tell me about it!" Sophie told Marigold about the encounter with Alfred at the Blue Boar. "But do you object, Mum?"

"No-o-o!" said Marigold hesitantly. "But be careful, Sophie!"

"Why?"

"It's just that you come from different cultures and..." she paused, then continued carefully, "...you know, men like that don't necessarily have the same attitude towards women as our men do."

She's thinking about those cases of Muslim men abusing girls in Rochdale and Oxford and places like that, thought Sophie.

"Don't worry, Mum! Ash isn't like that. And anyway, I can take care of myself."

Marigold turned and looked at Sophie. She was no longer a girl, but a young woman now, she thought. Five foot seven or so tall. Well developed breasts and hips; but slim and pretty, with blue eyes, long fair hair, pert nose and generous mouth. She takes after Alfred who, she remembered, had been good-looking when I first went out with him all those years ago, before drink had taken its toll.

"Yes, I'm sure you can, but be careful. Don't get hurt!"

Sophie walked over to her mother and kissed her cheek; something she hadn't done for a long time, reflected Marigold.

"Don't worry Mum!"

At ten, a Renault Clio drew up outside the cottage and Sophie went out to greet Ash. Her close fitting sweater flattered her figure, trim and firm from years of ballet dancing, and she noted Ash's approving glance from the driving seat.

"Hi, Ash! Are you coming in for a moment? Mum would like to meet you." Ash and Sophie went inside and after introductions and an exchange of courtesies, Sophie and Ash returned to the car.

"Where to?" he asked.

"Well, there's horse racing at..." and Sophie named a course in Leicestershire. "It's a point to point."

"What's that?"

"It's amateur racing, run by a fox hunt. It's good fun, especially on a day like today."

"Sophie, there's gambling at horse races. That's *harām*. Forbidden in Islam."

"But you don't have to bet, Ash. Lots of people don't."

"Yeah, and loads of Saudis own race horses. And they're Sunnis, like me." Sophie did not understand his reference to Sunnis, but thought that now was not the time to ask. Ash continued, "So that's alright then. Know how to get there?"

Sophie did and, an hour later, the car had been parked and they were standing below the stand. The first race was about to start.

"Ever been to a race meeting before, Ash?"

"Never."

"It's fun."

Later they bought hot dogs and Coca Colas and sat down at a picnic table.

"I'm surprised you're eating a hot dog," said Sophie.

"Why?"

"Well the sausage is pork and you're a Muslim, aren't you?"

"Yes, but not a serious one, Sophie."

"Aren't you?" Sophie raised her eyebrows in mock surprise. "But you're always going to those prayer meetings at the Academy on Friday afternoons, aren't you? With Zed and Ab, and Faz and Naz," she said, using the nick-names they went by at school. Ash was immediately on the alert.

"How do you know that?" he asked sharply.

Sophie laughed scornfully.

"Oh, Ash! Everybody at school knows about that. So what do you do in there? Pray?"

"Well, we do pray. But if I were a devout Muslim, I'd be praying five times a day."

"But none of the other Muslims at school do that," objected Sophie.

"No, that's true. We meet in the afternoon because we're older than the others and we're, like, a sort of club."

"Oh, so what do you talk about then at your club?" Sophie was smiling mischievously, her voice brimming with indulgent amusement.

"The usual things, I suppose. Football. Cricket, obviously. That sort of thing. Boy's talk. We're not fanatics or anything like that."

"I'm pleased to hear that. Mum wouldn't approve of me going out with a fanatic."

The conversation moved onto different ground and, once the tension engendered by the exchange had faded, onto the personal. They watched the racing until four o'clock, when they decided to go home. As they walked out of the race-course, Ash put his arm around Sophie's shoulder, feeling the softness of her upper arm under her cotton jacket and cashmere sweater. His boldness took him by surprise.

"Sophie, I like you."

"I like you too, Ash."

"Let's do something like this again, eh?"

"Yeah! Sure thing. I'd like that."

Back at Summerhay, when Ash leant over from the driving seat to kiss Sophie's cheek, she turned her head towards him and their lips met briefly. As they did so, what felt like a mild electric shock ran through Ash. It was unexpected, but, he thought, not unwelcome.

"See you tomorrow in church. And why don't you come to watch me playing cricket tomorrow?"

"In Pepynbridge?"

"No! We're playing away near Market Harborough."

"Can't. You go on the coach and I don't drive. I'll see you in church, anyway."

Sophie left the Clio and walked towards the door of the cottage. Ash watched her go and thought, I'd better tell Zed about using the prayer room; and, remembering Herbie, about the dead drop as well.

That night in bed in Abbey Gardens, Ash thought back over the time he had spent with Sophie that day. In his mind, he saw again the swell of her breasts through the thinness of her sweater and the slenderness of her legs encased in tight jeans and mentally he began to undress her. Since puberty, as an observant Muslim Ash had never been alone before with a girl of his own age. As his imagining progressed, he was surprised and disconcerted by the physical arousal that accompanied the images crowding his mind. As the strength of his attraction to Sophie took hold, he turned over in bed and buried his face in his pillow. And, what's more, he thought, she's nice with it. Sleep eluded him for a long time.

In bed at Summerhay, Sophie was also re-living the day. She decided that she liked Ash a lot. In fact, she admitted to herself, she would like to make love with him. She recalled the unsatisfactory couplings with boys her own age when she had been fourteen; and her fantasising about her and Herbie making a very different, but more interesting sort of love together last year. She had been a fool. She knew that now. An utter fool! And she wasn't going to make stupid mistakes like that again. Quite apart from the absence of any mutual fulfilment from any of those couplings, real or imagined, she had learnt, indeed it had been impressed upon her in The Templeton Mental Health Unit and later by Maisie, that anyone having sex with her before she was sixteen would be committing a crime. So she resolved, lying warmly but unaroused under her duvet, I'm not going to have sex with Ash, or anyone else for that matter, before my sixteenth birthday on the twenty-seventh of July, however tempting. A birthday which, she comforted herself, was not now that far off. You know what? she reflected, I'm growing up. Happy with her thoughts, Sophie fell into deep and untroubled slumber.

◆◆◆◆◆◆◆◆◆◆◆◆◆◆◆◆◆◆◆◆◆

Sunday, 31ˢᵗ May 2015

On the following morning, as High Mass progressed in the Abbey, Ash's gaze was persistently drawn to the features above the choir cassock in the stall opposite him; the long blond hair, the blue eyes, the pert nose, and the lips that had touched his own. And Leela, sitting next to Sophie, noticed. She knew that Ash and Sophie had been together for most of the previous day and she disapproved. Although since childhood Leela had never been alone in the company of a boy outside her immediate family, she read novels and was well aware of what went on between an unrelated boy and girl when no one else was around.

At the end of Mass, the choir recessed as it always did from the east end of the choir stalls down the chancel to the crossing and turned left towards the choir vestry in St Aidan's Chapel. As soon as the choir reached it, its members broke ranks and Leela saw that Ash had joined Sophie. In the vestry, they chatted together in low voices and left together. Leela followed them out of the Abbey and caught up with them.

"Hi!" she said, brightly.

"Hello Leela!" Sophie's voice was warm and friendly. She talked to her about the service and the music they had performed. Ash stood silently to one side. He wishes I wasn't here, thought Leela.

"Coming home, Ash? Lunch will be ready," Leela said after a while.

"Yes, but not for lunch. Pepynbridge are playing away. There'll be sandwiches on the team bus. 'Bye Sophie!"

"Bye! See you tomorrow on the bus to Medborough!"

Ash and Leela walked towards Abbey Gardens, while Sophie mounted her bicycle and began to pedal down Station Road towards Summerhay.

Ash changed into his whites and walked to the pavilion in Hall Park where the bus was waiting to take the Firsts to their away match. After her brother had left Abbey Gardens, Leela was thinking about him and Sophie. *It's obvious they're becoming close and I'm concerned about what might happen between them. After all, Ash is a Muslim. What bothers me is that he's not behaving as a good Muslim boy should. And yet I know he's observant, because he attends sessions every Friday in the prayer room with Zed and the others. Not only am I concerned, I'm confused as well. But I'll not say anything to Mum. At least, not yet. Not that Mum and Dad are observant Muslims anyway and they might not share my concern.* But, she reflected, *I am concerned because I'm very fond of Ash. Very fond indeed.*

◆◆◆◆◆◆◆◆◆◆◆◆◆◆◆◆◆◆◆◆◆

Friday, 5th June 2015

"Zed, we have a problem."

Ash was with the others in the prayer room. *Salāt* had been observed. Prayer mats had been rolled up and they were sitting drinking coffee.

"Why?"

Ash recounted how Herbert Onion had intercepted him as he had emerged from behind the reredos in the Abbey; and that Herbie had seen him going into the Abbey on his own on other occasions.

"You'll have to find a new dead drop."

"I already have, Zed. You know the bridge over the river in Pepynbridge?" Zed nodded. "Well, coming from Medborough, park just short of it. As you walk to the bridge, there's a path on the right that anglers use to go down to the riverbank. About thirty metres along the bank, there's a wooden seat on a metal frame?" Zed nodded again. "If you reach beneath the seat, there's a gap between the metal frame and the wooden slats. The slats are close together, so anything underneath them is hidden. I'll leave notes there under the left-hand end of the seat as you sit on it. Okay?"

"Yeah, fine! I'll inspect it this week and let you know what I think next Friday."

"And, Zed, there's something else."

Zed frowned. He resented unsolicited interventions in his leadership role.

"And what's that?" he enquired tetchily.

"Well, I've started to go out with Sophie Wicken. Know who I mean?"

"The blond girl in Year Ten?"

"That's her."

"Nothing wrong with that. It's what I told you to do. To get yourself a *kafir* girl friend."

"Yes, Zed. I know that. But she says the whole school knows about our meetings up here and she was asking me why we meet and what we do and what we talk about. I think people are getting suspicious."

"That's right, Zed. I've heard that too." The speaker was Ab; and Faz and Naz added assenting voices. Ab continued, "Zed, I think you've missed it because you're in

Year Thirteen and you don't have much to do with juniors."

"None of us in Year Thirteen do," observed Zed. "But that's serious. Or it could be. We'd better change where we meet." The others watched him expectantly. Then he said, "You know what? I don't think that we need to meet again this term. We've got to know and trust each other, haven't we?"

"Yes!" they chorused.

"Okay, then. Let's put off our next meeting until the training day on the twentieth of July" The others nodded. "You're all okay for that?" They confirmed that they were. "It'll be in Middlehay Wood. Ash, you said before that you know where that is and that you can borrow your mum's car, yeah?"

Ash nodded. "Should be alright. Otherwise, I'll cycle."

"To get there, Ash, go along the road from Pepynbridge to Corbury until you reach a turning to the right, signposted to Middlehay. Turn down there and after about two miles, there's a turning on the right with a Forestry Commission sign saying 'Middlehay Wood'. Turn up there. Take the first turning on the right along a track and, after a bit, someone will be waiting for you. Okay?" Ash nodded.

"We'll meet in the wood where I've just said at nine o'clock in the morning, okay? Have you all ordered your Fly Vests.? Not yet? Well, get on with it! And bring them with you. And you know the bits of paper I gave you with the video text on it?" More nods. "Bring them as well. And one more thing. Have you all got a prayer mat; or can you borrow one? Yes?" Nods. "Good! Make sure you bring one with you as we'll be there all day and we'll observe three ṣalawāt. All clear? Good! There'll be sandwiches and water laid on. Meantime, we'll either use the dead drops to keep in touch; or, if it's urgent, get hold of me here at the Academy. Ash, I'll check your new drop in Pepynbridge. If it's okay, I won't leave a note. I'll only do so if I think you need to find a different one. Okay"

Ash nodded. They finished their coffee, washed up, pronounced "*Allahu Akbar!*" and left.

◆◆◆◆◆◆◆◆◆◆◆◆◆◆◆◆◆◆◆◆◆◆◆

Sunday, 7th June 2015

In the Church's calendar, Sunday, 7th June, was the first Sunday after Trinity, when, apart from major festivals, the Church adopts green as its liturgical colour until the purple of Advent, four weeks before Christmas. Despite the lesser festive nature of Sundays after Trinity, Herbert made no concessions to informality. High Mass continued to be celebrated with all the panoply of Anglo-Catholic ceremonial; and the numbers of worshippers kept up. In August, when many would be on holiday, Herbert would dispense with the choir, although not the incense. On this Sunday, as the service progressed, Leela was unsettled by the almost constant gazing between Sophie and Ash.

Meanwhile, Zed, Raed, Waahid and Yaaseen were sitting at a table in a bar at the Grace Road cricket ground, home of Leicestershire County Cricket Club. The home side were playing Surrey under clear skies, but the four around the table were not interested. Cradling soft drinks in their hands, they were talking softly, so as not to be overheard.

One of the shortcomings of the way they arranged to meet was that there was no secure means of Raed letting Zed, Waahid and Yaaseen know in advance that there would be nothing to discuss at their next meeting. Today was just such an occasion. They agreed to meet again in the same bar on Sunday, 5th July, when Leicester would be playing Kent.

They finished their drinks and, as they were about to leave, Raed said,

"All sure you're not under surveillance, are you? You know what to look for?"

Each of them assured him that they were; that they knew what to look for.

"Good men. *Allahu Akbar!*"

"*Allahu Akbar!*" they replied and left.

Driving back to Medborough, Zed contemplated the mission and the planned meeting in July and felt a tide of excitement rising within him. It was what he wanted to do above all else. It helped, of course, that he was unmarried and did not have a girl friend. His parents and brothers and sisters would be sad that he would no longer be here for them, but they would be overjoyed, he felt sure, by the knowledge that he would be waiting for them to rejoin him in Paradise. And what's more, he thought, with luck his brothers and sisters might decide to follow in his footsteps when they were a little older. After all, the media was reporting that kids as young as fifteen were leaving England to join ISIL in Iraq and Syria. He paused on the way to inspect Ash's new drop on the bank of the River Pepyn and left no note.

Meanwhile, on the road to London, Raed was reflecting with satisfaction on the way things were going. He was pleased that they would only need to meet once more before their rendezvous in Middlehay Wood. All meetings carried risk. The more you gathered together, the more vulnerable you became to suspicion, or worse. Raed, who had undergone jihadist training in Yemen, was confident that, for the present, they were undetected. But that might not last. Constant vigilance was what he had been taught; and constant vigilance is what he practised; with applied ruthlessness in the face of any risk of discovery or betrayal. He had killed before and he would do so again without compunction if and when the need arose.

◆◆◆◆◆◆◆◆◆◆◆◆◆◆◆◆◆◆◆◆

Monday, 8th June 2015.

On Monday morning, Zed knocked on Francis Metcalf's study door.

"Come in!"

Zed entered.

"Mr Metcalf. I've come to thank you for letting me and my friends use the prayer room on Friday afternoons, but we've decided not to meet any more."

"Oh, why's that?"

"Well, as you know, this term I'm taking A Levels and the others are doing AS Levels and we're just too busy. We don't want to fluff our exams. You wouldn't want that, would you, Sir?"

Metcalf looked at Zed, his face expressionless, but inwardly irritated at Zed's unctuous tone. Was this a ploy?

He couldn't be sure. Zed might be telling him the truth, although he had never trusted the boy since he had arrived in Year 7. There was a deviousness about him; a self-assurance that he could deceive with impunity.

"Well, alright, Zed. That sounds sensible."

"Thank you, Sir," and Zed left.

Too busy to pray? wondered Francis Metcalf. He tapped the number of Andrew Hay's direct line into the telephone on his desk. When Hay answered, Metcalf reported what had transpired and his own uneasiness concerning Zed.

"Mr Metcalf, the question I ask is this. Do you think, or do you even suspect that this Zed...what's his name? Zaeem Zahra...that he's involved in Islamic fundamentalism? Islamism, it's called. The sort of thing that resulted in mayhem in Paris last January?"

"No, Sergeant Hay! I couldn't possibly say that I do. But I do wonder about him and just thought that you ought to know. If anything else occurs, I'll let you know."

"Thank, you, Mr Metcalf."

Andrew Hay put down the receiver and, looking out of the window over the tide of modern roofs that lapped around Medborough Police Station, he pondered for a while. Obviously something had aroused Metcalf's mistrust. In Hay's line of work, instinct was an important tool, not to be ignored. He turned to his computer keyboard and started to type a report, with the names, dates of birth and home addresses supplied by Francis Metcalf of the five Muslim pupils who had been meeting on Friday afternoons. When it was finished, he secure emailed it to Chief Inspector Guy Richards at the regional office of the Eastern Counter Terrorism Intelligence Unit. An hour later, he received by secure email, copied to Medborough Police's chief constable, an acknowledgement and a copy of an email from Richards to Paul Evans, a chief inspector with the Counter Terrorism Command within the Metropolitan Police Service, otherwise known as SO15, with Hay's own report attached. Later still, Guy Richards telephoned Andrew Hay.

"Andrew, SO15 wants us to keep an eye on Zaeem Zahra."

"Close surveillance?"

"Yes! Just as a precaution for the time being. If nothing results, we'll call it off. I've spoken to Medborough's chief constable. He'll give you his formal authorisation. Have you got the manpower?"

"I believe so. I'll check."

"Then, yes please. A close watch. But unobtrusive."

"What about the others who were meeting in the room at the Academy?"

"Not for now! We'll see."

"Okay Chief."

In his office a few minutes later, the chief constable of Medborough Police handed Hay a written surveillance authorisation, signed by him. Hay returned to his desk and made a number of internal calls. Zed would be kept under close surveillance from the next day, Tuesday, 9th June, 2015, except when he was physically within the Academy campus.

◆◆◆◆◆◆◆◆◆◆◆◆◆◆◆◆◆◆◆◆◆◆◆◆

Tuesday, 9th June 2015

At half past eight on Tuesday morning, when Zed left the house in Medborough he shared with his parents, brothers and sisters, he took no notice of a red Toyota Yaris parked in the street. There were many similar cars parked there and, if he had bothered to look at the driver reading a copy of the weekly *Garavi Gujerat*, he would have seen a man of South Asian appearance like nearly everyone else who lived, not only in that street, but in the neighbourhood. As he always did, Zed caught a bus that would take him to the Academy from the corner of the main road. The man in the Yaris folded up his paper, spoke into a mobile, started his car and followed the bus. At the Academy, from another small car parked within sight of the gates another police officer watched Zed alight from the bus and walk through the Academy gates. Zed did not suspect that he was under surveillance. He had been trained to spot watchers, but whether his guard was down or whether those observing him were too adept, he failed to realise that he was now of interest to the security services.

◆◆◆◆◆◆◆◆◆◆◆◆◆◆◆◆◆◆◆◆◆

Thursday, 11th June 2015

It was warm and close when Ash walked from Abbey Gardens to Abbey Close, skirted the Abbey and rang the front door bell of the Rectory. Herbert opened the door and welcomed him in. They turned right from the hallway into the study.

"Julie's making coffee. Alright for you, or would you prefer tea?"

stop him from hitting my wicket. And I cannot disengage and walk off the field of play, because if I do, he'll suspect I'm an Islamist.

"I'm not sure what to think," Ash said cautiously. Herbert sensed from his delay and calculated reply that Ash was either confused or, more probably because he was bright, being deliberately obtuse. An occasional fly fisherman, Herbert decided not to strike. It was too soon. He did not want to frighten his prey under the weeds.

"That's alright, Ash. We may return to Nawaz later. Now, back to Matthew's Gospel. What about the virgin birth?"

"There's something about that in the *Qur'ān*." Ash frowned. Then his features cleared as he remembered. "It's in the *sura* called *Maryam*."

"*Sura* nineteen," supplied Herbert.

"Yes! It says how an angel came to Mary and said that he would give her a son and she asked how could that happen since no man had touched her? And the angel, who looked like a man, said that it was easy for God and then she conceived Jesus and gave birth to him under a palm tree."

"And the Resurrection? What about that, Ash?"

Again Ash had to think. He recalled a discussion about this in the prayer room, when Zed had emphasised that whilst Jesus was special, a prophet and an apostle of *Allah*, he was not divine just because…and then it came to him.

"The *Qur'ān* says somewhere that *Allah* is so powerful that he can raise anyone from the dead if he wishes. I can't remember the *sura*…" Herbert consulted a paperback copy of the *Qur'ān* on his desk, adorned with an array of coloured and annotated highlighter flags.

"*Sura* forty-six, *ayah* thirty-three," he said.

"But that doesn't prove that Jesus was the Son of God, does it?"

"Well, that depends. It's what Christians believe for a number of reasons. But I don't want to focus on that. At least, not yet."

Ash eyed Herbert warily. I'm sure you're trying to convert me. Okay, Reverend, so bowl the next one!

"Have you any objection to talking about Islam, Ash?"

"Not at all!"

"What would you say is the defining characteristic of Islam?"

"The *Shahada*? There is no god but *Allah*; and Muhammad is the messenger of *Allah*."

"Apart from that?" Ash looked puzzled. "What determines how an observant Muslim should behave?"

"The *Qur'ān*?"

"Yes. The *Qur'ān* and the *hadith*, the sayings and teaching of Muhammad. That's the essence of your faith, is it not? *Allah*, as transmitted and elucidated by Muhammad, has laid down the law by which all observant Muslims should live. That's right, isn't it?" Ash nodded. Herbert continued, "Which is why Islamism has a problem with democracy, isn't it? Islamism holds that since *Allah* has prescribed how people should live, men and women have no right to make laws that contradict the *Qur'ān* and the *hadith*. That's true, isn't it?"

"Yes! As I understand it, that's right."

"Which is like the first five books of the Hebrew Bible, isn't it? You remember we discussed this last time? Have you read any of those five books, Ash? The Pentateuch?"

"No! But we've been taught something about them in RE and I've discussed them with Muslim friends of mine."

"Okay. Now, back to Matthew's Gospel. I'm going to chapter twelve, where Jesus and his disciples pluck ripe wheat on the Sabbath and begin to eat it because they're hungry. You remember that? Look it up, if you like."

"No! I can remember that."

"Well, in Mosaic Law the fifth of the Ten Commandments says this." Herbert opened a Bible on his desk and found the place in Exodus, Chapter 20. " 'Remember the Sabbath day and keep it holy. For six days you shall do your labour and do all your work. But the seventh day is a Sabbath to the Lord your God; you shall not do any work.' And, Ash, it extends that to all members of a household. Now in Luke's Gospel, Jesus heals a man with a withered hand; and a woman who had been crippled for eighteen years, probably by arthritis; and another man with dropsy; all of them on the Sabbath and he was criticised by Jewish leaders for doing so. Because, although Jews respect the sanctity of life and will always act to preserve it, it was against Mosaic Law to heal on the Sabbath. The point Jesus was making was this. The Two Great Commandments...remember those? To love God and to love your neighbour?"

"I do."

"Well, the point that Jesus was making when he healed on the Sabbath, was that the Two Great Commandments, which he endorsed in chapter twenty-two of Matthew's

Gospel, remember...?" Ash nodded. "...was that they override the rest of Mosaic Law. Do you follow me so far?"

"Yes, I do! But I don't see where you're leading."

"You will in a moment. If the Second Commandment is to love your neighbour, how do you know, in any given situation, how to apply it? Because, remember, there are no guidelines, Ash. But Jesus tells a good parable about how to recognise and love your neighbour."

"You mean the Good Samaritan? We've been taught about that in RE. But it's not in Matthew's Gospel."

"Yes, I do mean the parable of the Good Samaritan. It's in Luke's Gospel. The priest and the Levite feared that the man lying injured by the side of the road was dead. If he had been, it would have been against Mosaic Law to touch him. If they had, they would have been condemned as unclean. Had they known he was alive, they would not have broken the Law by going to his aid, but they didn't investigate. They passed by, leaving him for dead. Samaritans were despised by the Jews. Yet it was the Samaritan who obeyed the commandment to love his neighbour by caring for the injured man. You see, Ash, that's the problem. It's easy to live by a set of rules where everything is black and white; where every problem is solved by consulting a rulebook. But life's not like that."

"But that's what attracts me about Islam, Herbie. I need a clear set of rules about how to behave. Then I know where I stand."

"But to live in a society where people are not allowed to change the rules that govern them is totalitarian. It's like fascism and communism."

"Herbie, we discussed that last time, didn't we? But surely there can be good totalitarianism as well as bad; especially where the rules are made by *Allah*?"

"If *Allah* did make them, Ash. Non-Muslims don't believe he did. Many non-Muslim scholars consider that the *Qur'ān* was invented by Muhammad to justify his conduct. That it was his manifesto for conquest. The early verses, which, as you know, are the ones you find at the back of the *Qur'ān*, are non-violent, because when they were written or proclaimed, Muhammad's followers were few and he lacked the capacity to engage in military conflict. The violent ones, like the one that is termed 'The Sword Verse'..."

"*Sura* nine, *ayah* five," interrupted Ash, "the one about killing polytheists."

"Yes, that's the one! *Suras* advocating violence like that only occur later in the *Qur'ān*, when Muhammad was plundering caravans from Mecca and was on his way to capturing Mecca. Some scholars conclude that, far from the *Qur'ān* being dictated by God, or *Allah*, to Muhammad in the Hira cave before he embarked upon his mission, it was composed by Muhammad as he went from being just a preacher with a few disciples to conqueror most of the Arabian peninsular, in order to justify the brutal means he employed to do so."

Ash opened his mouth to protest, but Herbert waved it away.

"Just let me finish, Ash, and then you can have your say. Whatever the provenance of the *Qur'ān*, no set of rules can possibly cover every dilemma that confronts us in life. After Jesus ascended to heaven, and you may not accept that he did…" Ash shrugged his shoulders. "You remember Paul?" Ash nodded. "Paul spread the Gospel throughout the eastern Mediterranean as far as Rome. And what Paul preached was that if human beings wanted to have a relationship with God, they should ignore Mosaic Law. All they needed to do was to obey the Two Great Commandments. That meant that anybody could become a Christian. Now you see where I'm going? Your turn now!"

"Herbie, you're suggesting, are you, that the *Qur'ān* has taken Muslims back to where we were before Jesus came?"

"Well, where Judaism had been, anyway. I'm suggesting that's precisely where strict and uncritical adherence to the *Qur'ān* takes Islamists. But, as we discussed last time, moderate Muslims don't subscribe to that view."

Herbert paused for moment and decided to draw the conversation to a close.

"Ash, you wanted to say something earlier? No? Alright. Now, I want you to reflect on what I've said today and then come again and tell me what you think. I'd like to have another discussion with you. Is that alright?"

The imperative that had brought Ash to Herbert's study that afternoon led him to agree to do so again. They arranged to meet at six o'clock on Thursday, 25th June and in the meantime Ash agreed, at Herbert's suggestion, to read Luke's Gospel and Paul's Letter to the Galatians.

As Ash walked home with the slim volume of the New Testament and Psalms in his pocket, he could not rid his mind of what Herbert had just said. For now he was not equipped to dismiss it as the load of nonsense, he was sure, any *imam* would. But he realised that, by their next meeting, he was going to have to prepare a reasoned and coherent way of asserting, against what Herbert had said, the truth of what the *Qur'ān* and Muhammad, peace be upon him, had prescribed for mankind. And that, he sensed uneasily, was going to be quite a challenge.

When Ash let himself into the house in Abbey Gardens, only Leela was at home. She told him that Abi and Sabi had gone out to dinner with Dr and Mrs Maxey in Station Road.

"Where have you been, Ash?"

"With Herbie at the Rectory."

"What did you go there for?"

"Herbie wanted to talk about Islam and Christianity."

"He suggested you went, did he?"

"Yes, he did!"

"Was that the first time you've been to see Herbie?"

"No! I went once before."

"Why?" Leela sensed Ash's reticence. "Go on! Why? I'm interested."

"Because he'd seen me going into the Abbey at odd times when there was no service or choir practice and he wanted to know why."

"So, what did you tell him?"

"Oh, it doesn't matter, Leela. Really, it doesn't."

"Well, I think it does, Ash. You're a Muslim and you've just spent...how long?"

Ash looked at his watch,

"Nearly an hour."

"...nearly an hour with a Christian clergyman. And not for the first time, you say. We're brother and sister. I think I should know why you were going into the Abbey when you had no need to."

Unaware of Herbert's duty of confidentiality, Ash thought it better for Leela to hear it from him, rather than from someone else. So he said reluctantly,

"I told Herbie that I was going into the Abbey to pray."

"To pray?" Incredulity vied with contempt in Leela's voice. "To pray? But you're a good Muslim, Ash. Why on earth would you be going into a Christian church to pray?" She emphasised "pray".

"Well, maybe I'm not such a good Muslim, Leela."

"Oh, Yes you are Ash! Otherwise you wouldn't have gone to the prayer room after school every Friday with Zed and the others." She waited for a reply, and when there was none, she insisted, "Would you Ash?"

"Leela, it's a private matter. I really don't want to talk about it, okay?" Leela looked at her brother through narrowed eyes. There was, she was now sure, something very odd going on; something she didn't understand. And she began to feel just a little afraid.

"Okay, Ash," she said, resignedly.

"What's for supper?"

"*Biryani.* Mum's made it. It just needs warming up. When would you like it?"

"I've got some studying to do." Ash looked at his watch. It was a quarter past seven. "Eight o'clock?"

"Fine! So have I."

Later, as they sat at the table eating, Leela said,

"Ash?"

"Yes?"

"You're going out with Sophie, aren't you?"

"Sort of."

"What do you mean, sort of?"

"Well we went to the races the Saturday before last. It was cool."

"But you fancy her, don't you. I've watched you in the Abbey, looking across at her and smiling."

"She's a nice girl, Leela."

"If she were a good Muslim, she wouldn't be alone with you, would she?"

"No, she wouldn't! But she's not. She's a Christian."

"But as a good Muslim, Ash, don't you think it's immoral the way that girls and boys get together, like you are with Sophie? Shouldn't I be with Sophie when you're with her, Ash? That's our culture, isn't it?"

This is getting difficult, thought Ash. Living a double life is not easy. But, ironically, a word he understood, here I am, a better Muslim than Leela and a far better Muslim than Dad and Mum, having to justify my behaving in a way that is not only inconsistent with my religious principles; but contrary to my Islamist convictions. He was silent, while Leela watched him. Then he thought of Sophie and how he was attracted to her and, he admitted to himself, of what he hoped he could do with her one day soon. And he comforted himself that even if his going with her was contrary to his convictions, it was all of a piece with his deep cover. He sighed.

"Leela, we are living in England. Maybe we have to adapt our faith and our conduct to the culture we inhabit. Especially when we're living in a quiet English village where we're the only Muslims. Perhaps we shouldn't cut ourselves off from what's going on around us. After all, you're a member of the choir and attend Mass, even if you don't worship when you're in the Abbey."

Leela looked at him scornfully, screwed up her features and shrugged her shoulders. She is not, thought Ash, persuaded by what I've just said. And that, Ash reflected, is the problem for an ethnic outsider like me leading a double life in a small, rural, mono-cultural community like Pepynbridge. Easy enough to live under cover in the midst of a South Asian community in a big city like Medborough, or London, or wherever. But in Pepynbridge, it's proving well nigh impossible. The trouble is, he acknowledged, I'm too far in to pull out. It would be far too dangerous to resign from *IstishhadUK*, even if I wanted to; which I don't. My commitment to *jihad* is undiminished. Nor can I pull out of my involvement with the Abbey choir; and I certainly don't want to abandon my relationship with Sophie; not yet, anyway. Not until...he halted that line of thought. Anyway, if I resign from the choir and finish my friendship with Sophie, it might provoke awkward questions in Pepynbridge about me and my role, which is the last thing Zed would want. So, he concluded, I'm stuck where I am and I'd better make the best of it.

Ash and Leela finished their meal in silence and Ash went up to his room and accessed Islamist websites before going to bed.

◆◆◆◆◆◆◆◆◆◆◆◆◆◆◆◆◆◆◆◆◆

Sunday, 21st June 2015

Over the next ten days, Leela and Sophie sat next to each other chatting happily on the bus to and from Medborough. On Saturday, 13th June, Ash had played cricket for the Academy Firsts and Leela and Sophie had gone again to The Bathing Place and had read books in the gazebo. They had not swum, although Leela had brought her swimming costume. The weather in June had disappointed and the water, Sophie had assured her, was cold. When Leela had dipped her hand in the river, she had agreed. On Sunday, 14th June, they had watched Ash playing cricket in Hall Park. And on Saturday, 20th June, they had gone again to The Bathing Place and read, but not swum.

Leela welcomed and valued her time with Sophie, but in her spare moments she could not rid her mind of the conversation she'd had with Ash when he had returned from seeing Herbie. She did not share her misgivings about her brother with Sophie but, by Sunday, 21st June, she could contain them no longer. Mass in the Abbey was over and Leela had returned home. So had Ash, but he had not stayed as Pepynbridge Firsts were playing away. Abi was mowing the small patch of grass behind the house with a Flymo. Sabi was in the kitchen preparing the midday meal. When Leela said she had something important she wanted to discuss with her, Sabi washed and dried her hands and they went into the sitting room. There, sitting either side of the empty fireplace, Leela voiced her concerns. She recounted all that she knew: Ash's visits to the Abbey, apparently to pray; his deepening romantic attachment to Sophie; his protestations about not being an observant Muslim at odds with his attendance at the prayer meetings at the Academy.

"Which seem to have stopped now for some reason, but Mum, he told us about them didn't he?" Sabi nodded. "What worries me," Leela continued, "are not only the inconsistencies, but Ash's reluctance to talk about them. I just have the feeling that he's hiding something from me and from you and from Dad."

She paused, wondering whether she should spell out her growing fears. Sabi watched and waited, conscious that her daughter had something more to say. Leela looked at her mother and thought what a wise, sensible and loving person she was; and so she was emboldened to say,

"You know Mum, I think that Ash is living a double life. And you know what that might mean?"

"Leela, I do. I think we ought to talk to Dad, don't you?"

And Leela, greatly relieved, agreed.

When Abi came in from the garden, the three of them sat down to the salad that Sabi had prepared and Sabi said,

"Abi, Leela's been talking to me about Ash and I think that you ought to hear what she's being saying."

"Alright, Leela," said Abi. He smiled at Leela affectionately, but his clinical instincts were aroused. "What have you to say, then?"

Leela repeated what she had said to Sabi. When she had finished, Abi said nothing for a while, finishing his salad. Then Sabi made a pot of tea and they went into the sitting room. After they had sat down, Abi said,

"Leela, I think you have been absolutely right to share your concerns with Mum and me. Paris is fresh in our minds and I understand your fears and why you harbour them. I don't suppose for a moment that they'll be realised, but Ash's conduct since we've moved to Pepynbridge has struck me as odd. I think I should have a chat with Richard Maxey. He knows a lot about that sort of thing from when he practised in Newham. And his years as a GP have made him wise about the ways of people. If he thinks we're

worrying about nothing, he'll say so. But if he doesn't..."
and his voice tailed off as, for a moment, he contemplated
the dreadful prospect that his son had been corrupted by
Islamism.

Abi went to a telephone and tapped in a number.

"Hello, Richard! Abi here. There's something I'd like to
chat to you about. There's no match in Hall Park this
afternoon. Mind if I pop round to see you? No? Thank you!
'Bye!"

An hour later, Abi was sitting in the Maxeys' sitting
room in their cottage in Station Road. Over coffee, Abi told
Richard Maxey of Leela's fears and her reasons for them.

When he had finished, Richard Maxey said,

"Well Abi, as you know, I came across Islamism when I
was in Newham. There was a lot of it going on down there
then and, sadly, it resulted in someone being murdered. But
that was just a random act. Not part of a wider conspiracy
like al-Qaeda or ISIL. Abi, how much do you know about
Islamism; or jihadism as it's sometimes called?"

"Only what I read in the Press. I've never come across it
professionally."

"Well, in the light of what you've told me about Ash,
perhaps you'd like to know a little more?"

"Richard, I should welcome that. Thank you."

Richard Maxey paused, gathered his thoughts and
began.

"Islamism, like any simplistic ideology, can hold a
powerful attraction for the young; by which I mean anyone
from ten or twelve upwards into their mid-twenties;
vulnerable, often diffident youngsters seeking certainties.
They are easy prey for the really serious players. The sort of

people who were behind the atrocities in London, Madrid and Paris. Youngsters as young as fourteen are going off to fight for Islamic State in Syria and Iraq. They're foot soldiers in a master plan devised by some very dangerous people, like the leaders of Islamic State or ISIL, *al-Qaeda* in the Arabian Peninsular, and Boko Haram in Nigeria. Islamism offers simple solutions to what a Muslim commentator called Husain Haqqani, a former Pakistani ambassador to the United States, writing in the *Daily Telegraph* last January described as...I kept a copy of his piece..." He drew a cutting from a pile of papers on a table beside him, found the place he wanted and continued, "...'the collective Muslim narrative of grievance'. Many of us when we were Ash's age sought simple solutions to clean up the mess we thought our parents' generation and the one before it had made of the world. That was the attraction of Lenin, of Mussolini, and of Hitler. Each promised Utopia in return for a blinkered and fanatical obedience to an ideology that brooked no challenge or criticism. Well, Islamism has the same appeal. Just as fascism and communism played upon grievances, so Islamism does the same, as I'm sure you know, Abi?"

"Richard, I do! In Lahore, it was thrust down our throats at school. The collapse of the Ottoman empire, the colonisation of the Middle East, India and Africa, the occupation of Egypt and Sudan, the foundation of the State of Israel, the suppression by Moscow of Muslim majorities in the Caucasus and the Western invasions of Afghanistan and Iraq. It's deeply distressing and unwelcome. Islam can and should be about peace and harmony, not obsessed with grievance and revenge."

"It's a heady brew just as compelling as the humiliation of Germany by the triumphalist and vindictive Treaty of Versailles of nineteen nineteen," continued Richard Maxey. "It's hardly surprising that shy young men like Ash are attracted by Islamism. But even if Ash is, he's sensible enough and I very much doubt that he'd allow himself to be drawn into doing anything illegal. It's probably a passing phase he'll get over. And we can take comfort from the fact that at the moment there's no evidence that he has actually been recruited into anything like ISIL. That's right, isn't it, Abi?"

A relieved Abi replied,

"Yes, Richard it is. I'm so grateful to you for your analysis and I'm reassured that you think that there's nothing for Sabi, Leela and me to worry about. Thank you so much."

Abi left and, back in Abbey Gardens, he shared his re-assurance with Sabi and Leela. Like Abi, Sabi was ready to believe that her son was not involved in anything sinister. Leela was not so sure, but kept her own counsel.

Meanwhile, Richard tapped Jack Driver's home number into a telephone.

"Yes?"

"Jack, Richard here."

"Yes, Richard! What can I do for you?"

"Jack, will you be at choir practice tomorrow evening?"

"Of course!"

"Could you spare me a few moments afterwards?"

"Yes!" The tone was cautious. "Where?"

"At our cottage, if you wouldn't mind."

"Do I gather you would rather not go into detail on the telephone?"

"Yes!"

"I'll be there. Just after seven?"

"Fine!"

♦♦♦♦♦♦♦♦♦♦♦♦♦♦♦♦♦♦♦♦♦♦

Monday, 22nd June 2015

The following evening, Jack Driver was sitting in the Maxeys' sitting room. Tall, with a spare bony frame, large square head, bland, pale features and short, grey hair, Driver's pale grey eyes were focussed attentively on Richard Maxey as he repeated what Abi Malik had told him the previous afternoon.

"And what was the outcome of your conversation, Richard?"

"I re-assured Abi that it was probably just youthful enthusiasm and indiscretion."

"But, you're not sure, are you? Otherwise you wouldn't be speaking to me about it."

"No, Jack, I'm not. There's an element of subterfuge in Ash's presentation that I find disturbing. If he was just attracted by Islamism, he would be talking about it to his contemporaries to gauge their reaction to his new-found enthusiasm. But he's not. He attends mysterious prayer meetings with four other senior pupils at school, but is apparently unconcerned about joining the choir at St Aidan's and is happy to go out with Sophie, a Christian. It smacks of deceit and I ask myself, why deceive, unless it's for a purpose that he doesn't want to disclose. And if so, why doesn't he want to disclose it?"

"Why didn't you share your concern with Abi?"

"Because I don't want to create alarm within the Malik household. If I did and Ash is playing a double game, that would alert him, making it even more difficult to discover what he's up to. If he is!"

"Richard, I need to do some homework; legal homework. For example, if, which God forbid, Ash is involved in terrorism, we need to understand the implications. It's outside my normal field, so I need to do some research. I can do that at home on my computer. I'd rather do it there than in the office. Apart from anything else, I'm meant to account to my partners for every ten minutes that I spend at my desk. Chargeable units they're termed. I disapprove, but that's how it is these days. I shall be back in Pepynbridge on Wednesday evening for choir practice. Why don't I call in afterwards, like this evening?"

And so it was arranged.

◆◆◆◆◆◆◆◆◆◆◆◆◆◆◆◆◆◆◆◆

Wednesday, 24th June 2015

Two evenings later, a solemn Jack Driver was again sitting in Richard Maxey's sitting room.

"Richard, if Ash is mixed up with an Islamist or jihadist group intent on terrorism, then depending upon how far it's progressed, he could be in serious trouble." Driver unfolded a sheet of paper that he drew from a pocket. "Listen to this! 'A person commits an offence if, with the intention of committing acts of terrorism or assisting another to commit such acts, he engages in conduct in preparation for giving effect to his intention.' And, Richard, that conduct can include just the acquisition of information or articles. I read on; 'A person guilty of an offence under this section shall be liable, on conviction on indictment, to imprisonment for life.' That's Section Five of the Terrorism Act, Two Thousand and Six. Terrorism is defined by Section One of the Terrorism Act, Two Thousand. I've taken a copy for you, Richard."

He handed another sheet of paper to Maxey who studied it. Then Maxey said,

"So even if he's just been talking about a violent plot, he could be guilty?"

"It depends on how far it's progressed. If it's just been speculation: what if we do this? or, what if we do that? then probably not. But if, for example, he's been taught how to make or detonate an explosive device; or even how to conduct himself undercover, which you think he may be doing, then the answer could be: Yes!"

"What do you think we should do?"

"We have no firm information that Ash may be guilty of an offence under Section Five. We don't even have a well-founded suspicion that he is. He's been behaving oddly, but for all we know he may be acting out an adolescent fantasy. It would be premature, in my view, to report our concerns to the police. They probably wouldn't thank us if we did. After Paris, I imagine the security services are stretched as never before in detecting and preventing similar outrages in this country. No, what I think you and I must do is to keep an eye on Ash; and our ears open for any gossip about him in Pepynbridge."

"Sounds sensible, Jack. Maybe just a storm in a teacup, eh?"

"Maybe; but then maybe not." With which Driver left.

Over supper Richard Maxey told his wife, Mary, about his conversation with Jack Driver.

"Oh, Richard, here? In quiet, rural Pepynbridge? In Newham perhaps, but here in Pepynbridge?" Mary sounded incredulous.

"Well it hasn't happened yet, and it may never happen."

"I jolly well hope it doesn't."

"So do we all, darling. So do we all. But these are troubling times."

"They are, darling. They certainly are."

♦♦♦♦♦♦♦♦♦♦♦♦♦♦♦♦♦♦♦♦♦

Thursday, 25th June 2015

Following his last meeting with Herbert Onion, Ash had prepared carefully for their next encounter. He had read Luke's Gospel and Paul's Letter to the Galatians and decided that, rather than trying to justify Islam to an experienced and obviously clever clergyman, he would instead adopt an attentive and apparently receptive stance. It was with this in mind that, at six o'clock on a pleasantly warm Thursday evening, Ash rang the door-bell at the Rectory.

Herbert welcomed Ash in and they both went into the study where Julie had left two mugs of coffee and a plate of biscuits.

"Well, Ash," Herbert started, "have you read Luke and Paul's letter to the Galatians?"

"I have."

"Luke's Gospel, you probably gathered, is similar to Matthew; and indeed to Mark's Gospel. You remember I said that Matthew's Gospel was written by a Jew for Jews?" Ash nodded. "Well, Luke was not a Jew. He was probably a Greek and he was telling the story of Jesus from a non-Jewish perspective."

"Yes, Herbie! I discovered that." Herbert raised his eyebrows. "From Wikipedia," Ash explained. Herbert nodded approvingly and continued,

"And, of course, it's in Luke's Gospel that we find the Parable of the Good Samaritan, which we discussed last time. Another parable that's in Luke but not in Matthew is the Prodigal Son, where there are two sons and one is given his inheritance by his father and promptly squanders it. When he is destitute and returns home, his father rushes out to greet him and then holds a feast to celebrate his return. Remember?"

"Yes! And his older brother, who had stayed at home and had worked hard for his father, was upset because it was unfair."

"But was it unfair, Ash?"

"Yes, it was!"

"But the son who returned was sorry for what he had done, wasn't he?"

"Well, maybe, but he shouldn't have been rewarded by his father."

"But, Ash, that's not how Christianity sees it. If someone does something very wrong..." mentally Ash flinched "...but then repents; admits he has done wrong and seeks forgiveness, Christians hold that a loving God will do just that; and that we Christians should do likewise."

Herbert paused to let what he had said sink in. Then he said,

"What did you think of Galatians?"

"Well, it supports what you said last time about Christianity not being a rule-based religion as Judaism was when Paul wrote it."

"And as Islam, or at any rate Islamism is now, Ash, eh?"

"Yes, sure."

"Anything else?"

"Two things, Herbie. Paul stresses love a lot. And he talks about..." Ash glanced down at some notes he had made, "...he writes, 'it is no longer I who live, but it is Christ who lives in me'. What did he mean by that?"

"I touched on this the first time we chatted, Ash. He means what all Christians believe, or should believe, that every human being is made in the image of God. We are his children and so there is something inherited from God in each of us. To emphasise this, God came amongst us as Jesus, a human being, to demonstrate how he lives within us. We say that Jesus lives in us, but, despite what the *Qur'ān* says about Christians, we do not believe in three gods, but in one God; and that Jesus was God in a human body. So we believe that God indwells each human being and makes his nature evident when we demonstrate our love for others, as the Good Samaritan did."

Ash sat quietly, pondering this. He knew that the essence of Islam was encapsulated in the *Shahada*; that there was only one God and that Christian belief in three was heresy. But, consistent with the strategy he'd mapped out, he was not going to challenge what Herbert had just said. His reticence was not lost on Herbert.

"What was the other thing that struck you about Galatians?"

Again Ash glanced at his notes and opened the slim volume of the New Testament and Psalms that Herbert had lent him. He turned to Chapter Four of Galatians.

"Herbie, it's what's called here, 'The Allegory of Hagar and Sarah'."

"Ah, Yes! The mothers of Abraham's two sons. Sarah, Abraham's barren wife, as he thought, and Hagar, his Egyptian slave girl.   God had promised Canaan to Abraham and his offspring. When Sarah failed to conceive, Hagar persuaded Abraham to have a child with her and she gave birth to Ishmael. Then, miraculously, Sarah conceived and gave birth to Isaac. When Sarah saw Isaac playing with Ishmael, she told Abraham to send Hagar and Ishmael away. Now, why did that strike you?" asked Herbert mischievously, correctly anticipating what Ash's answer would be.

"Because Ishmael is regarded as the father of the Arab nation; and it is written in the *Qur'ān* that God's House at Mecca was established by Abraham and Ishmael."

"Precisely! *Sura* two, *ayah* one hundred and twenty-five, and *sura* three, *ayahs* ninety-six to ninety-seven, which prescribe the pilgrimage to Mecca; the *Hajj*, the Fifth Pillar of Islam," said Herbert, who had taken the trouble to look this up before Ash's arrival. "And what else does Paul say about that in Galatians, Ash?"

"He writes about Hagar and Sarah," and Ash started to read, " 'Now this is an allegory; these women are two covenants. One woman, in fact, is Hagar, from Mount Sinai, bearing children for slavery. Now Hagar is Mount Sinai in

Arabia and corresponds to the present Jerusalem, for she is in slavery with her children. But the other woman', Paul is referring to Sarah, 'corresponds to the Jerusalem above; she is free, and she is our mother.' Herbie, is 'Hagar, from Mount Sinai, bearing children for slavery' a reference to Islam? Was Paul predicting that Ishmael's descendants, the Arabs, would be enslaved by Islam as you contend they are?"

"No. Islam arrived about six hundred years after Paul was writing. He was referring to the enslaving of Mosaic Law and to disputes he was having with Jewish Christians in Jerusalem about the qualifications of Gentiles to be Christians. Whether they had to be circumcised first, which he mentions earlier in the letter. But, it's interesting, isn't it, in the light of the argument that Islam, the rule-based religion of the descendants of Ishmael, if that's what you believe, enslaves its believers? It deprives them of the freedom to develop as the West has developed since the Enlightenment. You understand what I'm saying, Ash?" Ash nodded. Herbert continued, "Let me boil it down. Islam is Arabic for submission. That's the essence of your faith, Ash, isn't it?"

"Yes, Herbie, it is."

"Well, submission enslaves. Just as it is submission that defines the relationship between a Muslim and *Allah*, or God...*Allah* and God are one and the same, you agree with that?" Ash nodded, "...so it is love that defines the relationship between a Christian and God. Submission denies human autonomy. Love respects it. That's why we Christians say that Jesus liberated men and women from the rigidity of Mosaic Law so that we can recognise and respond to the divine within ourselves. The trouble with Islam, it might be argued, is that it denies human autonomy and, by so doing, it enslaves men and women. That's what is argued, Ash. What do you think?"

Ash privately acknowledged that Herbie had neatly summarised the difference between Christianity and Islamism; between Western culture and the Islamist culture to which he, Ash, subscribed; between democracy and theocracy. More importantly, Herbie had made a powerful criticism of Islamism, which, with every Islamist fibre of his being, Ash wanted to challenge. But, he wasn't sure how. Herbert was observing him thoughtfully, wondering how he would respond. Ash decided not to engage and shook his head.

"Herbie, I need to think about that."

"Why?"

"Because you're striking at the heart of Islam; the religion of my childhood; my faith."

"So, why not just tell me that I'm wrong and we can talk about why you think that? You're not a fool Ash! You've been practising Islam in the prayer room at the Academy every Friday. You're not just a casual Muslim. You're a serious Muslim, aren't you?"

"Yes, but..."

"So you know about Islam, even if, until now, you haven't known much about Christianity? And yet you've been going into the Abbey to pray. And I ask myself: Why?"

"Herbie, would you like it if I became a Christian?"

"Ash, of course I would! But your conversion would have to be genuine."

"Suppose I said that it was?"

"I'd need to believe you. You'd have to persuade me. Ash, if you're serious about converting to Christianity, please let me know. I don't want to put pressure on you. The next move must be yours."

"Okay, Herbie."

"Alright, Ash, that's enough for today."

"Do we meet again, Herbie?"

"Not for now! I think we've gone far enough for the time being. There's one good thing though." Ash raised his eyebrows. "We're very pleased that you're singing in the choir, whatever your beliefs or your faith."

Herbert smiled at Ash, who smiled back, as much from relief as with warmth.

Ash left and began to walk back through Abbey Close. The tone and content of their concluding exchanges had disturbed him. Ash suspected that Herbie wasn't happy about him. It was a nuisance. If he hadn't chosen the statue of *Maryam* and *'Īsā* as a dead drop, none of this would have happened. Ash began to worry that his cover was beginning to crumble. And that, he thought, would be serious; not least for him. On the other hand, there was, he accepted, nothing that either he or Zed could do about it.

As, in the looking glass above his study door, Herbert watched Ash walking past the Abbey on his way back to Abbey Gardens, he reflected upon what had just transpired between them and Ash's reluctance to engage with him. As well as priest, Herbert had been a teacher before he had come to Pepynbridge. He could discern the thoughts of most adolescents and had come to the conclusion that Ash was not being honest about himself. Whether his dishonesty was internal or external, it was a cause for concern, especially in the light of the continuing threat of Islamism that attracted young men like Ash. Herbert was a long way from being convinced that, in his present state of mind, Ash was anywhere near abandoning Islam. Their final exchanges suggested that Ash might be playing a double game. And he, Herbert, didn't like that one bit.

Over supper that evening, Herbert shared his concern with Julie.

"Herbie, I believe you're right to be worried. I even think it's odd that, unlike Leela, whom we understand to be an observant Muslim, Ash is content to sing along with us in the Abbey without any expressed reservations."

"Of course, I may be worrying about nothing."

"You may be, but in these dangerous times, you can't be too careful. Why don't you have a word with Richard? He seems to know a lot about Islamic extremism."

"Thank you, Julie, I shall."

When supper was over and he had helped Julie wash up, Herbert telephoned Richard Maxey. They arranged to meet at the Rectory the next morning.

◆◆◆◆◆◆◆◆◆◆◆◆◆◆◆◆◆◆◆◆◆

Friday, 26th June 2015

In Herbert's study, Richard Maxey sat in one wing armchair and opposite him in the other sat Herbert. Herbert looked across the space between them, taking in Richard's handsome, if bluff features, his ruddy complexion and honest blue eyes, buried deep between creases of flesh. He was, thought Herbert, the epitome of reliability and common sense.

In turn, Richard Maxey was scrutinising Herbert. What a nightmare last autumn and winter had been! And what a blessing that catastrophe had been averted! Everything about Herbert, his gentle disposition, his musical expertise, his patent spirituality, reinforced Richard's view that the decisions taken by Alice Burton as patron of the living to present Herbert to the parish and by Julian Ross, the diocesan bishop, and the Parochial Church Council to appoint him, had been inspired. But now, as Richard took in Herbert's sensitive features, his dark brown eyes, magnified by black rimmed spectacles, and his generous but now pursed lips, he could see that this good priest was troubled.

As Herbert described his meetings with Ash, Richard was astonished to learn that Ash claimed he had been visiting the Abbey to pray. When Herbert had finished, Richard Maxey said,

"Herbie, I share your concern. And so does Jack Driver."

"Really?"

"Yes! We've already discussed Ash. Herbie, I don't believe for one moment that Ash was visiting the Abbey to pray. I can only think that he was either meeting someone there; or using it as a dead drop."

"He wasn't meeting anybody, Richard. I never saw anyone else go in or out at about the same time. And he was alone when I met him in there."

"Have you seen him go in since then?"

"No, I haven't!"

"He hasn't because he knows he's been rumbled. Which, to my mind, means he's up to no good. The only reason I can think of for Ash going into the Abbey alone was to leave or retrieve written messages hidden somewhere inside. Plenty of places to do that."

"Indeed, there are."

"That's one way people operating under cover communicate with each other. Herbie, I'll have another word with Jack. The trouble is that I like Ash. He's a good boy."

"I agree, he is."

"And, according to Jack, if he's got himself mixed up in something, he may already be guilty of terrorism. And if he is, he's in deep, deep trouble. Leave it with me, Herbie, okay?"

"Yes, Richard! Thank you. I knew I could rely on you and I'm relieved that Jack's involved as well. Goodbye." And Herbert left.

Richard rang Jack Driver and reported what Herbert had told him.

There was a long pause on the line. Then Jack Driver said,

"You, know Richard, I think it's time we told the authorities about Ash."

"The authorities, Jack?"

Another pause before Jack replied,

"Special Branch. Responsible for anti-terrorism. I'll give Medborough Police a ring on Monday. It's too late now."

"Thank you, Jack. That sounds right to me."

◆◆◆◆◆◆◆◆◆◆◆◆◆◆◆◆◆◆◆◆◆◆

Saturday, 27th June 2015

On Saturday afternoon, there was no Academy Firsts match, so Ash borrowed Sabi's car, collected Sophie and drove to the multiplex cinema in Medborough, where they watched *Jurassic World*. Now, they were sitting in a pizza restaurant nearby.

"Ash, I was talking to Leela the other day."

"What did she want?"

"She didn't want anything. But, Ash, she told me that she's worried about you."

Ash thought, I could do without this. He said,

"Why?"

"Well, you know how, at school, you used to go to the prayer room with Zed and the others to pray?"

"Yes?"

"Well, we all thought that you were serious about Islam."

"I am, Sophie, I am. Truly, I am."

"Well, Leela's worried about us."

"About us?" Ash's voice rose incredulously.

"Yes! Because she's told me that she wouldn't go out with a boy without a chaperone; who could be you."

"Does she want to go out with a boy? Has she got a boyfriend?"

"No! No! She was referring to us, Ash. She's worried about me. I told her that, in this country, there's no reason why a girl like me shouldn't be alone with a boy like you, like we are now. She agreed, unless one or the other was an observant Muslim. Like you, Ash."

"Well, Sophie, I think you have to adapt your faith to the culture you live in. Perhaps I wouldn't be going out with a white girl..."

"Just a white girl, Ash?"

"...oh, any girl then, without a chaperone if I lived in the South Asian community in Medborough. But I don't. I live in Pepynbridge. And Sophie?"

"Yes?" Sophie returned Ash's gaze.

"I think you're really fit; really cool. That's why I'm going out with you."

"Ash, I think the same about you." It was too far across the table to exchange a kiss, but they did so back in the car; and this time, it was not just a brush of lips and Ash became aroused. But, he told himself, this was neither the time nor the place. After they had drawn apart, he drew breath and said,

"I'd like to take you somewhere private, Sophie."

"I'd like that too, Ash. Perhaps on my sixteenth birthday?"

"When's that?"

"On the twenty seventh of July."

"Can we wait that long?"

"Oh, Yes! I'm sure we can! Ash, this is getting serious. I want to be certain we're doing the right thing. Know what I mean? I don't know whether anyone's told you, but when I was younger, I used to sleep around a bit. Having sex. There were three boys. Not a lot, but it was what I did; and what others like me did as well. Then, after last year...you know about what happened last year, do you?"

"Yes, I've heard."

"Well I ended up with a mental health problem. I'm still being treated for it. I'm okay now, but I decided that I was going to take life more seriously after all I'd been through. I promised Mum I would and I am doing. And I promised myself that I wouldn't have sex again until I'm sixteen when it'll be legal. I'm playing cautious; not letting my heart run away with my head. And I'm not promising we'll have sex on my birthday. All I'm saying is, not before. We'll see how I feel when we get there. Okay? You do understand, Ash, don't you?"

"Yes, Sophie! I do." They kissed again, and Ash drove back to Summerhay.

When Ash arrived back home in Abbey Gardens, Leela said,

"Where've you been?"

"Out with Sophie to the cinema."

"You don't give up, do you?"

"Why should I?"

Leela did not reply, but Ash knew what she was thinking. Not wanting to make things worse, he said nothing, but went up to his room and sat down in front of his laptop. He looked at the BBC News website and rejoiced that, the day before, an Islamist called Seifeddine Rezgui, using an AK47 and grenades, had killed 38 European tourists, 30 of them British, on a beach and in a hotel in Sousse, Tunisia, before he was martyred. Good for him! Ash thought. He'll be in Paradise now, lucky man! Then he ordered a Fly Vest from Katch & Kill at a cost of £29.99, using his debit card to pay for it. He looked at the script that Zed had given him of what he was to say in his *šahīd* recording and decided to add nothing to it. It made all the points that he would have made had he drafted it himself. He reflected, as he had often done, upon the professionalism that characterised Zed's leadership. Ash suspected that there were more than just the four co-ordinators orchestrating whatever he, Ash, and the others would be doing in due course. I wonder when? Well, we'll be told in Middlehay Wood on...when was it? He consulted his diary. Ah, Yes! The twentieth of July.

Later, when he heard his parents' voices downstairs, he went down to supper, and, in response to their enquiry, assured them that he and Sophie had enjoyed the film. Yes, they had each eaten a pizza, but he was happy to join them for supper.

◆◆◆◆◆◆◆◆◆◆◆◆◆◆◆◆◆◆◆◆◆

Monday, 29th June 2015

At half past nine on Monday morning, the telephone rang on Sergeant Hay's desk in Medborough Police Station.

"Yes?"

"A Mr Driver on the phone, for you, Sir."

"Put him through."

"Hello, Jack Driver here from Driver and Sickle, solicitors."

"Yes! Good morning, Mr Driver. Sergeant Hay speaking. What can I do for you?"

"I asked to be put through to Special Branch."

"You have been. Or more accurately, to the Eastern Counter Terrorism Intelligence Unit; Eastern CTIU for short. CTIUs are collaborative ventures involving several police forces. Amongst other things, they're an amalgamation of Special Branches. It's a programme that's been rolled out across the UK. The Eastern CTIU is not based here, but, as its officer seconded to Medborough, I am."

Then, adopting a cautious tone, Hay asked,

"So, what can I do for you?"

Jack Driver explained who he was and that, in addition to being a local solicitor, he was the organist at Pepynbridge Abbey.

"Sergeant, some colleagues of mine in Pepynbridge and I are concerned about a young man who lives in the village. He's originally from Pakistan. We think it would be prudent to share our concerns with the police."

"Very good, Mr Driver. Would you like me to come and see you?"

"That would be kind."

At three o'clock the same afternoon, Andrew Hay was sitting in Jack Driver's office, listening to Jack talking about Ash, whom he called by his full name, Aashif Malik, and making notes in a pocket notebook. When Driver had finished, Hay said,

"Thank you for telling me all that, Mr Driver. Very helpful. It will do no harm for you to be aware that we have already been alerted to a Muslim group that used to meet on Friday evenings at Medborough Academy; and, as you have told me, Aashif Malik is one of them They remain of interest to us, I can assure you, although I do not wish to disclose more for operational reasons."

"Of course not, Sergeant. I understand that; and I am re-assured that you have young Ash on your radar. As will be Dr Maxey and Reverend Onion. Do you mind if I tell them what you've just told me?"

"Provided it goes no further, Mr Driver."

"Of course not!"

Jack Driver left and later rang Richard Maxey and Herbert Onion and put them in the picture.

◆◆◆◆◆◆◆◆◆◆◆◆◆◆◆◆◆◆◆◆◆◆

Sunday, 5th July 2015

Zed, Raed, Waahid and Yaaseen were sitting in a bar at the Grace Road cricket ground where, under warm sunshine, Leicestershire were playing Surrey. The four around the table were not interested in the match.

"Bad news about the Chief," said Zed. "May *Allah* have mercy on him and grant him Paradise!"

On 12th June, it had been reported that Nasir al-Wuhayshi, leader of AQAP, had been killed in a United States drone strike in Yemen.

"Indeed!" responded Raed. Waahid and Yaaseen nodded in agreement. Raed continued, "Our new Chief is Qasim al-Raymi. I've already received an encrypted message from Yemen, instructing us to carry on with the mission and wishing us luck in the name of Muhammad, peace be upon him."

"But good news from Sousse in Tunisia!" said Waahid.

"Ye-e-s," said Raed, adopting a sceptical note. "ISIL says that Seifeddine Rezgui was one of theirs; so not an AQAP operation. And so maybe not something we should applaud. Things are changing in *Ash-Sharq al-Awsat*."

"Really?" said Waahid. "How so?"

"AQAP and ISIL aren't friends. Far from it! Yemen tells me that Saudi Arabia and the Gulf States are very worried about ISIL."

"Why?"

"Why, Waahid? Because ISIL has already carved out a huge amount of territory for itself in Syria and Iraq over which, if Iran defeats ISIL or with its ally, Bashar al-Assad, does a deal with ISIL, Iran would exercise effective control."

He paused to allow what he had just said register with the others.

Zed observed,

"Shiite Iran is no friend of Sunni Arabia."

"Indeed not," agreed Raed. "And neither is al-Assad a friend of Saudi Arabia. And there's something else that might surprise you. It certainly did me. I've learnt from our people in Yemen that Saudi Arabia has started to provide *al-Qaeda*, including AQAP, with money and arms. Basically, the Saudis want *al-Qaeda* to go to war with ISIL."

"And will we?"

"Early days yet, Zed. We must wait and see."

"But you said our mission continues?"

"Yes! If it changes, I'll tell you. But you know what? What we're going to do next December will put ISIL's effort in Tunisia in the shade. *Allahu Akbar!*"

"*Allahu Akbar!*" responded the others softly.

They went on to discuss the training day in Middlehay Wood, fifteen days hence. The mood was upbeat and they re-assured themselves that they were still operating beneath the security services' radar. Zed had not noticed the cars that had sequentially followed him from

Medborough to Leicester; and none of them were paying attention to two men who had entered the bar after them and were now sitting at a table at the other end of the room, dressed in chinos, open necked shirts and blazers, chatting and holding match programmes. They presented as unexceptional and, if the four jihadists had wondered about them, they would have assumed that they were cricket fans reviewing the morning's play. When the four left, one of the two men followed Zed at a distance, whilst the other, in his thirties, of medium height, with short dark hair and unmemorable features, approached the barman and asked to speak to the manager. The barman picked up a telephone, tapped some keys and spoke into it.

"The Secretary will be along in a minute."

"Thank you."

"Yes? You wanted to see me?" The speaker was a late middle-aged man, tall and lean, with a generous head of hair and wearing a blazer and a Leicestershire County Cricket Club tie.

"Good afternoon." The other reached into a pocket, drew out a credit card sized plastic card and shewed it to the Secretary. "I'm Police Constable Stuart Rally of Medborough Police. Is it possible to have a word in private, please?"

"Of course. Come with me!"

The two walked out of the bar, along a corridor and into an office. The Secretary sat at a desk and Rally sat opposite him in a high backed chair. The Secretary introduced himself as Jonathan Beckett and continued,

"How can I help you?"

Rally said,

"I'm sorry to bother you, Mr Beckett, but there were four men in the bar where I was just now that are of interest to me and my colleagues."

"Yes, officer?"

"I see that the bar has CCTV coverage."

"It has."

"I wonder if I might take away a copy of today's recording that covered the table where the men were sitting?"

"Shouldn't you have a warrant or something?"

"If you were to refuse then, yes, I would need a warrant. But I must warn you that I am investigating a possible terrorist offence and if you were to wipe today's coverage before I obtained a warrant, it would be regarded with the utmost seriousness."

Beckett pressed a button on his desk. After a short while, a man entered.

"Bill, can we make copies of the recordings on our CCTV cameras?"

"Yes we can, Jonathan."

"Would it be very inconvenient for you to make a copy of today's recordings from..." and he named the bar "...and give it to this gentleman?" Bill looked surprised, but said,

"No, Jonathan! No trouble at all. From which camera?" Rally described the table where the four men had been sitting. "No trouble," he said.

Rally and Beckett chatted until Bill returned with a CD-R in a cardboard slip which he gave to Beckett. Rally wrote and removed a receipt from a pad and exchanged it for the CD-R.

"Thank you, Mr Beckett."

"Are we likely to have to give any evidence?"

"Very unlikely, although I can't promise. I'll see you receive a formal letter from my boss confirming receipt of this disc and thanking you for your co-operation. Good day!" And Rally left.

Later, stills of Raed, Waahid and Yaaseen were made from the CD-R and circulated to SO15 in London and all regional CTIUs, with requests for intelligence. Within two days, responses had been received from SO15 and from the two regional CTIUs responsible for York and Lincoln respectively, with the names and addresses of Raed, Waahid and Yaaseen, together with print-outs from the Police National Computer. Unlike Zed, the others each had a history of minor delinquency. However there was no intelligence to suggest that any had previously engaged in Islamist activity and, as none had previously been of interest to the security services, there was no information about any visits they might have made to Pakistan or the Middle East.

In the light of the clandestine way in which the four had chosen to meet, taken together with prior suspicion about Zaeem Zahra, SO15 ordered that, with immediate effect, all four were to be put and kept under surveillance.

◆◆◆◆◆◆◆◆◆◆◆◆◆◆◆◆◆◆◆◆◆◆

Friday, 17th July 2015

On Friday, the last day of term, Zed asked Ash, Ab, Faz and Naz to meet him on the Academy sports ground during the mid-morning break. They walked casually around the perimeter in loose line abreast.

"End of term," remarked Zed.

"Yes!" the others responded.

"I'm leaving, so I won't be back next term. Everything okay with you?" They assured him it was.

"Okay. I'll see you in Middlehay Wood at nine o'clock next Monday morning."

They separated and at half past twelve, together with the rest of the pupils, they streamed out through the Academy gates under the sour gaze of Francis Metcalf at his first-floor study window.

When Ash arrived home, Sabi said,

"Ash, there's a parcel come for you by courier." She pointed to a plastic wrapped parcel on the kitchen table, with "Katch & Kill" on it. "What's that?"

"Oh, it's a sort of waistcoat."

"A waistcoat! Whatever do you want with something like that?"

"Well, fishermen wear them to keep their flies and that in."

"But, Ash," objected Sabi, "you're not a fisherman!"

Ash thought quickly. "No, Mum! I'm not. But my friend Zed is and it's going to be his birthday and I've bought it as a present for him."

The explanation did not satisfy Sabi; or Leela who was present; but neither thought it worth while challenging Ash, believing that, if they did, he would dissemble. But, thought Leela, it was all of a piece with the pattern of deceit that I keep seeing in my brother.

Sunday, 19th July 2015

The following Sunday after Mass, when Ash, Sophie and Leela left the Abbey, the sun had broken through clouds and the air was warm. A breeze was moving the tops of the trees in the grounds of Pepynbridge Hall.

"What shall we do?" asked Sophie.

"I'm playing away this afternoon," said Ash.

"Well, that leaves just us, Leela. What are you doing?"

"Well, I'm expected home for lunch and after that, nothing."

Leela was troubled that her friendship with Sophie, which had started so well, now seemed to be stalling in the face of the growing intimacy between Sophie and Ash.

"Why don't you come home to us for lunch and then we can spend the afternoon together?"

Sophie looked at Leela. She recalled their afternoons together at The Bathing Place and privately acknowledged guiltily that she had not nurtured their friendship as she might have done.

"Thank you, Leela, I should like that. I'll just phone Mum and tell her I won't be home for lunch. She won't mind. On Sundays, we eat in the evening."

Fifteen minutes later, Leela and Sophie were in the kitchen of 4 Abbey Gardens chatting to Sabi, while Ash was upstairs changing into his whites. A short while later he left the house and Abi, Sabi, Leela and Sophie sat down to lunch. Their conversation ranged over familiar topics like the Abbey choir and cricket. After lunch, Sophie and Leela went for a walk.

"Don't see much of you these days, Sophie."

"No! I'm sorry about that, Leela"

They strolled along Abbey Way and out of Pepynbridge between fields of ripening wheat, oil-seed rape and beans. The sun was shining now out of a clear blue sky. It had grown warmer and they talked. But their conversation was awkward. Ash had come between them, not deliberately, but it had happened. They turned back and as they approached Abbey Gardens, Sophie said,

"Leela?"

"Yes?"

"Don't worry about Ash and me. We've got something going between us. I don't say that we're in love, but if or when we are, then love solves all problems, doesn't it?"

"But, Sophie, it doesn't! Ash is, or is meant to be, a good Muslim. Look, I don't blame you, Sophie. You're behaving entirely in accordance with your culture. But he's not. I just feel that I'm losing him. And not just me, Mum and Dad feel the same way."

"Leela, I promise you won't lose him. I respect your faith and your culture. But we are living in twenty-first century England. You need to adapt like Ash, otherwise you'll be lonely."

Quietly and unemotionally, Leela responded,

"But that's just what I am, Sophie. Lonely."

Sophie could think of nothing to say, but she felt sad. When they reached Leela's house, she kissed Leela on the cheek and noticed that her friend's eyes were brimming with tears. Leela went inside and Sophie mounted her bicycle and started pedalling. She was, she acknowledged, fond of Leela and she understood her dilemma. In a funny sort of way, thought Sophie, her parents are no help to her when it comes to her faith. Ash and I shall just have to do our best to include her. She paused...but only when it's appropriate, which it won't be on my birthday, a week on Monday.

♦♦♦♦♦♦♦♦♦♦♦♦♦♦♦♦♦♦♦♦♦♦

Monday, 20th July 2015

On Sunday, when he returned home from playing cricket, Ash had secured Sabi's agreement to him borrowing her car for the whole of the next day.

"Where are you going, Ash?"

"Oh, I'm meeting some friends from school," Ash had replied truthfully.

"And, if you don't mind me asking, what will you be doing with your friends from school?"

Ash had resented her curiosity, incorrectly assuming that it was born of a mother's natural anxiety for her son, rather than prompted, as it was, by the concerns that Leela had shared with her.

"We're going to spend the day in some woods, nature walking."

Nearly true! Ash had thought.

"All right, Ash."

Sabi hadn't believed him, but decided not to probe further.

"Thanks Mum," he had said.

Now, at a quarter to nine on a warm Monday morning, Ash drove out of Pepynbridge towards Corbury and after two miles turned right down a narrow lane, signposted to Middlehay. Two miles along the lane, there was, as Zed had said there would be, a turning to the right, with a green

Forestry Commission sign that announced: 'Middlehay Wood'.

The trees in the wood were oak and spruce divided into blocks, with hard tracks separating the blocks. The oaks were laden with leaves and swelling acorns. On a quiet day, faint rustling of fallow deer in undergrowth could sometimes be heard, but today there were vehicles moving in the wood and the deer were still.

Raed had arrived early and driven down to the disused bomb store he had chosen. It was brick-built with a concrete roof, about ten metres wide, five metres deep and open on the side facing the track. The doors that had spanned the opening had long gone. The shed was set back several metres from the track and reached from it along a narrow earthen path, flanked by brambles. The entrance of the path was obvious, but the path curled and the shed was concealed from the track. Raed had fastened to one wall of the shed a black flag with the *Shahada* in white on it. In front of it, he had laid a rug on the bare dry earth. On the eastward facing wall, he had marked a *qibla* with charcoal.

Ash drove into the wood and, as instructed, turned onto the first track on his right. After half a mile, he saw a figure standing in the middle of the track. As he approached, the figure waved him down. Ash drew to a stop and Raed walked to the driver's side window, which was open.

"Hello. Who are you?"

"I'm Ash Malik."

"Hi, Ash! I'm Raed. A friend of Zed's. Are you here because Zed invited you?"

"Yes, I am!"

"Good. See that path that goes into the trees?" He pointed to the opening in the undergrowth to Ash's left.

"Yes!"

"That leads to the shed where we're meeting. Zed's told you about the meeting?"

"He has."

"Good! Well, drive on about fifty metres and there's a grass clearing on your right. The ground's firm and dry. Park there under the trees. Come back here and walk down the track till you come to the shed. Okay?" Ash nodded. "Zed's already here with the others from Medborough."

Five minutes later, Fly Vest and prayer mat under his arm, Ash walked into the shed. He greeted Zed, Ab, Faz and Naz. Others were there to whom Ash was introduced. After a few minutes, more arrived. By a quarter past nine, there were twenty young South Asian men in the shed.

There followed a brief introduction by Raed. He explained that the day would start with *salāt*. There would be another *salāt* at lunchtime and a third before they left. After the first, each cell member would be interviewed outside by a co-ordinator from a cell to which they did not belong. Then he, Raed, would address them and tell them about their mission.

"Okay? Now, we cannot perform *wudū* here, but so sacred is our mission that *Allah*, Most Gracious, Most Merciful, will forgive us." He pointed to the mark he had made on one of the walls. "That's our *qibla*. It's as near as I can place it in the direction of the *Ka'aba*. So, unroll your prayer mats and we'll begin." They did and observed *salāt*.

When it was over, the co-ordinators started to interview. Ash was spoken to by Waheed a few metres away from the shed. He could hear low conversations going on nearby, although the speakers were hidden by dense undergrowth. Waheed conducted the interview rigorously, probing the depth of Ash's faith and his conviction that *istishhad* was what he really did want to do. Ash reflected ruefully afterwards that it had been rather less challenging than his sessions with Herbie. Finally Waheed said,

"Ash, in a little while, Raed is going to tell you about the mission. Up until now, you haven't known and although betraying us before today would have been damaging, it would not have been nearly as damaging as if you were to betray us after today. Even if you withdrew now, we should treat that as very serious and we might have to take severe action against you. You know that. Don't you?"

"Yes, Waheed, I do!"

"But if you betray us after today, you know what will happen, don't you?"

"I'd be killed, wouldn't I?"

"Yes, you would! No second chance! Understand?" Waheed's tone was menacing.

"I do understand, Waheed. And don't worry. No chance!"

"Better not be!"

Ash returned to the shed. After the interviews of all sixteen ordinary members were over, the co-ordinators conferred outside. Then they entered and Raed said,

"Okay, everybody. We're happy. Are you?" This was greeted by a chorus of, "Yes!"

"Okay. Now, everyone sit down!" Everyone sat cross-legged on the ground except Raed, who stood facing them.

"Zed, Waahid, Yaaseen and I are satisfied that all of you are true Muslims, obedient to *Allah,* and loyal followers of the Prophet, peace be upon him. I'm going to remind you of why you're about to be asked to perform *istishhad* in the sacred cause of *Allah,* Most Gracious, Most Merciful. First of all and most importantly, our Holy Book commands all observant followers of the Prophet, peace be upon him, to kill polytheists wherever they are found, unless they repent and give charity, for *Allah* is Forgiving and Merciful. So it is written in *sura Al-Mā'idah, ayah* five. Our mission will strike at the heart of the Christian community in this country. I remind you of what our Holy Book says about Christians. Together with Jews and Sabians, they are termed People of the Book. But Christians persist in the heresy that Jesus, or *'Īsā,* was more than God's apostle; that he was God's son. And they also say that God is one of three; that *'Īsā* and the Spirit are also gods. Our Holy Book tells us that it is a sin to speak of God as one of three. There is but one God, as we assert when we pronounce the *Shahada.* That is the truth; the only truth. Those who deny that, like the Christians, will be severely punished unless and until they willingly pay the *jizya,* the unbelievers' tax, after they have been humbled. So it is written in *sura al-Mā'idah, ayah* seventy-three and *sura At-Tawbah, ayah* twenty-nine. And we, as loyal and obedient Muslims, have a duty to put into practice the will of *Allah,* Most Gracious, Most Merciful."

Raed paused to allow his listeners to digest what he had said, before continuing,

"As Sayyid Qutb, peace be upon him, wrote in *Ma'alim fi al-Tariq,* or Milestones, *jihad* is to liberate every human in the world from servitude to other humans; in other words, to free mankind from the yoke of democracy, so that every man and woman, and I quote from the English translation..." Raed glanced down at a sheet of paper he was holding, "...'can serve his God, Who is One and Who has no associates'." He looked up. "That, Sayyid Qutb declared, is by itself sufficient reason for *jihad*. And that, and nothing less, brothers, is the sacred mission upon which we are engaged. Sayyid Qutb emphasised that once we have accepted the way of Muhammad, peace be upon him, we must fight unbelievers until we are martyred or victorious. Islam, he wrote..." he looked again at the sheet of paper, "...is entitled to remove obstacles by force; and obstacles are institutions and traditions that prevent people from walking in the way of *Allah* and his Prophet, Muhammad, peace be upon him. In Lahore in April 1939..." Raed continued, still looking at his note, "...Abul a'la Maududi, another great follower of *Allah*, Most Gracious, Most Merciful, and his Prophet, Muhammad, peace be upon him, told us that we must establish a new Islamic order in the world by the sword and that to do that, we Muslims must be prepared to use every asset at our disposal; all the powers of our bodies and souls, our belongings and our lives in the fight against evil. It is our duty to rid the world of evil by force of arms." Raed looked up. "That," he said with emphasis, raising a clenched fist, "is our sacred duty."

Raed next reminded his listeners of the history of Islam. Of the greatness it had achieved by the twelfth century in Baghdad and Toledo; how it had defeated the Crusaders over and over again, liberating the holy places in Jerusalem; but how it had been systematically humiliated ever since by the forces of the Christian and Jewish heretics. He reminded them of the conquest of India and the defeat of the Mughals by the British; of the colonisation of Egypt by the British; and of the Maghreb by the French and the Spanish; of the division of the *ummah* in the wake of the destruction of the Ottoman Empire by the British and the French following the treacherous Sykes Picot agreement of 1916; of the displacement of 700,000 Muslims from Palestine on the establishment of the State of Israel in 1948; of the invasion of Afghanistan, first by Russian Christians and then by American and British Christians; and of the occupation of Iraq. Raed told his listeners that all these humiliations were being avenged by jihadists like them.

"And our Holy Book promises," he concluded, "that your sure reward for *istishhad* will be instant translation to Paradise. When you detonate your *šahīd* vest, you will feel and hear nothing; no pain; no noise; instantly you will be in Paradise, as it is written in *sura 'Āli 'Imrān, ayah* one hundred and sixty-nine. So, go forth from here today, secure in the knowledge that you are about to strike a blow in the name of *Allah*, Most Gracious, Most Merciful; a blow that will strike terror, not just in this country, but around the world; and your names will be revered in every mosque and in every household of the faithful. *Allahu Akbar!*" To which everyone present dutifully responded, "*Allahu Akbar!*"

All of which, thought Ash, excitement welling up within him, is music to my ears and food for my heart. I could go out of here right now with an AK47 and kill the first policeman I see; preferably dozens of them.

Surveying the eager expressions ranged in front of him, Raed thought, So far so good!

In the lane near the entrance of the wood, four nondescript, unmarked cars were parked on a roadside verge and eight police officers in plain clothes, amongst them Stuart Rally, were chatting quietly amongst themselves. They had not followed the vehicles of the jihadists, if that's what they were, into the wood, because there was only one vehicular entrance and exit. As soon as the sound of an approaching vehicle was heard from within the wood, they would disperse. Stuart Rally had already reported by radio to Andrew Hay that extra assistance was needed, not to make arrests, but to search the wood after the jihadists had left. He had been assured that it was on its way.

Inside the shed, Raed continued,

"This is our mission. We're going to target Christians. They may be People of the Book, but in this country they pay no *jizya* and they support democratic institutions that defy the authority of *Allah*. They are legitimate targets. Now what you may not have been told yet is that this operation is under the direction of *al-Qaeda* in the Arabian Peninsular, based in Yemen. You may have heard it referred to as AQAP." There were several nods. "AQAP has approved our selection of targets. Cathedrals and churches."

Raed paused to allow this to sink in. Then he went on,

"We are going to set off *šahīd* vests simultaneously in twenty places of Christian worship at midnight on Christmas Eve, the twenty-fourth of December, when they will be full. The cathedrals, for which Zed, Waahid,

Yaaseen and I will be responsible, are Saint Paul's in London; York Minster; Lincoln Cathedral; and Medborough Cathedral. Churches have been chosen for each one of you, which I am now going to read out."

When he came to Ash, it was with no surprise, but some apprehension, that Ash learnt that his target was to be Pepynbridge Abbey.

"At midnight on Christmas Eve, the infidels will be queuing to take communion, as they call it. You will queue with them and that's where and when you'll detonate your *šahīd* vest. In the cathedrals, there will be one or two archbishops, at least three bishops and maybe more; and many important citizens as well as lesser folk. In the other churches we have chosen, there will be community leaders like Lord Lieutenants and High Sheriffs and titled landowners. We shall be striking at the heart of the British Establishment. All clear?" There was a forest of nods.

Raed paused again, this time to gauge the reaction of the sixteen in the room, none of whom had previously had any inkling of the mission. Their features displayed a mixture of surprise and pleasure at the enormity of what they were being asked to do.

Ash thought about the Abbey, about Leela, about Sophie, and about all those he had come to know since his family had moved to Pepynbridge in March. Like the others, as he learned later when they broke for lunch, he had thought that there might be raids on shopping centres, or police stations and the like. But this was far greater than anything he had imagined. Ash became uneasily aware of a scintilla of misgiving within him. He firmly banished it and concentrated on what Raed was telling them about the Fly Vests

"Have you all brought them with you?" They held them aloft. "Good! Now I'm going to shew you how to use them." He held up some small brown slabs. "These are plastic dummies, the same size as the explosives that you'll pack in your *šahīd* vest. You'll receive the real explosives a few days before Christmas. Your co-ordinator will tell you where to collect them nearer the time. Now, watch!"

Raed demonstrated how to pack and wire up the slabs in the pockets of the Fly Vest, designed to keep boxes of artificial flies, rolls of nylon, scissors and all the other paraphernalia that accompanies the dedicated angler when he, or she, ventures onto the banks of rivers and streams. Having packed one vest, Raed then shewed them a battery powered detonator; where to conceal it in the vest; how to wire it to the explosives; and how to trigger it.

"All clear?" he asked. It was. "Okay, break for *salāt* and lunch."

After performing *salāt*, sandwiches and bottles of water were passed around and as they ate, there was low murmuring, as the ordinary members discussed the mission. There was talk of immediate transition to Paradise when they triggered the *šahīd* vest that would blow the *šuhadā* and the infidels into fragments of shredded flesh and splintered bone. Openly, everyone was eager to express what a privilege it was going to be. Raed, Zed, Waahid, and Yaaseen were encouraged by what they interpreted as enthusiasm for the mission. Although the ordinary members' private thoughts were impossible for Ash to gauge, he was uncomfortably aware that the misgiving he had earlier tried to banish was still lurking at the back of his mind.

As the others ate and drank, Raed, Zed, Waahid and Yaaseen went outside. They arranged to meet at the King Power Stadium on Saturday, 22nd August, when Leicester City was scheduled to play Tottenham Hotspur.

Then Zed asked,

"Raed! Did you see the article in last Saturday's *Spectator*?"

"I did," said Raed.

"Yes, well, I don't normally buy it," Zed went on, "but I was in a newsagents and noticed its cover with an Arab warrior on a horse and something about *al-Qaeda* coming to the rescue. So I bought it and when I read the article, it said what you told us, Raed, when we last met, about ISIL, Iran, Saudi Arabia and *al-Qaeda*. Did you read it?"

"I did," repeated Raed, guessing what was coming next.

"Well I mention it because it said that Ayman al-Zawahiri has called off attacks on America. Is that right?"

Raed was anxious to dispel the risk the article presented to the morale of *IstishhadUK*.

"Two points, Zed. One, I don't believe it. It's probably disinformation planted by Western security services. And two, Ayman al-Zawahiri does not command AQAP. He's the head of *al-Qaeda*, to which AQAP is affiliated but that's all. We take our orders from AQAP, not from al-Zawahiri and, at the moment, as I told you last time we met, AQAP is expecting us to go ahead with our mission."

"Isn't there a danger," broke in Waahid, "that some of the others inside may have read the same article and misunderstood what it means? Perhaps you'd better repeat in there what you've just told us."

Raed agreed and, when they went back inside the shed, he did precisely that. "Beware of false information, planted by our enemies in the West," he told them. He was in regular communication with Yemen and the suggestion that AQAP was calling off operations like theirs was rubbish. Then he sat down to eat his sandwiches.

When lunch was over, Raed stood up again.

"The next thing is to make your videos. Each of you was given a text, Yes? Have you cleared any amendments with your co-ordinator? None of you have made any? Good! See the Black Flag there with the rug in front of it? I want each one of you to put on your *šahīd* vest, sit cross-legged on the rug and read out the words on your sheet, but looking at the camcorder lens as much as you can. Okay? And while one of you is recording his message, the rest of you can practise preparing *šahīd* vests using the dummy explosives and detonator."

The twenty each recorded the reason for their *istishhad*; revenge for the insults to *Allah*, Most Gracious, Most Merciful, to Muhammad, peace be upon him, and to the *ummah*. Each concluded with a warning that their mission was but a step in a series that would continue until the West in general, and the United States and the United Kingdom in particular, admitted the gross errors of their ways, repented and submitted, as all faithful people should, to the authority of *Allah*, Most Gracious, Most Merciful, and of his Prophet, Muhammad, peace be upon him.

When all twenty recordings had been made, Raed announced,

"These will be encrypted and transmitted by a secure electronic route to AQAP and released to the world's media on Christmas Day. We estimate that the operation should account for at least two hundred dead, and with luck double that; and there will be thousands injured. *Allahu Akbar!*"

"*Allahu Akbar!*" came the unanimous response.

There followed another *salāt*, after which, Raed said,

"Okay, that's it! May *Allah* be with you!"

As they walked towards the cars, Zed stepped alongside Ash.

"Ash, we're going to go on meeting regularly between now and Christmas. I've spoken to Ab, Faz and Naz and we shall meet on the first Monday each month after term starts on the third of September."

"Okay. Where?"

"At my house in Medborough. My parents won't mind or even care. They're devout and if I tell them we're friends meeting for prayers, that'll be fine." Zed gave Ash a piece of paper. "My address is on there. Don't lose it!"

"I shan't."

"Okay then. It's on the number four bus route from outside the Academy. See you there on Monday the seventh of September at half past five. Okay?"

They continued to their cars.

At the entrance to the wood, when the police officers heard vehicles approaching from within it, they dispersed to resume discreet surveillance. The four cell leaders were followed back to their home cities.

Later, a team of police officers entered the wood. After a while, one of them found the shed and evidence of its recent use, including the crude *qibla* marked on one of the walls. He radioed the others and they searched it, but recovered nothing of significance.

"Don't know why they were praying in here," remarked one.

"Oh, they do that anywhere and everywhere. Doesn't do them much good," responded another.

"Well," said Rally, who knew more about Islam than some of the others, "if nothing else, it means that they're observant; even devout. And that to me, at any rate, means that they must be taken seriously."

"We'll put that in our report to the Boss," said another.

"Indeed we shall," said Rally.

Driving back to Pepynbridge in bright, but fitful sunshine, the misgiving Ash had suppressed resurfaced. What he was expected to do had taken him by surprise, as, it was clear, it had the other ordinary members. In the shed there had been no airing of doubts; nor could there have been. But now, alone at the wheel of the Clio, Ash was seeing in his mind those who were likely to be in the Abbey at midnight on Christmas Eve: Sophie; Leela; Herbie; Julie; Jack Driver; and the others in the choir with whom he had grown friendly. It wasn't the same for the other *IstishhadUK* members. They wouldn't know any of those whom they would be killing and maiming. But, for me it's different. Of course there was the beguiling promise of an immediate translation to Paradise, but Sophie wouldn't be there; she was a *kafir*. And Leela...there would be no short cut to Paradise for her. As he turned into the parking space in front of the twin garages at 4 Abbey Gardens, Ash was troubled. But, he told himself firmly, even if I did withdraw…he paused…but there was plenty of time to think about that between now and Christmas. Put it out of your mind, he told himself. He parked the car in one of the garages and went inside. It was a quarter to six.

"Had a good time, Ash?"

"Yes thanks Mum!"

But had he really? he wondered a few minutes later as he walked to the Abbey for choir practice.

The recording to raise money for the Abbey roof was to be made the following week. The programme had been finalised. There would be excerpts from Handel's *Messiah*; Allegri's *Miserere* and Mozart's *Laudate Dominum*, with Leela singing the solo soprano parts in both; and Gordon Jacob's arrangement of *Brother James' Air* which would be performed unaccompanied by Leela and Sophie. The performance would conclude with the *Spatzenmesse*, or Sparrow Mass, by Mozart, for which Herbert had hired professional musicians to play the parts for trumpets, trombones, timpani and strings; but not the organ, which was tuned to a pitch that was incompatible with orchestral instruments. One day, Herbert thought, I'll remedy that. That Monday, Herbert reminded the choir that they would try and make the recording a week on Thursday; failing which on the following Friday. The recording would start at ten o'clock on the Thursday evening, to avoid the risk of intrusion of traffic noise and emergency vehicle sirens, which, if they did occur, would necessitate a retake the following evening. The technicians, he told them, would be in the Abbey next Monday to site recording equipment.

"As I think you all know," he continued, "I have hired instrumentalists for the recording and they will be here to rehearse with us next Saturday. Everyone available to do that? Good. At three o'clock, then. And, because the technicians want unrestricted access to the Abbey next Monday and they don't know for how long, there'll be no rehearsal on Monday. We'll rehearse again on Tuesday, Wednesday and Thursday in the mornings and afternoons. I warned you some time ago that I wanted that to happen. Are you all happy with that?"

As everyone said that they were, Ash looked across the chancel at Sophie and winked and they exchanged happy smiles. Next Monday was Sophie's birthday. They would have the whole day to themselves.

Herbert continued,

"On the Thursday evening, we'll meet in here at nine o'clock to start recording at ten. Now, this evening I want to rehearse the programme, or at least as much of it as we've time for."

As Ash listened to Leela and Sophie singing *Brother James' Air*, the sublimeness of the music struck him and for the first time he wondered whether Western culture was really as evil as Islam contended. Damn doubts again! he reflected, firmly banishing them, this time, he hoped, once and for all.

◆◆◆◆◆◆◆◆◆◆◆◆◆◆◆◆◆◆◆◆

Tuesday, 21st July 2015

Tuesday was damp and Ash and Sophie spent the day at Summerhay, watching television and reading. At one point, Sophie said,

"You okay, Ash?"

"Of course I am. Why do you ask?"

"Oh, you just seemed a bit...." she searched for a word.

"Pre-occupied?" suggested Ash.

"Yes, that's it. Pre-occupied. Well, are you?"

"Not really! Just thinking."

"About what?"

"About us," lied Ash. His doubts about *IstishhadUK* and the mission were proving obstinately persistent.

"Oh don't worry about us," retorted Sophie, "everything'll be alright."

"Really?"

"I expect so," she said, unwilling as yet to commit herself.

But she realised that what was going for her with Ash was quite different to anything she had previously experienced. Certainly not with those boys two or so years ago with their hurried couplings in her father's fields. It wasn't how she'd felt about Herbie, either. In therapy, she'd learnt that her fantasising about him had been a reaction against her father's rejection of her, fuelled by the powerful eroticism that was part of her make-up. But this was more important that that, she knew. The eroticism might prove useful, but not to be deployed unless she felt more than just physical attraction to this boy. And, she conceded privately, even if I do, I don't want to tell him or even shew him yet. Not just yet, she told herself. No harm in waiting and seeing. And if, as Ash put it, he was pre-occupied with her, well no harm in that either.

What Sophie did say was,

"Ash, we must be careful not to shut Leela out. She's feeling very lonely in Pepynbridge."

"Yes, I know she is! We must make an effort to include her."

Sophie took Ash's hand and squeezed it.

◆◆◆◆◆◆◆◆◆◆◆◆◆◆◆◆◆◆◆◆◆

Thursday, 23rd July 2015

On Wednesday, there was another choir practice at which Herbert was satisfied that the performance was shaping up. Sophie had been inspired by Leela's singing and, with Herbert's help, she had improved. Although her voice was not as limpid as Leela's, it was not quite as strong either and Herbert was content that they were well matched to sing *Brother James' Air* together.

On Thursday, Ash borrowed Sabi's car and he, Sophie and Leela drove around the countryside, which, to her surprise, Sophie discovered meant more to her than she had realised. They talked about music and ballet; and, for the first time, about farming. Leela sat quietly in the back of the car, saying little, but happy to have been included. Sophie explained that the next day, she would like to shew Ash around Pepynbridge Farm and would Leela be interested? No, Leela would not. She had some holiday homework for next term which she would do at home.

"Have a nice time," she said.

"Thanks, Leela."

During the week, the doubt that had lodged itself in Ash's mind on Monday had lingered. Over and over again he had tried to ignore it and during the day, had largely succeeded, only for it to return to haunt him after he had gone to bed, depriving him of untroubled slumber.

Friday, 24th July 2015

Friday was overcast, but dry, and at eight o'clock, when Sophie knew Alfred would be out on the farm and to avoid encountering Shirley on the farm's land line, she called his mobile.

"Hello?"

"Hello, Dad!"

"Sophie! What the hell do you want?"

"Dad, I'd like to shew Ash around the farm. Would that be alright?"

"Your Paki boyfriend, eh?"

Sophie said nothing. A long pause followed.

The trouble with Sophie, thought Alfred, is that she's never been interested in the farm; never helped with the bullocks. Never driven a tractor as a son would have done, if he'd had one, but bloody Marigold had undergone a hysterectomy after Sophie had been born and that had been that. He and Shirley were trying hard enough, whenever, Alfred reflected, he was sober enough to perform; but nothing had happened yet. And now here was this waster of a daughter wanting to shew a bloke round the farm. Well, he thought, bugger me! Pity he's black, but better than nothing, I suppose. And then he thought, his dad's a doctor. So not riffraff, then. Better not bite off my nose to spite my face!

"Yeah, okay then. If that's what you'd like to do."

"Yes, please, Dad!"

"You can go anywhere. Shirley and the kids and I are going out for the day. Shut the gates, won't you!"

"'Course I will! And, Dad?"

"Yes?"

"Thanks!"

Alfred grunted and ended the call.

Sophie and Ash left Sabi's car at the farmhouse and spent the day walking around Alfred's fields. Sophie had brought a picnic which they ate sitting at the table in the farmhouse garden where, a year ago almost to the day, she had fantasised about drinking gin and tonic with Herbie and then...She banished the shaming memory from her mind.

Ash had never been on a farm. Before he had moved to Pepynbridge, his whole life had been spent in an urban environment; in Lahore; in London; and then in Medborough; although he had uncles and cousins who farmed in the Punjab on both sides of the border between Pakistan and India. As the day wore on, he became aware of a growing fascination with, and an affinity for the fields, carpeted as they were with yellow wheat, replete with hanging ears of grain, and dark green potato plants, bearing purple flowers. Sophie pointed to lines of stalks, where oil seed rape had already been cut. She told him that the wheat was nearly ready and that it too would soon be harvested. Bending down to a raised ridge of potato plants, she said,

"Ash, look!"

She dug in with her fingers and drew out a small tuber.

"I've only ever seen raw potatoes in the shops and Mum's kitchen," he said, wonderingly. "I never knew that's how they're produced."

"Well, there you are, Ash! You're learning."

"Certainly am."

At the end of the afternoon, when Ash dropped Sophie back at Summerhay, he said,

"Thank you, Sophie. I can't remember when I enjoyed a day more."

"Oh, you've seen nothing yet!" laughed Sophie coquettishly. She kissed him fleetingly on the lips. "I must go," she said and left the car.

As Ash drove home, he told himself that he had not decided to withdraw from *IshtishadUK*. But even if I wanted to, he reflected gloomily, I have no idea how on earth I can.

While Sophie was shewing Ash around Pepynbridge Farm, five men and two women were sitting around a table in a small conference room at Medborough Police Station. As well as Andrew Hay, there were four other counter-terrorism police officers present; Chief Inspector Paul Evans and a sergeant from SO15 in London; and inspectors from the CTIUs responsible for Lincoln and York respectively. In addition, there were two officers from MI5; one from Thames House, London; the other from one of the regional offices set up following 7/7. A buff coloured file, notepad and glass of water were in front of each. Paul Evans, the 'Boss' referred to by the police officer in Middlehay Wood, was in the chair.

"Just to summarise where we are," he started, after thanking them for their attendance. "We know that between January and early June this year, five IC4 male pupils at Medborough Academy met every Friday afternoon in a room there, ostensibly for Islamic prayer and theological discussion. In January, the head teacher..." he glanced down at a paper "...Francis Metcalf, as matter of routine reported that to Andrew. We know the identities of the members of the group. The one who approached Mr Metcalf about using the room is Zaeem Zahra, Zed for short, aged 18. The others are..." he glanced down again and read, "...Aashif Malik, Aabdar Ranjha, Faazil Chaudry and Naasir Khokhar, all then aged 17 and a year below Zed at school. In June, Zed told Mr Metcalf that they no longer needed to use the room. Metcalf was uneasy about him and reported that to Andrew. Andrew sent me a report and it was decided to keep Zed under surveillance. On 5th July, Zed was followed to Leicester, where he met three other IC4 males, whom we have identified from CCTV stills as..." and he read out the full names and addresses of Raed, Waahid and Yaaseen. "Since then," he continued, "all four have been kept under surveillance. Last Monday, they were followed to Middlehay Wood. From that we gathered five vehicle index numbers. Two vehicles are registered in Medborough and the others in London, York and Lincoln. I'll come to the identities of their registered keepers in a moment. With one exception, those attending from each city arrived in one vehicle. The exception was..." he glanced again at the paper in front of him, "...a Renault Clio registered to a Saabirah Malik of Forty-One Elmgrove Gardens, Medborough."

"She lives in Pepynbridge now," broke in Andrew Hay. "She's married to a consultant psychiatrist based in Medborough General Hospital. They have two children. Aashif Malik, known as Ash, whom you have already mentioned, and a daughter, Jaleela, aged fifteen. The Renault Clio was being driven by an IC4 male, who I assume was Ash. Not long ago, I had a word about Ash with a Mr Driver, a local solicitor who plays the organ in

Pepynbridge Abbey. He told me that Ash's father, Dr Malik, and the Reverend Onion, rector of Pepynbridge, and a retired doctor in the village by the name of Maxey were concerned about Ash. They suspected that he might be mixed up in something illegal. From what Mr Driver told me, there are grounds for believing that Ash is acting under cover."

"Thank you, Andrew. The other vehicle from Medborough," continued Paul Evans, "was a 2006 Ford Escort registered to a Raafat Zahra, of..." he named another address in Medborough.

"He's a taxi driver," supplied Andrew Hay. "He has five children. The eldest is Zed who we know was the driver of the Escort."

"Okay," resumed Paul Evans. "The vehicles from London, York and Lincoln have also been traced to the other three IC4 males who were with Zed in Leicester on the fifth of July, but we don't know the names of the other twelve IC4 males who accompanied them to the meeting in Middlehay Wood. Discovering their identities and details is a priority. A search of the building in the wood where they met, a World War Two bomb store, revealed nothing beyond evidence of recent use, namely some blue tack on one wall and a broad, black arrow on another wall with an indented tail and a drawing of a square on it."

"A *qibla*," said Andrew Hay.

"Yes!" interpolated Cedric Fane, the MI5 officer from London. He presented as absurdly young for one employed as he was. Slender, with a boyish face and a shock of straight mousy hair falling over his forehead, he looked as though he had just left university; which he had done, but five years earlier. "For the benefit of any of you who don't know, it's a sign indicating the direction of Mecca, towards which Muslims are meant to face when they pray."

"So where do we go from here?" asked one of the others. Everyone looked at Paul Evans, who in turn looked at Cedric Fane.

"It's going to be difficult to place someone within one of the cells as they're probably complete by now," began Fane. "I've been looking at the information we have. With one exception, those whom we have traced are resident in and, we must assume, firmly rooted in their local ethnic communities. The same may or may not be the case with the other twelve whose identities at present we don't know. The exception is Aashif Malik, or Ash, as I shall refer to him. Andrew Hay's people have done some useful background work on him. As Andrew has already said, Ash lives in Pepynbridge. Andrew, you know the village. Perhaps you would describe it for us?"

"Sure! It's a typical Northamptonshire village. It's big, with a population of about two thousand. It mainly comprises old stone buildings but there are two recently built private housing estates. The central feature of Pepynbridge is St Aidan's Abbey. You may have heard of it?" The others nodded. "There was an issue there last year, when a fourteen year old girl called Sophie Wicken, the daughter of a farmer in Pepynbridge, made a false allegation against the rector, Herbert Onion. You may remember the case? It attracted national media coverage?" He paused, noting the assents of the others. "That's got nothing to do with this investigation except we have information that Sophie Wicken and Ash are close. As well as that, Ash sings in the Abbey choir, which is famous. It produced a highly acclaimed CD last year. And Ash plays cricket for the village First Eleven. So, despite being, as we have heard, an apparently observant Muslim, he's deeply embedded in what for him is a culturally alien environment."

"Thank you Andrew," Cedric Fane continued. "The provisional conclusion that I draw is that, if Ash is engaged in violent *jihad*, he is maintaining deep cover. But doing so in a village like Pepynbridge will present a presumably impressionable young man with a considerable challenge. He might be a target for turning. Andrew, you as the local CTIU officer, and I, as the MI5 officer assigned to this case, should keep an eye on that possibility."

"Any point in approaching his parents? Or his sister?" suggested the other MI5 officer.

"Certainly Bob," replied Andrew Hay. "Another possible approach might be through the rector. Both Ash and his sister sing in the Abbey choir which is very much the rector's baby. He's an accomplished musician."

"Or the cricket club?" suggested another.

"Indeed."

"Or his girl friend?"

"Maybe."

The discussion moved onto possible means of identifying the other twelve who had attended the meeting in Middlehay Wood.

"Cedric, what about obtaining a warrant for intercepting the emails and telephone calls of the four cell leaders from London, York, Lincoln and Medborough?" asked Andrew Hay. "That might lead us to the others."

"Telephone records may help and will be made available by telecom companies at the request of a chief constable. I suggest that written requests are made by each relevant chief constable. Emails and telephone intercepts require warrants from the Home Secretary and I doubt whether we have enough evidence yet to persuade her to grant them. I'll talk to my legal people at Thames House about that and let you know the answer. But, as I say, given the present state of our knowledge, don't count on it."

"Remind us, if you will please, of the criteria," said Paul Evans

Cedric Fane glanced down at a briefing paper he had brought with him.

"We have to convince a senior civil servant at the Home Office that we need to intercept telephone calls and emails on the ground of national security, or of preventing or detecting serious crime or of safeguarding the economic well-being of the UK. If and when we have done, the civil servant will ask the Home Secretary to sign the warrants. It's then up to the Home Secretary whether to do so."

He looked up.

"As I say, I doubt we have enough to trigger that yet. I'll see what our lawyers say and keep it under review."

After more discussion about liaising with one another, the meeting broke up. Andrew Hay returned to his office and tapped in a number on the telephone on his desk.

"Yes?"

"Susan?"

"Yes?"

"Andrew Hay here."

"Yes, Andrew?"

"Could you come and see me, please?"

"Sure!" A minute or so later, there was knock on the door and, in response to Andrew Hay's invitation, a woman in her thirties, of mixed race, slim, with dark brown hair, a round face, darkish skin and brown eyes, came in and sat down on a straight backed chair opposite him. Susan Armstrong was a police constable and child protection officer with the Medborough Police.

"Susan, you were involved in that investigation in Pepynbridge last year, weren't you?"

"Yes, Andrew, I was."

She had been the child protection officer detailed to investigate Sophie Wicken's allegations of sexual abuse against Herbert Onion. Andrew Hay told her about the investigation that was now on-going into Aashif Malik's suspected involvement in Islamist terrorism; and of his known connection with Sophie Wicken.

"Susan, we need to know a little more about Aashif, or Ash as he's known. What he's doing. What he's thinking. If he really is engaged in terrorism and acting under cover, he's playing a very difficult game in a community as sturdily rural and English as Pepynbridge. Are you still in touch with Sophie?"

"No, I'm not Andrew. You know she tried to commit suicide after the trial of Reverend Onion was stopped?"

"Yes, I remember something about that."

"Well, she's been under mental health care since then and we thought it as well to keep out of her way. In fact, we had no need to contact her once the CPS had made a decision on public interest grounds not to prosecute her for attempting to pervert the course of justice and perjury. She was too unwell for that and there were extenuating circumstances. The consultant psychiatrist who was treating her made that very clear."

"Okay. I understand. But if you could create an opportunity to have a chat with her about Ash?"

"I will try, Andrew. But I can't promise. Sophie's an apple cart I don't want to upset."

"Thanks. Susan. And follow any other leads you discover. For example the rector and Ash plays cricket for the village, so the cricket club as well. And keep me informed?"

"Sure!"

◆◆◆◆◆◆◆◆◆◆◆◆◆◆◆◆◆◆◆◆◆◆

Sunday, 26th July 2015

On Sunday, the choral performance in the Abbey during High Mass so inspired Ash that, for a brief moment, he wondered how he would feel if he approached the communion rail to be blessed; and if he had the courage to do so, which he lacked, what Herbert's reaction might be.

That afternoon found Ash on the cricket ground. Unseasonably heavy rain that had soaked Pepynbridge the day before had given way to clearing skies accompanied by a cool, north-easterly breeze. Pepynbridge's opposing team was high in the Rutland League. By tea, they were all out for 176.

"Do-able," one of the other members of the Pepynbridge team said to Ash as they walked off the pitch. And it was done, with help of a brisk eighty runs, not out, from Ash's bat against aggressive fast bowling.

As Ash made his way back to the pavilion at the close of play, the crowd of spectators, mostly seated on canvas chairs in front of and for several metres to either side of the pavilion, was the largest he had seen in Hall Park. He knew that the enthusiasm of Pepynbridge for its First XI cricket team had been fuelled, in part at least, by his own performances, accounts of which had been disseminated throughout the village. As Ash approached, the spectators rose to applaud him. It was, thought Ash, a quintessentially English scene; nowhere near as hot as it would be in Lahore; a warm sun shining through gaps in the clouds onto the green grass of Hall Park; cricketers in whites walking off a pitch after a day of enjoyable and wholly innocent fun; and applauding supporters, amongst whom he recognised Alistair and Augusta Pemberton-Smith, Dr Maxey, Herbert, a now obviously pregnant Julie, Alice Burton, Sophie, his parents, Leela and others. All of whom with the exception of his father and mother, Ash reflected bleakly, would be in St Aidan's Abbey on Christmas Eve. Or would be unless he could engineer their absence. How he was to do that without alerting someone like Herbie that he was a jihadist, Ash could not imagine. As he always did, Ash acknowledged the applause with a slight raising of his bat, but as he walked up the steps of the pavilion out of bright sunshine into the gloom within, the reality of what he had been ordered to do struck him with a terrible force. What price now his loyalty to Zed; to Muhammad, peace be upon him; and even to the Islamic *Allah*?

In the changing room, Oliver Standard approached him.

"Ash, could you spare me a moment? There's someone I'd like you to meet."

Suppressing his bleakness, Ash followed Oliver upstairs and onto the balcony, where committee members were nursing drinks and chatting. A tall middle-aged man, lean with white hair and a kind, aquiline face, watched him as he approached.

"Kevin," said Oliver Standard, "let me introduce you to Ash Malik. Ash, this is Kevin Wood."

Wood held out his right hand and took hold of Ash's. It felt warm and dry.

"How do you do," Wood said.

Ash sensed that "Good!" would not be an appropriate response.

"Good afternoon, Sir!"

"Mr Wood is Northamptonshire's head coach," said Oliver.

"Ash," said Kevin Wood, a gentle smile playing about his features. "Well played!"

"Thank you, Sir."

"Good bowling and bold but careful batting. Impressive. And I've been looking at your figures in the club's score-book. Fancy a county trial?"

Ash's face registered astonishment. It was the last thing he was expecting. Would he like it? You bet he would! What he said was,

"Thank you Sir. That would be wonderful!"

"Yes! Well, if you're free, Ollie will bring you to Northants Cricket Ground tomorrow morning and we'll have a session in the nets with some club professionals."

"I'm sorry, Sir. I can't come tomorrow."

Ash explained that it was a friend's birthday and that he had promised to take her out. Kevin Wood smiled.

"I quite understand, Ash. Mustn't let a special friend down on her birthday, eh? How about the following Monday, the third of August? Ollie, would you be free then?"

"Yes, Kevin! I would."

"And I shall be as well, Sir."

"Good. That's settled then. Turn up at the ground at eleven o'clock. No need to wear whites. Track suit or shorts; that sort of thing will do. And bring your bat and pads. See you then, Ash!"

"Yes, Sir. And thank you."

Ash left the balcony as if in a dream. What will Mum and Dad say? And Leela? And Sophie? He felt jolted. It's all happening at once, he thought. It's as much as I can handle. His mind went back again to the previous Monday in Middlehay Wood and the bleakness flooded back. What the hell should he do?

◆◆◆◆◆◆◆◆◆◆◆◆◆◆◆◆◆◆◆◆◆

Monday, 27th July 2015

A narrow ridge of high pressure accompanied by a southerly wind had brought a brief interlude of heat to a July that had been almost as disappointing as June. Imagining and anticipating what he hoped would happen with Sophie on her sixteenth birthday, Ash had slept poorly through an uncomfortably warm night. Sophie had told him they would spend the day at Summerhay, so as Sabi's car was not available for him to borrow, Ash set off on his bicycle dressed in jeans and a T-shirt. As he pedalled, the heat of the day began to send rivulets of sweat down the valley of his spine into the cleft of his buttocks. Half way up the hill between the bridge over the River Pepyn and the turning to Summerhay, Ash dismounted and walked to minimise his embarrassment at arriving drenched. At the junction at the top of the hill, he remounted and, as he free-wheeled down into Summerhay, the breeze of his passage cooled and dried him so that, when he arrived at midday, he felt fresh. Sophie answered the door with the information that Marigold had gone to Medborough for the day, she didn't say why. Bra-less, a T-shirt sculpted her breasts and nipples; and shorts revealed slender and exquisitely shaped thighs and calves. As Sophie had intended, Ash took in her appearance with mounting excitement that set a lump in his throat and aroused a stir in his groin.

"Happy birthday, Sophie!" he said, unsteadily.

"Thanks!" She pointed to a cool box at her feet. "I thought we'd go out for a picnic."

"Great!" They kissed, fleetingly. That could wait, thought Ash. No point in forcing the pace. He took hold of the cool box and Sophie locked the front door.

"There's somewhere nice I want to shew you," she said, and they walked away from the cottage and The Mill across the lawn beside the River Pepyn.

"Mrs Burton lives in The Mill," explained Sophie, "and she owns all this land. She doesn't mind us using it. One of her gardeners looks after the river bank, keeping it mown; and the place I'm going to shew you."

After a hundred metres, they entered the wood and walked along the narrow path beside the river until they emerged from shadow into The Bathing Place. From a cloudless sky, the sun was bathing the glade in shimmering light.

"Wow!" exclaimed Ash.

Sophie felt deep satisfaction. You've got this right, girl! Let's hope the rest goes alright. She invited Ash into the gazebo, where, earlier that morning, she had laid on its floor a rug from her bedroom in the cottage. She invited Ash to put the cool box down and, when he had done so, she moved towards him and put her arms around his waist.

"Okay?" she asked.

"You bet, Sophie! This is marvellous. Will anyone come by?"

"No chance! Mum's in Pepynbridge and Mrs Burton's in France." She smiled at him and raised her face. Their lips met and this time, their kiss was driven by fierce sexual desire. Sophie's hands slipped round and began to undo the buckle on Ash's belt. He did the same. A few moments later, they were both locked in a naked embrace, lips apart and tongues working. Sophie reached down and gently caressed his erect penis.

"Do the same to me, Ash!"

He slipped his hand between her thighs and felt wetness. He inserted a finger between her labia and, although he had never done anything remotely like it before, nor even read about it, instinctively he knew what to do. Sophie began to moan.

"Let's lie down!" she said.

"Will it be safe?" Ash asked.

"I'm on the Pill," was Sophie's reply and she lay down on the rug on her back and Ash laid on top of her. She opened her legs and he entered her and began to thrust urgently.

"Ash! No!" said Sophie sharply. He continued thrusting. "Ash! Listen to me!" Her tone was peremptory. "Ash, stop!" He paused inside her, his deep brown eyes, their pupils dilated by excitement, gazing uncomprehendingly into the blue wells of hers.

"Why?"

"Ash, you've not done this before, have you?"

"No, I haven't!"

"Take it slowly! Gently, now! Gently! Ash, we have the whole day to ourselves. No need to hurry."

He began again.

"Like this?"

"Yes, Ash! Just like that."

After several minutes of rhythmic moving in unison, Sophie pressed her finger tips hard into Ash's muscled buttocks and cried out; and they came together. Slowly they relaxed and a few moments later, Ash rolled off her.

"Sophie, that was amazing!"

"It was!" she agreed.

They lay quietly for what seemed like a long time, holding hands but alone with their thoughts. That, thought Sophie, really was something special. She looked across at Ash's body, noting the muscled arms and chest, the flat stomach, the slim hips and the long slender legs, all the colour of what? Of an espresso with a dash of cream, she decided. He's fit, she concluded. Fit and just right. He, in turn gazed at Sophie, taking in her whiteness, her firm breasts, smooth rounded arms, the slight dome of her stomach and, below it, a mysterious thicket of pale curls before the gentle swell of her thighs. After a while, Sophie sat up, leant over Ash, came down on his groin and began to fellate him. When he was erect, she said,

"Again?"

Ash's response was to lie on her and enter her again. This time the coupling took much longer before they both climaxed with unexpected intensity.

"I love you," said Ash, after he had rolled off her.

"Ash, I love you too."

"We can do this forever, can't we? For the rest of our lives?"

"Don't rush things, Ash! We've got to be sure of more than this. But this is okay, isn't it?"

"It certainly is."

"Let's swim!"

"What?"

Sophie sat up and clasped her knees. The heat of the day was almost tangible inside the gazebo.

"This is called The Bathing Place," she said. "Come and see!"

"Shall I put on my boxers?"

"Heavens, No!"

Naked, Sophie ran down to the decking at the stream's edge and dived in. Ash followed her. The freshness of the water caressed his skin, flushed with the day's heat and their love-making.

After they walked up the steps out of the water, Sophie produced towels she had put in the gazebo earlier. She had made baps filled with salad and egg; and there were cans of apple juice. The sun had grown stronger and when they had finished eating, Sophie took the rug and laid it on the grass outside. Then, from the cool box, she produced a plastic bottle of sun block and offered it to Ash.

"Don't need it!" he replied and they laughed. Sophie anointed her front with it and asked Ash to do the same to her back. And so they lay in the sun on the rug on the grass and made love and swam until the sun began to dip towards the tops of the tall trees across the river. They talked about themselves, what they had done in the past, where they had been brought up. Ash spoke about Lahore and, then London; and about moving to Pepynbridge.

"You like Pepynbridge?"

"Of course I do! Especially this afternoon!"

Sophie laughed; but then she said,

"Remember my telling you when we went to the cinema about Leela being worried about you? Saying, on the one hand, that you're a good Muslim, and yet on the other hand, you're going out with me without a chaperone?"

Ash's thoughts were brutally translated from the idyll of the present to the shed in Middlehay Wood.

"Yes?"

Sophie sensed his guardedness. A shaft of darkness had come between them.

"Ash, you're not mixed up in anything..." she paused, searching for an appropriate word, "...wrong?" she concluded lamely.

"What do you mean, wrong, Sophie?"

"Oh nothing. It's just that there's a lot of talk about Muslims since Paris and Tunisia. You're not involved in anything like that, are you, Ash? Not hiding anything from me?" Her voice was pleading.

"Of course I'm not!" responded Ash firmly, guiltily conscious that he had just lied to someone who, at that moment, he loved more than anyone or anything else in the world.

"Good!" was Sophie's response.

A little while later, Ash said,

"Sophie?"

"Yes?"

"You know when you took me round your dad's farm?"

"Yes?"

"Would you take me round again? I'd really like that."

"Of course I shall!" said Sophie happily. She leant over and kissed him on the lips. "Let's make love again!" And they did. When they had finished, Sophie looked at her mobile where it lay next to her shorts and T-shirt.

"Heavens!" she exclaimed, "It's half past six. We'd better go back or else Mum'll come looking for us."

They both dressed and made their way back to the cottage. Marigold opened the front door.

"Hello, you two! Had a nice day?"

"Yes, thank you, Mrs Wicken," responded Ash.

Marigold looked at their faces, glowing with happiness. I bet you have, she thought, with a pang of envy. But no harm in that. He's a nice boy and one hell of an improvement on the lads Sophie used to hang out with. And have sex with too, she had learnt in Medborough Crown Court last December.

Ash made his apologies and began to cycle home. Inside the cottage, Marigold said,

"It's good to see you looking so happy, Sophie. You haven't looked as happy for as long as I can remember."

"I am happy, Mum. Very happy. In fact I feel so good, I don't think I need any more therapy."

"What do you mean, you don't need any more therapy!? Unless I'm very much mistaken, you've just been engaging in excellent therapy. And, I suspect, it's done you a lot more good than the sessions at the clinic." Mother and daughter smiled knowingly at each other, "But when you tell your therapist about Ash...." she paused, "...you will tell Maisie, won't you?"

"Of course, Mum."

"Well, when you tell her about him and you, see if she agrees that you've done enough with her. Oh, and Sophie?"

"Yes, Mum?"

"You're still...?" she paused again.

"Oh, Yes, Mum. Don't worry about that. No chance!"

Sophie was delighted and relieved that Marigold knew what was going on and didn't object.

"He seems a nice boy."

"Oh, Mum. He is. And you know what?" Marigold raised her eyebrows interrogatively. "He wants to go round the farm again. He really likes it."

"Don't know what your father will make of that. He's not exactly tolerant of ethnic minorities."

"Don't tell me, Mum!"

As Ash pedalled up the hill towards the junction with the main Medborough to Pepynbridge road and the immediate enchantment of Sophie faded, he reminded himself that he was a warrior of *Allah* on a mission; a mission to strike a grievous blow for Islam, which would transport him straight to Paradise. Mind you, he reflected ruefully, I'm not sure that the seventy virgins, or any of them, will be any better at making love than Sophie. And his thoughts went back to the river bank. No! He told himself. That's not the way! Not the *sunna*! He remembered how Zed had emphasised more than once in the prayer room at the Academy that jihadists should demonise their enemies.

"It doesn't matter how nice they seem," Zed had said. "They are enemies of *Allah*, Most Gracious, Most Merciful; and of the Prophet, peace be upon him. You must regard those you are about to destroy as less than human."

He's right! thought Ash with relief as he reached the main road. He turned right and began to freewheel down the hill towards Pepynbridge. That Sophie Wicken is just like any other Western girl. White trash, that's what she is. No good Muslim girl would have behaved as she'd done that afternoon.

Then his mind went forward to Christmas Eve and he envisioned the flawless body he had made love to being reduced to shredded flesh and splintered bone. Whatever Zed had said, Ash found that prospect profoundly disturbing and he resolved that, regardless of who else would be there, he'd do everything within his power to make sure Sophie was not in the Abbey when he detonated his *šahīd* vest.

"Did you have fun with Sophie?" asked Leela mischievously.

"None of your business!" Ash replied.

"I'm not sure you should be going out alone with a girl. Don't you agree, Mum?"

"Oh Leela! Don't keep on about it! We have to fit in with the culture we're living in. Don't you like it in Pepynbridge, Leela?"

"'Course I do, Mum."

Leela decided to leave it there, but her concern was not lost on Ash.

Later, in his bedroom in front of his laptop, he attempted to bolster his enthusiasm for *istishhad* by browsing Islamist websites. The trouble was, he acknowledged reluctantly, they didn't arouse half as much enthusiasm in him as the prospect of another love-making session with the delightful, flawlessly beautiful and eminently desirable Sophie Wicken. It was impossible to banish what had happened that day at The Bathing Place from his mind and his final thoughts, before he fell asleep, were not about *istishhad*; nor even about his coming trial with Northamptonshire, but rather about making love again with Sophie; and about how much he was looking forward to going round her father's farm with her again; and about how much he'd like to marry Sophie and work on the farm and learn about growing stuff and harvesting it.

◆◆◆◆◆◆◆◆◆◆◆◆◆◆◆◆◆◆◆◆◆

Tuesday, 28th July 2015

It was seven o'clock in the evening of the following day and Herbert was conducting the *Spatzenmesse* with his customary *brio*. The members of the choir, whom he had trained the previous summer for the first recording, were by now well accustomed to performing with him. They adored him and their performances shewed it. They put everything they had into them and this Mass by Mozart was eminently suited to their considerable musical skills, honed as they had been by Herbert. The sacred space of the Abbey was saturated with the composer's melodies and harmonies. They echoed off the vault of the nave and curled around the Gothic columns, and yet, at the same time, the precision of Mozart's music and its superb cadences shone through. And the whole was executed with a feeling and an enthusiasm that would have gladdened the composer's heart. As the closing chords of the *Agnus Dei* subsided around the medieval stonework, a beaming Herbert said,

"Wolfgang Amadeus would be proud of you!"

"And you!" boomed a bass voice from a back row choir stall to general laughter. Herbert waved away the compliment.

Wires wound around the Abbey, linking microphones and cameras. Two technicians were busy adjusting a bank of equipment, festooned with dials, switches and sliders.

"Was that alright?" called out Herbert, addressing them.

"Yeah! Fine Reverend! Fine! You're doing alright."

"We'll rehearse again tomorrow and then have a first run through on Thursday, okay? Mr Cohen will be here then."

"Okay by us. What time on Thursday?"

"We'll start recording at ten o'clock in the evening. With luck, there'll not be much traffic then and no emergency vehicle sirens."

"Hope not!"

"Otherwise, we'll have another go on Friday evening."

The rehearsal over, the choir began to file out of the south porch. Sophie, Ash and Leela were together. An overcast, cool day had yielded to evening sunshine and Ash said,

"Let's go for a drink at the Blue Boar?"

"Rather not!" replied Sophie. She looked at her mobile. "Dad'll be there. Always is at this time. How about the Pemberton Arms?"

The Pemberton Arms was at the bottom of Station Road, just before the bridge, with lawns reaching down to the banks of the River Pepyn.

"Sophie, why don't we go and talk to your dad about going round his farm again?"

"Really?"

"Yes! Really, Sophie."

"Well, prepare to be insulted."

"I can cope with that."

"If you two don't mind," said Leela, "I'll go home."

After her earlier encounter with Alfred Wicken, Leela had no wish to be in his company. Pepynbridge was challenging enough without being subjected to racial abuse. She turned left and walked past the Abbey towards the gates of Pepynbridge Hall and into Abbey Gardens. When she let herself in, her mother was preparing the evening meal.

"Hello, Leela! Where's Ash?"

"Gone to the pub with Sophie. Where's Dad?"

"At the clinic. He should be home..." Sabi looked at the clock on the wall, "...in about half an hour."

"Mum, I know I've said it before, but I really am worried about Ash."

"I know you are, Leela, but what can we do?"

"I suspect that he and Sophie are..." Leela paused, reluctant to articulate what she believed.

"Yes, Leela, I know what you mean, but the boy's nearly eighteen. He has to make his own life choices."

"He's getting interested in farming. I think he might marry Sophie and go and work on her dad's farm."

Sabi put down a pan she was carrying, wiped her hands and looked directly at Leela.

"Do you regret coming to live in Pepynbridge?"

"In a way, I do. I love the singing, even though I know it's disapproved of by Islam. But I feel so isolated here. My only friend is Sophie, but she and Ash obviously want to be alone together most of the time when they're free. So, Mum, I'm lonely."

"I'll have a word with Dad and we'll have to see what we can do about it. But, Leela?"

"Yes, Mum?"

"I can't see us moving from here."

"I know that, Mum. I'm not expecting you to. It's just..."

"Leela, it's a hard thing for me to say, my love. But I believe that you should make more of an effort to integrate in Pepynbridge. Sophie's not the only girl..." she paused, "...and Ash isn't the only boy."

"Mum!" exclaimed a shocked Leela.

"Just reflect on what I've just said. We'll have a word with Dad when he comes in and see what he says."

When Abi came in and the conversation was renewed, as Leela anticipated he would, Abi endorsed Sabi's advice. Well, she concluded reluctantly, it might be good advice after all. I'll have to think about it; which is what she said to her parents, bringing the conversation to an end.

When Sophie and Ash arrived at the Blue Boar, every table in the garden was taken, but Ash found a bench seat against a fence.

"I'll get the drinks," said Sophie. Ash looked around him. "If you're looking for Dad, you won't find him out here. I'll go inside and ask him if he'll talk to you. Okay?" Ash nodded. Sophie disappeared inside and, after a minute or two, re-appeared. She nodded and gestured to Ash to come inside. The evening was soft and most customers were in the garden. The bar was nearly empty, but in one corner three men were sitting at a table with partly drunk pints of beer in front of them. Ash followed Sophie over to the table. He recognised Alfred Wicken. Of medium height and heavy build, watery blue eyes beneath a carpet of wiry, curly, straw-coloured hair appraised Ash from a face, puffy and red from prolonged alcohol abuse.

"Pull up two more chairs!" Wicken instructed them.

She and Ash did so and sat down.

"Ash," said Sophie, "this is my father."

"Hello, Sir!" said Ash. Alfred grunted.

"And this is my granddad, Reg."

"Hello!" said Ash. Reginald Wicken nodded. He looked much like his son, only older; the same hair in tight curls, but grey; and features that also betrayed heavy drinking.

"And this is Mr Callow. He used to be the head teacher at St Aidan's Church of England Primary School before Mrs Onion took over from him three years ago."

Ash absorbed a frail, elderly, sad-looking man, very nearly bald with a few strands of hair carefully arranged across the dome of his skull. One eye was lower than the other and the corner of his mouth below it sagged a little.

"Good evening, Sir!" he said.

"Hello, young man," Callow replied, his speech slightly distorted.

"Norman had a stroke in January," explained Alfred. Annoyance crossed Norman Callow's features. Alfred continued, "Ash, is it?"

"Yes, Sir!"

"You're interested in farming are you? Not many of your ilk are."

"Oh, but with respect, Sir, that's not quite right."

"Really? What do you know about it, then?"

"Well, Sir..."

"Oh call me Alfred, will you!" Wicken was irritated by this foreigner's good manners and formality. I can do without that!

"Alfred," started Ash again, "I come from Pakistan; from the Punjab. I was born in Lahore, a big city. But the Punjab is one of the most fertile places on earth. They grow all sorts of crops there. Wheat, rice, cotton and so on. And if you went there..."

"No chance of that!" growled Alfred.

Ash ignored the interruption, "...you'd see great big fields, grain silos and, during the harvest, huge combine harvesters. We have relations who farm in the Punjab, both in Pakistan and in India. Although we're not allowed to visit India, I know from letters and photographs from family members who live and farm there what their farms look like. My great uncle is one of the biggest farmers in India. He drives a Range Rover."

Alfred looked at Ash with narrowed, shrewd eyes. Bigot Alfred may be, but he was an opportunist. This lad, he thought, seems bright. He's good looking too. Pity about the colour of his skin, but you can't have everything.

"So, you'd like to take another look around my farm, would you?"

"Yes please, Alfred!"

"So how serious are you about farming, then?"

"I'm exploring it. I shall be eighteen in October and leaving school next year. I need to work out where to study after that. Perhaps at an agricultural college?"

As Ash said this, he realised that he would not be alive after Christmas Eve, but, he told himself, it's all part of maintaining cover. And anyway, if I hadn't been going to martyr myself, what I've just said would have been the truth.

"And you two are going out together, are you?"

"Yes, Dad!"

"Serious, are you?"

"Could be," Sophie said.

Funny that, thought Alfred. This darkie's not the son-in-law I would have wished for, but only because he's a Paki. Otherwise, it could be quite promising, seeing as how my own attempts to impregnate Shirley are bearing no fruit. And anyway, if Shirley did bear me a son one day…His train of thought tailed off.

"Okay then," he said. "When?"

Ash looked at Sophie.

"After the performance on Thursday?"

"Yes, I think so," replied Sophie. "One day next week, Dad?"

"Go!"

And they did.

After the performance of each piece and whilst the next was proceeding, a technician took what had been recorded into the museum in the ambulatory, which had been temporarily sound-proofed, and gauged its quality through headphones.

It was during the awesome double solo rendering by Sophie and Leela of *Brother James' Air* that, without warning, Ash found himself out of his body, looking down as the person below that was him detonated his *šahīd* vest. There was a blinding flash and an ear-splitting report. The chancel was filled with smoke and, when it cleared, Ash made out, amidst the chaos, the limbless naked torsos and severed heads of Sophie and Leela.

It was all that he could do not to stand up and shout,

"No! No! I can't do it!"

But with painful sharpness, Ash's mental turmoil was pierced by an apprehension of incalculable repercussions.

Ash felt his cheeks wet with tears. The tenor next to him laid a comforting hand on his thigh. Ash turned and responded weakly to his sympathetic smile. He pulled out a handkerchief, dried his eyes and cheeks and turned back to the girls, who were still singing. I haven't made that decision, he told himself. Not yet I haven't! I've got to think it through very carefully.

But the *istishhad* dam was crumbling and, like Ash's tears, rivulets of *ridda*, of apostasy, were seeping through its cracks. When Sophie and Leela finished and the technicians nodded that the equipment was switched off, the choir broke into applause. When it had subsided, Ash's neighbour turned to him and said,

"I'm not surprised you were moved, Ash. Your sister and your girlfriend, eh?" Ash nodded, not trusting himself to speak.

By midnight, the performance was complete. There had been no intruding noise and Joshua and the technicians declared themselves delighted. It had been, Herbert Onion and Joshua Cohen agreed afterwards, outstanding.

♦♦♦♦♦♦♦♦♦♦♦♦♦♦♦♦♦♦♦♦

Friday 31st July to Monday 3rd August 2015

The next day, Friday, Ash and Sophie both slept in until noon. They had agreed not to meet. Saturday was damp and overcast. Ash was unable to borrow the Clio, so he cycled over to Summerhay where he and Sophie watched television. On Sunday in the Abbey, as most of the members of the choir were going on holiday in August, the last fully sung Mass before September was celebrated. The liturgy cast its usual spell over those present; and, for the first time, Ash felt it weaving a mysterious magic within him, born, he was now willing to concede, of its divine inspiration. This time, he was seized by an impulse to join Sophie at the rail and receive a blessing from Herbert. But he held back. He was not yet convinced that he should betray Zed. Later, Ash reflected that, oddly, it now seemed to be Zed for whom he felt any residual loyalty, rather than *Allah* and Muhammad, after whose name, for the first time that he could remember, Ash declined mentally to append its customary invocation.

That afternoon, Pepynbridge Cricket Club played away and it was past eight o'clock before Ash returned home.

Monday was overcast but dry when Oliver Standard collected Ash. At the County Ground in Northampton, Ash passed an hour in the nets, batting against, and bowling to, club professionals under Kevin Wood's watchful eye. Afterwards, he talked to Wood about his life and cricketing experience. Ash felt that his performance in the nets had matched his proven ability in the field, but when they left, Wood gave no indication of what he thought. He'd let Ash know, he told him, after he had consulted the club professionals who had been in the nets with Ash and reported to the Club Committee. He couldn't say at the moment what he would recommend, but the decision would be the Committee's, not his.

On the way back, Ash asked,

"So, what do you think, Ollie?"

"Ash, I thought it went well. Very well, in fact. You should be all right."

"You really think so, Ollie?"

"I do. But, Ash, you heard what Kevin Wood said. I'd be hopeful, anyway. You didn't blow it!"

"Thanks, Ollie."

Later, at supper Ash sought and was granted his mother's consent to him borrowing her car the next day.

"Off to spend another day with Sophie then, Ash?" asked Leela disapprovingly. Ash ignored her. Later, in his bedroom, he called Sophie on his mobile. Would Tuesday be a good time to look around the farm?

"I'll ask father in the morning and ring you. No point now. He'll either be in the pub or out harvesting. How did the trial go?"

"Alright, I think."

"When will you know?"

"I'm not sure. Keep your fingers crossed, Sophie!"

"Don't worry! I shall. Love you!"

"Love you too!"

◆◆◆◆◆◆◆◆◆◆◆◆◆◆◆◆◆◆◆◆◆

Tuesday, 4th August 2015

At eight o'clock Sophie rang Alfred on his mobile. Then she rang Ash.

"That'll be fine. Dad will meet us at the farmhouse at ten."

At ten o'clock, Ash and Sophie drove up the gravel drive and parked in front of Pepynbridge Farmhouse. As they got out of the Clio, Alfred emerged from the front door.

"Hello!" he growled, his voice and features distorted with anger.

"Dad! Whatever's the matter?"

"Shirley's walked out on me, the bitch!"

"How come?"

"Came in this morning for breakfast and found a note saying that she was bored with me and the farm and was going back to London with the kids. And her car's gone."

"Yes, well Dad, Pepynbridge is rather different from Peckham. I did wonder how long it would last. You may be better off without her."

Alfred Wicken looked at his daughter and, for the first time she could remember, a genuine smile of pleasure transformed his features.

"You know, girl, you may well be right. Hello, Ash! I forgot about you."

"No problem, Alfred."

Ash thought it as well not to comment on the collapse of Alfred's Wicken's domestic arrangements.

"Right! Where do you two want to go? What do you want to see?"

"Well, Alfred, first of all, I'd like to watch some combining."

"Too early, my boy." Sophie was astonished at her father's affectionate tone. "Still dew on the wheat," he added.

"Well, how about the cows?"

"Bullocks, Ash! Bullocks! Cows are female. No cows here. I've done with cows. Bullocks are castrated males we're fattening up for the abattoir." Seeing Ash's expression of incomprehension, Alfred thought, Bloody hell! The boy knows nothing. "Slaughterhouse," he explained. "Sophie, why don't you shew Ash the fattening shed and then the beasts in the paddocks out the back?"

"Okay, Dad."

"And when you've done that, drive out to Butler's Mede. You know where that is?" She nodded. "We'll be combining in there by then. The tracks are dry. You'll be alright in the car."

Alfred went back inside the house.

Sophie and Ash inspected Alfred's cattle. First, she took him to a large shed, covered in at the sides.

"This used to be the dairy," she explained. "Dad went in for milk when I was four. He lost a packet and had to sell land for housing in Pepynbridge to stop going bust. That's Abbey Gardens where you live, Ash. And Hall Close, over the road from you. Anyway, in October, when the grass stops growing, he brings the bullocks in here and feeds them on barley and barley straw over the winter."

After walking through meadows where Alfred's bullocks were lying down, "...because it's going to rain," explained Sophie, glancing up at dark clouds gathering above them, they returned to the house and drove along the main road before turning through a gateway half a mile further on towards Corbury. As they drove down a track between fields, Ash saw ahead a green combine harvester, with a green tractor and high-sided trailer alongside it, moving slowly through ripe wheat and leaving a carpet of shredded straw behind it. As he watched, a pipe swung slowly out from the combine until it was over the trailer and a brown stream poured from it.

"Wheat," explained Sophie. "When the trailer's full, it'll go back to the dryer. There'll be another tractor and trailer at the dryer now. When it's emptied its load of wheat, it'll come back and take over from that one."

"What happens to the straw?" Ash asked. "It's all cut up."

They had drawn to a halt and were standing beside the car, watching the combine harvester going away from them across the field.

"It's no use. You can't feed cattle with wheat straw. Too tough. You could save it for thatching, but that's a lot of trouble." Sophie went on, "Or you could bale it and sell it as fuel to a power station, but there isn't one round here that'd take it, so we don't."

"You seem to know a lot about farming," said Ash. "Alfred doesn't think you're interested."

"Well, I'm not really, but you can't live on a farm all your life as I did till last December without learning something about it. Come on, I'll shew you something else."

They climbed back into the car and Sophie directed Ash further along the track. It began to climb and on the skyline ahead woodland stretched for three hundred metres away to their right. They stopped at the end of the wood and got out. The wood was narrow and on its far side, and parallel to it, was a strip of green maize, thirty metres wide.

"What's that for?"

"Shooting."

"Shooting?"

"Yes, shooting. This is tenanted land. Mr Templeton-Smith...you know who I mean? He lives in the Hall?"

"Yes."

"Well, Mr Templeton-Smith shoots over the land that Dad rents from him. And Dad lets the sporting rights over the land he owns to Mr Templeton-Smith."

"So, why...? What's that?" He pointed at the maize.

"It's maize. Corn on the cob." They started to walk along a narrow corridor of roughly mown grass between the maize and the wood. As they went, Sophie explained that Alastair Templeton-Smith employed a gamekeeper, who would soon be releasing pheasant poults into a pen in the wood. When they could fly, they would leave the pen; and the wood and the maize would provide them with cover and food.

"They'll be fed from hoppers as well," she said, pointing to small blue plastic barrels sitting on short legs along the edge of the wood. "That's how the gamekeeper knows where the birds are. On a shoot day, people with sticks called beaters walk through the wood and the maize and drive the birds out. You see how the ground slopes down from here? See the big wood at the bottom?" Sophie pointed. Ash looked and nodded. "Well, the shooters stand in front of that and the birds fly over them."

"And they shoot them?"

"They do, if they can."

"Is it difficult?"

"Can be, I'm told, but I don't really know, I've never done it; or even seen it done. But Dad's told me about it."

They stopped and faced each other. Sophie tilted her head back and Ash kissed her lips.

"It's okay. We can," she said, reaching down and placing her hand against Ash's crutch. Moments later, their naked bodies were moving slowly and rhythmically together on the grass. Ash remembered The Bathing Place and held back until he felt Sophie's fingers digging into his buttocks and she said,

"Now!" And then, "Oh, Ash!" and they climaxed together. After a little while, he rolled off her and they lay side by side in the shadow cast by the wood. After a long silence, because for his part Ash was unsure what to say, Sophie said,

"Ash?"

"Yes?"

"Would you be interested in farming?"

Ash was silent for a long time.

"Ash?"

"Sophie, I'm thinking." And then, after another pause, he said, "Yes, Sophie, I would be!" As the words escaped, it struck him with almost tangible force that he might just have made probably the most important decision of his life. "Why do you ask?"

"Dad's family have farmed in Pepynbridge for over two hundred years. Apart from Dad and Granddad, I'm the only one left. That's what the trouble was up until Mum and I left him."

"What was the trouble?"

"The fact that I'm a girl; and that I'm keen on music and ballet. All Dad wanted was a son to carry on the farm when he retires. He's only forty-one now, so that'll be a long way off, but when it comes, he'll have to sell the farm. Ash, it'll break his heart. And I doubt whether he'll get a son now. He might do, but not with Shirley; and certainly not with Mum."

"Why not with your mum?"

"She's had a hysterectomy."

Ash thought again, and Sophie, guessing what was going through his mind, did not interrupt. Finally, he leant over her, kissed her gently on the lips and said,

"Sophie, do you think we should get married?"

"Yes, Ash, I do! But not yet! Not until you've been through agricultural college."

"And if I do and we get married, do you think your dad would treat me like a son."

"Yes, I do! Of course, he might have another son one day, but you're nearly eighteen. If he had a son, say next year, it would be twenty or more years before he could take over the farm and Dad will be over sixty…" she paused and added "…if he hasn't killed himself with booze by then. In the meantime he needs someone like you to help him run it. Would you?"

At that moment, with total clarity and resolve, Ash knew that it was what he wanted to do more than anything else, whatever price he would have to pay for his *ridda*. He would have Sophie as his wife and the farm as his living. Perfect! But, first he would have to tell Sophie about *IstishhadUK*. And he would have to work out how to withdraw from it and survive.

"Sophie, there's nothing in the world I'd like better." Sophie smiled. "But there's something about me that you don't know and I need to tell you about that. Let's get dressed and go back to the car." As they did, it began to rain.

In the Clio, Ash said,

"Sophie? Remember the other day at The Bathing Place when you asked me if I was mixed up with anything that was, as you put it, wrong?"

"Yes, I do! And you said you weren't."

"Yes, well, Sophie, it wasn't the truth. I'm involved in terrorism." The colour drained from Sophie's face, her eyes widened and she made to speak. "No, Sophie! Please let me finish!" He told Sophie about Zed and the others; and about the mission. As he was talking, she put both hands against the sides of her face and when he finished, she cried out,

"Oh, No, Ash! It can't be true! Tell me it's not true!"

"Sophie, I'm afraid it is true. And the reason I lied to you at The Bathing Place was that I wasn't sure then what I should do. But now I am!"

"Ash, it's awful! Terrible! We can't let it happen."

Sophie's face crumpled and tears streaked her cheeks.

"Sophie, we mustn't let it happen. I won't let it happen, whatever the cost. But didn't you suspect anything?"

Sophie sniffed.

"Leela did and she hinted to me that she did, remember? But I didn't want to believe it. But now, you're finished with it, Ash. Aren't you? Promise?"

"Yes, I am! But I've got to find a way of getting out of it. If they find out that I've betrayed them, they'll kill me." Sophie looked stricken. She remained silent for a while. Then she looked at Ash and said, quietly and deliberately,

"So, what are you going to do?"

"I'm going to tell Herbie."

"When?"

"This afternoon."

"Shall I come too?"

"No, Sophie! And please listen to me! Don't breathe a word of what I've just told you to anyone else! As I said, if Zed finds out that I've betrayed him and the others, my life won't be worth a cent; and maybe yours won't be either. At the moment, what I've told you must remain a big, big secret, okay? I'll tell Herbie and when I have done, I'll ask him to tell you that I have, so that you'll know that I've told him. Okay?"

"Yes, Ash! I trust you." And then, "Ash, I love you."

"I love you too Sophie. Think what it'll be like when we've got out of this mess."

"We're in this together, aren't we?"

"I'm afraid we are."

"And we'll be together for the rest of our lives, however long or short."

They kissed again. Ash started the car, turned it round and drove back to Summerhay.

Herbert and Julie had been shopping in Medborough. Julie's pregnancy had just entered its thirty-fifth week and she had told Herbert that it was time to buy a cot and a pushchair.

"But the baby's not due for another six weeks," he had protested.

"Could come at any time now, Herbie. We must be ready."

"How are you feeling?"

"Hot and tired."

Herbert paid at a checkout for a cot, a pushchair and a steriliser and feeding bottle that Julie had assured him would also be needed. As they walked together towards the multi-storey car park, Julie remarked,

"I'm so pleased the recording went well. Have you heard from Josh?"

"I have. He rang me this morning. He's delighted with it. He's already put it on YouTube and sent it to Amazon."

Awkwardly they loaded their purchases into their estate car and drove back to Pepynbridge.

In the Rectory, Julie made a pot of tea and they sat at the kitchen table, talking about the baby and what it was going to mean for them.

After Ash dropped Sophie in Summerhay, he drove back to Pepynbridge, parked the car at 4 Abbey Gardens and straightaway set off to see Herbert. The shower had passed and, as Ash walked the short distance to the Rectory in hazy sunshine, it felt as though fetters had been struck from his wrists and his feet; and a great weight lifted from his shoulders. His whole being felt so light that he could barely sense the ground beneath him. The net of obligations that, he now recognised, were not only wrong, but oppressive; oppressive of himself; and oppressive of everyone else unfortunate enough to be entangled in them as he had been; that net was gone from him; gone for ever.

Recalling his discussions with Herbie, Ash felt liberated from *Shari'a* just as the first Christians must have felt when they had been liberated from Mosaic Law. Whatever he wanted to do with his life, and whatever consequences might follow from his *ridda*, nothing could ever take away from him these precious moments when joy was coursing through him like a mighty, unstoppable flood. However long he lived, whatever life had in store for him and whatever faith, if any, he might embrace, he was and would remain forever unchained from Islamism and the *Qur'ān*. Euphoric, he rang the bell of the Rectory front door.

In the kitchen Julie said,

"I wonder who that is?"

Herbert went to the front door and opened it.

"It's Ash," he called out and added, "We shall need another pot of tea."

RIDDA
(Apostasy)

Wednesday, 5th August 2015

It was six o'clock the following evening and Herbert Onion, Richard Maxey and Jack Driver were in Herbert's study. Sitting at his desk, in measured and calm sentences, Herbert relayed everything that Ash had told him. When he had finished, a long silence followed. The thoughts of Richard Maxey and Jack Driver went back to June and their discussions about Ash.

Then Richard Maxey said,

"You know, I'm not altogether surprised."

"Frankly, Richard," said Herbert, "nor am I. Jack, what do you think we should do?"

"Herbie, it's difficult. When Richard and I last discussed Ash in June, I warned Richard that if Ash were mixed up in something like this, he could be in serious trouble." He glanced down at some notes he had brought with him. "In the light of what you have told us, Herbie, I'm afraid that Ash is undoubtedly guilty of an offence of terrorism under Section Five of the Terrorism Act Two Thousand and Six, for which the maximum penalty is life imprisonment."

Another silence followed while Herbert and Richard digested this unwelcome news. Then Driver continued,

"It's also a crime under the Terrorism Act, punishable with up to five years imprisonment, for anyone who knows about a terrorist conspiracy not to report it to the police. I've done some research on this, just in case things turned out as they have. And I've spoken to a colleague in London who is more familiar with this field of criminal law than I am. There is no doubt that disclosure to the police must be made, but there is debate about when and in what circumstances. Ash's disclosure was made to you, Herbie, in confidence. However you would be guilty of an offence if you didn't report what Ash told you yesterday to the police, in the words of the Terrorism Act, 'as soon as reasonably practicable'. And the same now applies to you, Richard..."

"But Jack," interrupted Herbert. "What about you?"

"What about me, Herbie?"

"Aren't you subject to the same duty to disclose?"

"Possibly not, Herbie. Although I'm not yet formally instructed to act as Ash's solicitor, if I were, I would be protected by something called legal professional privilege. So far as concerns you and Richard, the position is not straightforward. Christmas Eve is a long way off, which means there's time to play with and the expression, 'as soon as reasonably practicable', admits to elastic interpretation. So far as I'm concerned, I'll do everything I can to protect Ash, consistent with my duty to disclose what I know to the police, however that's interpreted, and without compromising their investigation. A possible way forward is for me to secure Ash's immunity from prosecution in return for his co-operation with the security services. If I do that and he tells the police all about the conspiracy, anyone else's failure to disclose it to the police will become academic."

"Can they do that, Jack? Grant immunity from prosecution?"

"Yes Herbie. It's possible under Section Seventy-One of the Serious Organised Crime and Police Act Two Thousand

and Five. The offender is given a written notice to that effect. In a case like this, the notice would be issued by the Director of Public Prosecutions."

"Is it likely?"

"Herbie, I simply cannot say. After you spoke to Richard about Ash in June, I spoke to a Sergeant Hay at Medborough Police Station. Hay told me then that he had been interested for a while in the group of Muslim students, including Ash, who had been meeting on Friday afternoons in Medborough Academy. Beyond that, I don't know how much the security services know. If they don't know much more than I told Sergeant Hay, then they would welcome Ash's co-operation. If so, then a grant of immunity might be forthcoming. I need to discuss the situation with Sergeant Hay or someone else in authority. But before I do, I need Ash's consent."

"And Abi's?"

"As Ash is under eighteen, normally I should. But in these circumstances I don't think so. This is far too sensitive to disseminate any wider than it already has been. Herbie, what did you say to Ash about that?"

"I told him that he must not say anything to anyone. He promised he wouldn't, but then he said he'd told Sophie Wicken. He asked me to tell Sophie what he'd told me."

"So what, if anything, did you do about that?"

"After Ash left me, I drove to Marigold's cottage in Summerhay. Sophie was there alone. She told me that she had been expecting me. I told her what Ash had told me, and she said that it was the same as he'd told her. I warned her that it was more than her and Ash's lives were worth to say anything about it to any one else, not even Marigold. Sophie said she understood and that she wouldn't."

"Good! Then I need to see Ash."

"When?"

"As soon as possible! Now?"

Herbert tapped a number into a telephone on his desk.

"Hello, Sabi! Reverend Onion here. Is Ash there? He is? Please may I have a word?" A pause, then, "Hello, Ash! Are you free to pop down and see me? I'm at the Rectory." Another pause, then, "When? Now?" Another pause, followed by, "You are? Good! See you in a minute or two."

The doorbell rang and they heard footsteps in the hall. The study door opened and Julie said,

"Ash to see you, Herbie."

"Hello, Ash! Come in! Mr Driver would like to have a word with you about what you told me yesterday."

Herbert fetched in another chair and Ash sat down. A discussion followed, during which Ash registered shock when he learnt of the risk of prosecution and its possible consequences that now hung over him. When Jack Driver invited him to instruct him to approach the police to try and secure immunity from prosecution, Ash asked,

"What if I don't, Mr Driver?"

"Ash, we should have to report to the police what you told Herbie. We'd have no choice. It's our legal duty."

Silence followed while Ash reflected. Then he said, very calmly,

"Thank you, Mr Driver. Please would you try to get me immunity from prosecution?"

"Ash, you do realise, don't you, that the security services may wish you to act for them under cover?"

"Yes!"

"Would you be willing to do that?"

With a wry smile, Ash replied, "Mr Driver! I'm used to doing that."

"Okay, Ash. Leave it with me."

"But, Mr Driver?"

"Yes?"

"What about your fee…"

Driver interrupted, shaking his head. "Don't worry about that for now. We'll see what happens and then think about it. I shan't do anything for which I would charge without warning you first. Alright?"

"Yes! And thank you, Mr Driver."

"You're on holiday at the moment, aren't you?"

"Yes! I go back on the third of September."

"When do you next meet Zed and the others?"

"On Monday, the seventh of September. Zed's left school and we're meeting at his house."

"And you're not planning on going away between now and then?"

"No!"

"Got a mobile? You have? Number please!"

Ash gave Jack Driver his mobile number and the meeting ended.

♦♦♦♦♦♦♦♦♦♦♦♦♦♦♦♦♦♦♦♦♦♦

Thursday, 6th August 2015

Jack Driver rang Andrew Hay the next morning and, at ten o'clock they were sitting either side of Hay's desk in Medborough Police Station.

"Sergeant Hay, I am in possession of information about a terrorist conspiracy, provided to me by someone who's involved in it, but now wishes to resile from it and help the security services. That person has instructed me to act on his behalf. For obvious reasons, I do not wish at present to disclose my client's identity."

"Mr Driver. Are you acting for that young man you told me about? The one who lives in Pepynbridge?"

Driver made a quick assessment and wondered how much more Hay knew than he, Jack Driver, had told him last June. He decided that he certainly knew something.

"I couldn't possible say," he replied.

Hay swivelled to his left, tapped on a keyboard on a table beside him and looked at a computer screen. Then swivelling back to face Driver, he said,

"Mr Driver, let's not beat about the bush. I know that something is going on. I know that it's serious. I don't know much more than that at present and I'd dearly like to know more. What I do know is that Aashif Malik, the son of Dr Malik, who is attached to Medborough General Hospital, is amongst those involved. If he is your client and if I were to authorise his arrest, what would your advice to him be, were he to be interviewed under caution?"

"I should advise him to exercise his right to silence, Sergeant."

"Well, that doesn't surprise me, Mr Driver. I should have expected no less of you. Let's approach the matter from a different angle, then. Whoever is your client, Mr Driver, can he…"

"Or she," interrupted Driver.

"Or she," acknowledged Hay, "provide details of what is planned; the target or targets; the timing; and who is involved?"

"Yes, my client can."

"How imminent is the threat?"

"Not very. I can disclose that the acts are not planned to take place for some months."

You are being careful, Hay thought. And I don't blame you. He appreciated the hazardous situation of Driver's client as well as Driver did.

"Let's be clear!" said Hay, swivelling back to look at the text displayed on his screen. "So far as you can judge, Mr Driver, is your client able to provide all the material that the security services might reasonably need to identify and arrest everyone involved in plenty of time before the action is perpetrated?"

"Yes, my client is able to do that, Sergeant."

Hay made a written note on a pad beside the keyboard.

"I need to ask you a few more questions, Mr Driver."

"I cannot guarantee that I'll answer them."

"Sure. I understand that." Hay tapped again and, looking at fresh text displayed on the screen, he continued,

"If you were in my position, or the position of the Director General of MI5, would you consider that, in the interests of justice, it would be of more value to have your client as a witness for the Crown than as a defendant?"

"Yes, I would!"

"Would your client give evidence for the prosecution?"

"I can't guarantee that, but in my judgement, that would be highly likely."

"In your opinion, would your client be a credible witness?"

"Yes, my client would be."

"In your opinion, in the interests of public safety and security, is the obtaining of information about the planned action of greater importance, than your client's conviction of terrorist offences?"

"Incomparably so. The scale of what is planned is as serious, if not more serious, than the London bombings in July two thousand and seven."

As Driver had answered each question, so Hay, his face a mask, added to his hand-written note. He continued,

"If your client were not offered immunity..." he swivelled again and looked at Driver, "...because that's what you're after, isn't it?"

"Yes it is!"

"I think that you have already made this clear, but is it right that if immunity were not offered, your client would not be willing to tell us about the conspiracy."

"If my client acted on my advice, that's correct Sergeant."

"Apart from the offenders, does anyone else know about the conspiracy?"

Driver appreciated the danger in the question.

"Sergeant, I'm not in a position to answer that."

"Mr Driver, I'm sure you're aware of the duty to disclose information under Section Thirty Eight B of the Terrorism Act Two Thousand?"

"I am, Sergeant and, at the moment, I decline to discuss it further."

Sergeant Hay reflected that if anyone else apart from Driver had been told about the conspiracy, it might be difficult to discover their identity. Anyway, it would be far more valuable to have the information direct from Driver's client, because it would be admissible as evidence in a trial of the other terrorists, rather than hearsay evidence from others whom he'd told, which would not.

He swivelled back to the screen and contemplated the final circumstance in which, as the then Attorney General had informed the House of Commons as long ago as November 1981, immunity should be granted. Hay concluded that there was not enough evidence at the moment to prosecute Aashif Malik, for whom he was convinced Driver was acting; or any of the other IC4 males who had been in Middlehay Wood on 20th July. Whether we acquire any more evidence is a matter of chance as things stand. So, if young Malik can help, that would be extremely valuable. He swivelled again and looked at Driver.

"Mr Driver, as you are aware, there is already an investigation into the conspiracy I believe your client is involved in. The question of immunity from prosecution is not a matter for me alone. I need to speak to others. As soon as I have done and a decision has been made, I'll be in touch with you."

"Thank you Sergeant!" Driver rose and left.

That evening, after telephoning Ash, Herbert and Richard, Jack Driver drove to Pepynbridge and all four gathered in Herbert's study. Jack recounted his conversation with Sergeant Hay.

"So," said Ash, "they're already on our tracks."

"They are, but I don't think that they know very much at the moment and it's clear they need to find out a whole lot more. Ash, I would expect to hear from Sergeant Hay, or someone else, within the next week or so. In the meantime, be very careful what you say to anyone. But I just need to check one thing with you, Ash."

"Yes, Mr Driver?"

"If the others are arrested and charged, would you be willing to give evidence against them at their trial?"

"Do I have a choice?"

"Not really, if you want to be granted immunity from prosecution. And if it is granted, I imagine that it will be a condition that you give evidence for the prosecution. If so and you refuse, your immunity would lapse." Ash raised his eyebrows interrogatively. "It would be null and void; of no effect; and you would be prosecuted for terrorism and in all likelihood convicted on your own admissions."

"And if I gave evidence for the prosecution, would I be protected afterwards?"

Jack Driver thought for a moment.

"I would hope so. We'd have to find out."

"Well, if that were guaranteed, I would give evidence against the others."

"Thank you, Ash!"

"Oh, Ash?"

"Yes, Dr Maxey?"

"I heard you had a trial with Northamptonshire Cricket last Monday. How did it go?"

"Oh, alright, I think. Mr Wood, that's the head coach, said he'd let me know. If they invite me to join, it wouldn't be until next season. All this will be behind me then, I hope."

Jack Driver thought that the trial of the terrorists, if it happened, would be unlikely before this time next year. And whenever it happens, if Ash needs protection, I doubt he'd be able to play county cricket. But he kept his misgivings to himself.

"Oh, and one more thing, Mr Driver."

"Yes, Ash?"

"Would it be alright if I told Sophie about what you've said this evening?" Jack Driver thought for a moment, and the others looked at him. Then he said,

"Yes, you may. In the circumstances, I think that you ought to keep Sophie in the picture. You and she are in this together, aren't you? After all, you decided to involve her."

"True," responded Ash. "And we intend to be together for the rest of our lives."

"Well, maybe," said Herbert.

"No, Herbie! For sure!"

"We'll have to see." And then, to lighten the mood, Herbert added, "Ash? When you want a wedding, just let me know. Although, perhaps you'll not be wanting a Christian marriage?"

"Well, Herbie, as you just said; we'll have to see."

◆◆◆◆◆◆◆◆◆◆◆◆◆◆◆◆◆◆◆◆◆

Friday, 14th August 2015

For Ash and Sophie, the week that followed seemed longer than they'd ever spent before. Their mood was sombre and when they were alone together, there were few joyous moments, much watching of television and no love-making. They found it easier to include Leela in their company because, when they did, they were constrained from talking about the trouble they were in. And, they calculated, the more they treated Leela as a chaperone, the less anxious she would be about their relationship.

Alfred had rung Sophie to ask her how the second visit to the farm had been and Sophie had replied that Ash's enthusiasm for farming was growing, but that, for the moment, he was tied up and she could not say when they would visit the farm again. Perhaps when the drilling of next season's crops began in September? By which time, Sophie privately and fervently hoped, their immediate situation would have been resolved.

The week felt even longer because, as well as hearing nothing from Jack Driver, there was no news from Northants.

Then in his office on the morning of Friday, 14th August, Jack Driver took a call from Sergeant Hay.

"Can you come over, Mr Driver? Any time to suit you."

"Sure. I'll come straight away."

In Hay's office, Hay said,

"If you provide me with the name and address of your client, I am in a position to provide him…" he paused, "…or her with the immunity that you've requested."

"Sergeant, you were correct. My client's name is Aashif Malik and his address is 4 Abbey Gardens, Pepynbridge, MD5 7PQ."

"One moment, please!" Hay noted down Ash's full name and address, swivelled, typed into his computer and, moving his mouse, clicked on "Send". Then he said, "The immunity notice is being prepared now. I understand that the DPP will sign it as soon as it is ready and then it will be scanned and a copy emailed to me. The original will be brought here by one of the investigating team from London."

They waited in silence for several minutes until an alert sounded from Hay's computer. He opened an email, downloaded its attachment, printed it and handed it to Driver. Under a heading that read:

The Crown Prosecution Service,

Head Office, Rose Court,

2 Southwark Bridge,

London, SE1 9HS

it recorded that immunity from prosecution was granted to Aashif Malik, with his address, for any offence committed by him under the Terrorism Acts before the date of the notice on condition that, first, he rendered every assistance to the security services in their investigation into all terrorist offences in which he was, or had been, complicit; and, second, in the event of any other person being prosecuted for such an offence, he would give evidence on behalf of the Crown against that person, if requested to do so by The Crown Prosecution Service. It was dated 14th August 2015 and, Driver verified, signed by the Director of Public Prosecutions.

"Sergeant Hay, in the light of this, I am in a position to advise my client, Aashif Malik, to provide the security service with all the assistance in this matter as he is able."

"Thank you, Mr Driver. Together with colleagues, I wish to conduct an interview under caution with Aashif Malik, which you may attend. And after that, to take a witness statement from him."

"Of course, Sergeant. When?"

"Tomorrow for the interview, please."

"Saturday?"

"Yes, Saturday! We're taking this investigation very seriously. You have told me that the planned acts are not to take place for some months, but our priority is to arrest those concerned as soon as possible. In all probability, when we have done, Aashif Malik will be relatively safe."

"Wait a moment, Sergeant! Do you mind if I telephone my client?"

"Not at all! In here?"

"Not a problem."

Jack Driver tapped Ash's number into his mobile. Yes he would be able to attend Medborough Police Station tomorrow. Noon was fixed.

"There's another matter, Sergeant."

"Yes, Mr Driver?"

"Obviously Ash has disclosed the details of the conspiracy to me. As he's my client, I maintain that I'm protected by legal professional privilege from prosecution for failing to disclose it to the police under Section Thirty Eight B of the Terrorism Act Two Thousand."

"Mr Driver, that's been discussed with the DPP. We take the view that you are."

"What about anyone else Ash may have told, Sergeant?"

"Provided your client makes full disclosure tomorrow, there will be no investigation of anyone who may be in breach of Section Thirty Eight B. If, on the other hand, your client doesn't..." Hay broke off and looked at Driver.

"Sergeant, in such a circumstance, I and, I am confident, anyone else able to do so, would make full disclosure to you without delay. One way or another, you will have the information you need by tomorrow evening. However, as you will be aware, evidence in court against the offenders will have to be given by Ash, rather than by someone he's told."

"I'm well aware of that, thank you, Mr Driver."

"Thank you, Sergeant," said Driver and left.

That evening in his flat in London, Raed noted with satisfaction an internet media report that Hamza bin Laden, a surviving son of Osama bin Laden, had issued a call on behalf of *al-Qaeda* to its followers in Kabul, Baghdad and Gaza to carry out lone wolf attacks in Washington, London, Paris and Tel Aviv. That, thought Raed, should lay to rest any concerns within *IstishhadUK* prompted by the article in *The Spectator*.

◆◆◆◆◆◆◆◆◆◆◆◆◆◆◆◆◆◆◆◆◆

Saturday, 15th August 2015

Ash parked Sabi's Clio in Driver and Sickle's car park and he and Jack Driver travelled in Driver's car the half mile to Medborough Police Station on the outskirts of the city. Driver parked in the Visitors' Car Park and he and Ash walked round to the front of the building and into the foyer. A civilian sitting at a counter behind a screen recognised Driver and spoke into her head set. Moments later Hay entered the foyer and led Driver and Ash upstairs to a small conference room, furnished with a rectangular table and eight chairs. Two men were sitting at the table on the side away from the door.

"Mr Driver and Mr Malik, this is Chief Inspector Paul Evans of the Metropolitan Police Service and Cedric Fane from MI5."

Hay sat down on the same side of the table as Evans and Fane. Ash and Jack Driver sat opposite them. In front of Hay was a microphone with a wire from it leading beneath a side table on which there was a screen and a keyboard. Hay passed to Driver the hard copy of the notice of immunity. Driver satisfied himself that the signature was hand-written. He turned to Ash.

"Ash, this is the original of the copy notice of immunity that I shewed you in my office. It's genuine and, as I have advised you, provided you give evidence against the jihadists if requested to do so, you may answer any questions that Mr Evans and Sergeant Hay ask you without fear of being prosecuted for the things you told Herbie Onion last week. You understand that, don't you?"

"Yes, I do!"

"Well, now Ash. That's what you're called isn't it?" Cedric Fane's tone was friendly.

"Yes, Sir!"

"Call me Cedric, okay?"

"Okay."

"Ash, has Mr Driver explained to you that your immunity depends upon you giving us all the information in your possession about the conspiracy or plot in which you're concerned?"

"Yes, he has."

"If any of the others involved are taken to court, would you be willing to give evidence of their involvement against them?"

"Yes, I would, Cedric!"

"Another thing before we begin. Ash, it is absolutely vital that you tell us the truth; everything. That you hold nothing back. Let me explain. We believe that, from now on, your life may be in danger from the other jihadists. Do I need to explain why?" Ash shook his head. "We are here to protect you, but we can only do so if we have the full story; or, at least, as much of the full story as you know. Alright?"

"Yes, Cedric! But Cedric?"

"Yes, Ash?"

"If I tell you everything and the others are arrested and prosecuted as a result, will I be protected?"

"Ash, I promise we shall do our very best to do so. Sergeant Hay?"

"I agree. Ash, at the end of this, I'll discuss your protection with you. I may not be able to tell you today the precise measures we shall adopt to look after you. That will depend to some extent upon what you tell us; but we shall do our best to keep you safe from harm. Alright?"

"Yes, okay!" replied Ash, nodding.

"Mr Driver, there's a formality we must observe before we start."

"Yes, Sergeant Hay?"

"I need to caution your client. Of course, if he gives evidence against the others, it will be irrelevant because he won't be prosecuted."

"Of course. I quite understand." Driver explained the caution to Ash. "Yes, Sergeant?"

"Aashif Malik. You do not have to say anything, but it may harm your defence if you do not mention when questioned something you later rely on in court. Anything you say may be given in evidence. Do you understand that, Ash?"

"Yes, I do."

"Good! Yes, Cedric?"

"Well then, Ash..." started Fane. The interview, recorded onto the computer beneath the side table and converted into text by means of software, took two hours. Sandwiches and soft drinks were brought in at one o'clock. Ash recounted everything he knew about *IstishhadUK* and answered every question truthfully. When he had finished, Hay tapped into his keyboard, clicked on 'File' and then on 'Print'. A printer in the corner of the room clattered. When it stopped, Hay collected five bundles of printed script and stapled each bundle. He placed three bundles in front of Fane, who passed one to each of Ash and Jack Driver.

"Ash, this is a transcript of the interview we have just conducted. Please read through it and tell me if everything there is correct."

All five in the room read the transcript. At the bottom was printed,

> Everything said by me and recorded in this document is true to the best of my knowledge and belief. I know that I shall be liable to prosecution if I have wilfully stated anything recorded in this document which I know to be false or do not believe to be true.

Beneath there was a space for Ash to sign and date it. After half an hour, Ash looked up and said,

"Mr Driver, shall I sign and date it?"

"Is it the truth, Ash?"

"Yes, it is!"

"Then you should sign and date it, Ash."

Ash did so. The deed was done.

"Mr Driver?"

"Yes Sergeant Hay?"

"We shall convert that into a formal Criminal Justice Act witness statement later, which Ash will be asked to sign. I'll run it past you first, alright?"

"That's fine. What next, Mr Fane?"

"Mr Driver, Ash lives with his father, mother and sister in Pepynbridge, doesn't he?"

"He does."

"Do they know anything about this?"

"No! I advised Ash to say nothing about it to anyone except his girlfriend, Sophie Wicken, who knew about it anyway." Fane raised his eyebrows. "He told her before he told Reverend Onion." Fane nodded. "Sophie lives with her mother in Summerhay and she's been told not to say anything to her mother, or to anyone else."

"Andrew?"

"Thank you, Cedric. At the moment, there's no specific threat to Ash. We've had no indication that any of the four main suspects know that they're under surveillance."

"I didn't know they were!" exclaimed Ash.

"Precisely, Ash, you didn't; and they don't. But we know who they are and we've had them on our radar for some time. We also know the names and addresses of the other three who used to meet with you and Zaeem Zahra on Fridays in the Academy. We don't know, and Ash you've told us that you don't know, who the other twelve are from London, York and Lincoln. As a result of the information you have provided, we should be able to discover their identities and bank details from Katch & Kill in Lincoln. However, until any of them realise they're on our radar, I don't envisage there being any immediate threat to you. Without going into detail, we should know if and when there is. But Ash, for the moment, there's no need for your parents or for your sister to know what's happening; or Mrs Wicken, for that matter. Okay?"

"I understand."

"What about Reverend Onion and Dr Maxey?" asked Driver. This was greeted with silence, which Paul Evans broke.

"Well, as Ash has told us, they're in the picture anyway. For my money, it would be sensible to let them know what has happened today. What do the others think?"

They agreed.

"As a precaution, Ash..." Hay picked up something resembling a mobile phone, "...I'm going to give you this. It's both a phone and a radio alarm permanently connected to this police station." He passed it across the table to Ash. "You see the red button? If at any time you need assistance, press that. It goes through to a dedicated slot on the switchboard that tells us, not only that it's been activated, but because it's also a tracker, where it's been activated, so we can find you, or it. If you press the green button, you'll be voice-connected to the switchboard at Medborough Police Station. You see the five bars at the top of the screen? When less than two are shewing, you'll need to charge it up." He passed a charger and plug to Ash.

"Ash, you've told us your next meeting with Zed is on September the seventh at his home address," said Fane. "You happy about attending that?"

"Yes, I am!"

"Good. We want you to go on acting as you would have done if you'd never been here today and told us what you have. And we need to talk to you on a regular basis. When we do, I or Andrew Hay will phone you. I'm not going to give you my contact number in case you lose your mobile. If you need to speak to one of us, then use the phone that Andrew Hay's just given you."

"Ash," said Hay, "I'll need to see you again to obtain more background information about you, okay? When I do, it won't be here. Too public, but in the child protection unit. It's a bungalow on the other side of Medborough. Anything else?" He looked at the others, all of whom shook their heads. "Okay then. Mr Driver, I'm going to take you and Ash to a back door that opens directly onto the Visitors' Car Park. More discreet."

Back at the offices of Driver and Sickle, Jack Driver and Ash parted company, but not before Driver had squeezed Ash's shoulder.

"Well done, Ash. Not easy for you."

"No! But I don't blame anyone but myself."

They smiled at each other and Ash left and drove back to Pepynbridge.

Back in the conference room, Paul Evans said,

"In the light of what we now know, we shouldn't have a problem, should we, with the Home Office over a warrant to intercept emails and to monitor telephone calls of everyone who's on our radar?"

"No!" replied Cedric Fane. "The applications will be at Marsham Street first thing on Monday morning. I'll secure email drafts through to you, Paul and Andrew, tomorrow for you to check their accuracy. GCHQ will do the monitoring. If and when I hear anything from them, I'll let you know. Meanwhile, Andrew, can I leave it to you to investigate the Katch & Kill connection? You should be able to discover from them the names and credit card details of everyone who ordered Fly Vests..." he paused and added "...ingenious that!"

"Yes! So simple," responded Andrew Hay. "I'll get someone onto that on Monday morning."

"Thanks. Well, keep in touch!"

"We shall."

The meeting broke up and Fane and Evans drove back to London.

Andrew Hay, using a search engine, located Katch & Kill in Lincoln. He sent an email to the East Midlands Special Operations Unit, the CTIU responsible for investigating suspected terrorism in Lincoln, informing it that DC Stuart Rally of Medborough Police would be making enquiries at the premises of Katch & Kill on the following Monday.

Then Hay tapped a number into his telephone.

"Yes?"

"Susan Armstrong? Andrew Hay here."

"Oh, hello! I'm afraid I've not got round to seeing Sophie Wicken yet. Or anyone else in Pepynbridge."

"Don't worry about that, Susan. Not necessary now."

"Why not?"

"Operational secret, I'm afraid."

"Oh! I hope Sophie's not in trouble."

"I can assure you that she's not."

"Oh, good!"

Hay ended the call.

♦♦♦♦♦♦♦♦♦♦♦♦♦♦♦♦♦♦♦♦♦♦

Monday, 17th August 2015

Perched on a limestone escarpment, Lincoln Cathedral and Castle dominate the city beneath like feudal overlords. On the plain below them, nineteenth century terraced housing and shops and twentieth century industrial units beyond spread out untidily. Just after ten o'clock on Monday, 17th August, an unmarked car drew to a halt outside one of the industrial units and Stuart Rally got out.

The day before, Sunday, Andrew Hay had read secure emails from Paul Evans and the East Midlands Special Operations Unit. He had approved by secure email the wording of the applications to the Home Secretary for interception warrants; and had been pleased to note that the East Midlands Special Operations Unit raised no objection to Stuart Rally making enquiries at Katch & Kill.

Under a sign identifying the unit as the premises of Katch and Kill, Rally pushed open a door marked 'Entrance'. Inside, the whole of one wall consisted of a glass-fronted cabinet displaying an array of shotguns and sporting rifles. Rally negotiated stands holding fishing rods and outdoor clothing and stopped in front of a low counter. Behind it sat an overweight, middle-aged man, balding and wearing a check shirt encasing a generous stomach that overhung a belt securing a pair of jeans. He smiled at Rally.

"Yes? Can I help?"

Rally shewed him his warrant card. The other's face fell.

"Firearms?"

"No! I'm from Medborough; not Lincoln. Is there somewhere where we can talk in private?"

"Yes! Come into the office!"

Rally stepped behind the counter and followed the other through a door into a tiny office. A plump, kindly-faced woman was sitting at a desk, looking at a computer screen.

"I'm Geoff Fletcher," said the man, "and this is Joan, my wife and book-keeper. Joan, Mr...?" he paused and looked at Rally, who obliged with,

"Rally."

"Yes! Mr Rally and I need to have a private chat. Could you look after the shop for a moment?"

"No need for your wife to leave, Mr Fletcher."

"Someone's got to mind the shop."

She left and Fletcher closed the door.

"Yes?"

"You sell a piece of clothing called a Fly Vest, do you not?"

"I do!"

"I'm investigating a serious offence and I'm interested in anyone who may have bought Fly Vests from you on-line between the first of January and the twentieth of July this year."

"Okay, officer. I've got no problem with that, but I'll have to ask Joan to look it up in the records. I'm not good with computers."

"Alright."

Fletcher called Joan in.

"Mr Rally is a policemen and he's interested in the identity of anyone who bought a Fly Vest from us on-line between...?" he paused.

"Between the first of January and the twentieth of July this year," supplied Rally.

"Oh, Yes!" said Joan. "It was odd. A lot of people did. Nearly all of them had..." she paused, searching for the right words, "...foreign names. You, know, Asian-type names? Don't you remember, Geoffrey? We laughed about it."

"I do! I said I thought they might need them for suicide vests."

He broke into loud laughter at his recycled joke. Rally smiled thinly and said,

"Don't worry Mr Fletcher. Nothing like that, I can assure you."

"Yes! But why would a load of Pakistanis suddenly want to buy Fly Vests?"

"Perhaps they had entered a charity fishing competition?" suggested Rally, mischievously.

Joan Fletcher sat down in front of the screen and, after a few seconds, she said,

"Between the first of January and the twentieth of July this year we sold twenty-four Fly Vests on-line. Twenty of them to people with foreign names. One of them was Yaz, Geoff. Remember?"

Fletcher made no reply.

"Could you print out their details, please?" said Rally.

Joan looked at Fletcher.

"Yes! That's alright, Joan. We must help the police with their enquiries."

"What details do you want, Mr Rally?"

"Names and card numbers, please."

"Is it alright for me to go back into the shop, officer?"

"Of course, Mr Fletcher!"

Joan Fletcher printed off a sheet with the information that Rally had requested. He looked at it, thanked her and returned to the shop.

"Got what you came for, officer?"

"Yes, thank you."

"You a fisherman then?"

"'Fraid not."

"A shooter?"

"No."

"Pity! Thought we might do some business. 'Bye!"

"'Bye!"

Rally left, got into his car and drove back to Medborough.

As he heard Rally's car drive away, Fletcher tapped a number into a telephone on the counter.

"Yes?"

"Yaz?"

"Yes?"

"Geoff here from Katch & Kill. Yaz, there's something I think you ought to know, mate…"

On the same Monday morning, Sabi's Renault Clio drew up outside the cottage in Summerhay. Sophie and Marigold had gone away early on Saturday morning to stay with Marigold's sister who lived in Clacton-on-Sea with her husband and three children. They had returned late on Sunday evening and Ash was anxious to see Sophie. He pipped his horn and she came out. Out of the vehicle, Ash took her in his arms, kissed her and said,

"I've missed you."

"Me too."

"Can you come out?"

"Of course I can. I'll tell Mum." She went back into the cottage and emerged a minute later. "That's fine," she said. "Where shall we go?"

"The Bathing Place?"

"It's not that hot; and there's no rug or towels there."

"No, it's just somewhere private where we can talk."

"Oh, okay then."

They walked along the river bank, through the woods and sat down in the gazebo and Ash brought Sophie up to date.

"Do your parents know any of this?"

"No!"

"Or Leela?"

"No, again. I've been told not to tell anyone. Apart from the police and MI5, only you, Herbie, Dr Maxey and Mr Driver know."

Ash shewed Sophie the personal alarm he had been given and explained how it worked. They were quiet for a while, until Sophie said,

"Ash, I'm scared."

"Sophie, so am I. But there's nothing we can do about it. It's all my bloody fault for getting mixed up with Islamism in the first place. Sophie?"

He turned and looked at her. She met his gaze.

"Yes?"

"Do you really want to go on seeing me?"

"Of course I do! I love you! For better or for worse, eh?" They kissed, with affection but without passion. "How about going to the farm again?"

"Great idea!"

They walked back to the cottage, got in the Clio and Ash drove to Pepynbridge Farm. There was no one at the house. Behind it, lay a large concrete yard on which there were two rectangular sheds, a square tower and a round silo, all constructed from aluminium.

"What are those?" Ash pointed towards them. "I've been meaning to ask."

"That's where the harvest is dried and stored. Look, I'll shew you. Come with me!" Sophie walked through a wide opening into one of the sheds, followed by Ash. There was a similar opening on the other side of the shed.

"See that?" she said, pointing to a metal grille in the floor between the openings.

"Yes?"

"Tractors come in through that doorway with a trailer-load of grain, which is tipped through that grille into a pit below. From there..." they walked outside and Sophie stopped next to the silo "...it goes into this..." she patted the side of the silo "...called the pre-store."

"And what happens in there?"

"From there it goes into this..." she said, pointing at the square tower next to the pre-store "...where it's dried."

"Why?"

"Because, if the grain is too damp, it spoils. Dad stores it at fourteen percent moisture."

"Why not dry it in..." Ash paused, recalling, "...the pre-store?"

"Because it has to be dried very slowly. It passes down through filters from the top of the dryer and, as it does, warm air is pumped through it. You couldn't do that in the pre-store."

"But why dry it at all? Why not harvest it when it's fourteen percent?"

Sophie smiled.

"This isn't the Punjab, Ash! We have to take the crop when we can; sometimes between showers." She pointed up. "Look at those clouds! Sometimes the harvest comes in at over twenty percent moisture, so we have to dry it."

Ash noted with pleasure Sophie's use of the first person plural pronoun. He suspected that last year, when speaking of her father and the farm, she would not have said, "we".

Just then, a tractor drawing a trailer drove across the yard into the shed, stopped, and tipped its load of wheat into the pit. A man in orange overalls climbed down from the cab.

"Hi Sophie! How you doing?"

"Good, John! John, this is Ash."

"Ah, Yes!" said John, "I've heard about you. You're interested in farming aren't you?"

"Yes, I am!"

"Know what's happening here?"

"Not really. Sophie was explaining it to me."

"Well, I've just tipped wheat into that pit. It's about ten metres deep. From there it goes into the pre-store..." he pointed, "...and then into the dryer." He pointed again.

"Sophie's just told me that. But how does it get from the bottom of the pit into the pre-store?"

"By a chain and flight." Ash shook his head gently. "Inside that..." John explained patiently, pointing to metal casing about 15 centimetres square that emerged from the side of the shed and rose to the top of the pre-store and the dryer "...is like a bicycle chain with flighting, like cups, attached to it. When it's switched on, which I'll do in a moment, the chain inside moves and the flighting carries the grain up and into the top of the dryer."

Ash nodded understandingly.

"Clever!" he said.

"Yeah! Bit like an augur; like on the combine to transfer grain from it into a trailer."

"An augur?"

"An augur does the same as a chain and flighting, but it's round, not square, with a pole inside it and continuous flighting coiled round it from the bottom to the top. When the pole turns, the flighting carries the grain up. Invented by a Greek bloke a long time ago, called Ark..." He stopped, uncertain of the name.

"Archimedes?" said Sophie.

"That's it, Sophie! Archimedes. Clever chaps those ancient Greeks! Anyway, when the grain's dry, it's carried by a chain and flight from the dryer back into the pre-store and then over there..." he pointed to the other, much larger, shed "...where it's stored till it's taken away by lorries."

"Thank you for explaining all that," said Ash.

"Not at all!"

"Is Dad in the fields?" asked Sophie.

"Yes! He's in Long Meadow. He's nearly finished. He'll be pleased to see you."

Makes a change, reflected Sophie, which she decided not to voice. Ash and she resumed their places in the Clio and she directed Ash to another part of the farm. They parked on the road and walked through a gateway. Apart from a narrow strip of wheat on the far side where a combine harvester was moving slowly forward, the field was empty. They walked across to another tractor and trailer. Alfred Wicken climbed down from the cab.

"Hello, you two. Good to see you!"

Wow! thought Sophie.

"Hi, Dad!" she said.

"We're nearly done. Only one more load to go. That's why I'm waiting here. Been to the dryer, Ash?"

"Yes, Alfred! Very interesting. What's the...you know, the wetness?"

"Moisture content? It's sixteen at the moment, which isn't bad." Alfred looked up to the sky. "But for how long, I couldn't say." As if in response, a raindrop struck his forehead. "Bugger!"

"We'll go back, Dad, if that's alright?"

"Yeah. Sure. We might have to stop, if the rain continues." Ash and Sophie walked back across the field. As they did, Ash said,

"Sophie, I've made up my mind what I'm going to do if I get out of the muddle I'm in at the moment. When I go back to the Academy, it'll be the beginning of my last year and I'll have to make a choice about where I go after that."

"And?"

"I'm going to apply to an agricultural college. I'm predicted four 'A's at A level. I should get an offer."

"I'm sure you will Ash. And Ash...?"

"Yes?"

"I'm so pleased," and she stopped him, pulled him to her and kissed him. This time, there was passion in it.

"Not here, Sophie!"

"Of course not! At my place!"

"What about your mum?"

"It's Monday. She'll have gone shopping by now."

So they went back to Summerhay and made love on Sophie's bed. By the time Marigold returned, Ash had left.

"Been with Ash, Sophie?"

"Yes, Mum! We went down on the farm again. They were harvesting in Long Meadow and we saw Dad."

"Did you now. And how was he?"

"You know, Mum, he's changed."

"What do you mean, changed?"

"Well, did I tell you that Shirley's left him?"

"No, you didn't, but I heard she had in the village shop. Do you know why?"

"Dad told us that it was because she was bored. She's gone back to London."

"Not surprised. But how has Alfred changed?"

"He's much more friendly, especially since he's met Ash."

"Well, that does surprise me. Your father was never one for coloured people, amongst his other pet hates."

"Yes, but Ash is interested in farming."

Marigold looked at Sophie thoughtfully.

"Is he now? Well that might explain it. The one thing your father values above all else is the Wicken link with Pepynbridge. Does he think you and Ash are serious?"

"Mum, we are serious and, yes he does. You know what? Ash told me today that when he leaves school, he's going to go to agricultural college."

"Does your father know that?"

"No, not yet."

"Sophie, you say you're serious about Ash. How serious?"

"When Ash has finished college, we're going to get married."

Marigold turned away and looked out of the window in the kitchen where the conversation was taking place. Would she mind having a Pakistani son-in-law? No, she wouldn't! Would she mind having coffee-coloured grandchildren? No, she wouldn't!

"Early days," is what she said.

"Yup! Early days."

"Does Alfred know you two are going to marry?"

"Well, we haven't told him, but, as I just said, he knows we're serious."

Well, the thought ran through Marigold's mind, if that happened and Alfred was happy about that, I might...she calculated...I might just consider going back. Hmmmm! We'll have to see.

Sophie knew her mother well enough to read her mind, but she decided it was not the time to explore with her the possibility of them returning to live at Pepynbridge Farm. But, Sophie thought approvingly, it is a possibility, what with Ash wanting to take over the farm from Dad and us providing him and Mum with lots of grandchildren. And there would be lots of them, she decided; at least four. We could live in the farm cottage. It had been empty for as long as she could remember, but it was wind- and water-tight. There were only three bedrooms and one bathroom, but we could see to that. Extend it, we could. And modernise the kitchen.

"I think you ought to tell Dad about Ash's decision to go to agricultural college."

"Don't worry, Mum. I shall when I next see him."

"Good," responded Marigold, ruminatively. There was, she thought, a lot to think about just now.

That afternoon, Stuart Rally was sitting in Andrew Hay's office.

"Twenty-four names. Four of them are European. We won't need to bother with them," said Hay. "I'll scan this and secure email it to Paul and Cedric in London. The card numbers will tell us the banks involved. They should be able to provide us with home addresses; and with luck email addresses as well."

"Five of them from Medborough, including Ash and Zaeem Zahra. Apart from the four prime suspects, do we place the others under surveillance, Andrew?"

"We'll see what London says. Anyway, we don't know their addresses yet."

The information was not long in coming. A secure email to Andrew Hay and to the CTIUs responsible for Lincoln and York supplied the names and home and email addresses of all twenty. Surveillance of the four cell leaders would be maintained. Warrants had been issued authorising the interception of telephone calls and emails of all twenty. A strategy meeting was fixed at Medborough Police Station for Friday, 21st August at 2pm.

Friday, 21ˢᵗ August 2015

On Friday morning, Ash received by post an envelope containing a distilled version of his interview in Medborough Police Station, with a covering letter from Jack Driver advising Ash to read it and, if content with it, to sign and date it. When he had done so, would he please return it to Driver and Sickle in the stamped addressed envelope enclosed and he would forward it to Sergeant Hay. Ash read, signed and dated the statement and posted it in the post box at the corner of Abbey Way and Abbey Gardens.

At two o'clock, the six who had met in Medborough Police Station four weeks earlier were again assembled in the small conference room. As he had done previously, Chief Inspector Paul Evans was leading the discussion.

"So, now we know the offenders' identities and where to find them, what's our next step? Arrest them? Or wait and see?"

"I think we should wait and see." The speaker was Cedric Fane. "Bob..." he indicated the other MI5 officer sitting beside him "...and I have been talking and we agree on tactics. The bombings are not planned to take place until Christmas Eve and, given the nature of the plot, I doubt that will change. Even if it did, Ash Malik would tell us. So, there's no immediate danger. At the moment, apart from Ash's testimony, which a court would discount to an extent because he is, or was an accomplice, and any Fly Vests that might be recovered from the offenders, there's no other evidence upon which to charge and try them. That would be a slender thread upon which to seek convictions."

"I agree with that," said one of the other police inspectors. The others added their assents.

"So do I," concluded Paul Evans. "Andrew, you're going to handle Ash Malik?"

"Yes!"

Further discussions followed dealing with remoter contingencies, but when the meeting finished, the strategy agreed upon was to wait, maintain surveillance and see what transpired.

In the Rectory, Herbert was cooking a light supper; a task for which his bachelorhood before his marriage to Julie had well prepared him.

Julie's pregnancy was approaching its thirty-seventh week and she was wishing it was over and done with. At antenatal classes, she had been advised to rest as much as she could; advice she followed. Term had ended five weeks ago, for which both she and Herbert were grateful. As the choir was on holiday, Herbert was spending more time at home, relieving Julie of tasks she found tiring. She would take the next term as maternity leave. She and Bishop Julian Ross had decided that sadly, Norman Callow was not well enough to cover for her, so the bishop had arranged for another retired head teacher to do so until Christmas.

The Rectory was equipped with four bedrooms, one of which Julie and Herbert shared. Herbert had painted out the smallest, which now contained the cot. Herbert and Julie had happily accepted Harry and Joy Swift's offer to come and stay after the birth, due on 14th September. The choir would be back before then and there would be much to be done in the Abbey; Harvest Festival in October; the Feast of Christ the King on 22nd November; and then Advent and Christmas, with a ticketed Christmas Concert like last year, Crib and Carol Services, Midnight Mass, which Herbert had decided would be a *tour de force*; as well as a Book of Common Prayer Holy Communion service for the Puritan Remnant on Christmas Morning. For Herbert to be relieved of chores at home would be very welcome. And, he then remembered, if everything went alright, there would be a baptism as well. In his mind Herbert provisionally fixed the 25th October when, all being well, their son or daughter would be about six weeks old. Herbert held to the Catholic view that infants should be baptised within a few weeks of birth.

Herbert and Julie sat down to eat at the kitchen table.

"Oh, Herbie, I forgot to tell you."

"Yes?"

"I went for a check up today, and the midwife said that, as this is my first pregnancy, it would be better for me to have the baby in the maternity unit, rather than at home. Do you mind?"

"Mind?" said Herbert. "No, I don't mind. In fact, I'm relieved."

"So that's alright then." They looked across the table, smiled at each other and separately and privately counted their blessings.

When they finished their supper, Julie went upstairs to bed and Herbert to his study to prepare a sermon for next Sunday.

◆◆◆◆◆◆◆◆◆◆◆◆◆◆◆◆◆◆◆◆◆

Saturday, 22nd August 2015. Morning

Marigold Wicken knew that the wheat harvest at Pepynbridge Farm was over and that Alfred would not start harvesting potatoes or drilling winter wheat and oil-seed rape until September. It was 9 o'clock on Saturday morning, far too early for him to be in the Blue Boar, so a good time to ring him.

"Yes?"

"Alfred? Marigold here!" There followed a long pause, which, thought Marigold, was out of character. Maybe Sophie is right and he has changed.

"And what would you be wanting?"

"I hear that Shirley's done a runner..." and before he could reply, "...Want any help with the paper work?" Another long pause. And then,

"Are you free, Marigold?"

"I am Alfred."

"Can you drop round for a chat?"

"Sure! When?"

"Any time that suits you."

Marigold decided that to name a time after opening hours would be unnecessarily provocative.

"I could come now?"

"Okay. See you in a few minutes."

Ten minutes later, Marigold and Alfred were sitting across the kitchen table in Pepynbridge Farm, nursing cups of coffee. That's a change, thought Marigold. He'd never have made me a cup of coffee in the old days. Yes, Alfred would like her to do the books. They'd got a bit behind since Shirley had left. Did Marigold want paying?

"No, Alfred! I'll do it as a favour." Alfred looked surprised. What's got into her? he wondered. Marigold continued, "Do you know about Sophie and Ash Malik?"

"What about them?"

"Well, it seems they're an item."

"I gather so."

"Do you now?"

"Yes, I do, Marigold. And Sophie rang me this week and told me that Ash wants to go agricultural college and learn how to farm. Not that he will of course!" Marigold looked at him quizzically. "Oh, he may go to college, but he'll not learn how to farm there. He'll learn theory at college but what matters is practice. Here's where Ash will learn how to farm."

"Here?"

"Yes, Marigold, here! Unless I'm very much mistaken, our Sophie's going to hitch up with him."

"Alfred, has she told you that?"

"No, but it's my hunch."

"Well, if you want to know, that's what she told me the other day."

"Well there you are, you see. Mud-coloured kids, they'll have."

"Do you mind?"

"Mind? Me? I don't mind so long as a Wicken goes on farming here and Ash is the nearest thing to a male Wicken that I'm ever going to find."

Marigold looked at Alfred in astonishment. She'd known him before he'd got her pregnant when she'd been seventeen and their respective parents had insisted that they married. Then he'd been pleasant, if a little over-fond of the booze, but that's young farmers for you. The trouble was that he'd changed when she'd had the hysterectomy. He'd become resentful and over-bearing; bullying and contemptuous of Sophie. And his drinking had got out of hand. She hadn't seen the side of him she was seeing now since before she'd lost her womb fifteen years ago.

"What about doing your books, Alfred?"

"That's very kind of you, Marigold. When can you start?"

"Today. Right now!"

And she did. When twelve o'clock came, she expected Alfred to go to the pub, but he didn't. At one o'clock, she finished what she was doing and decided to go back to Summerhay. She walked from the office into the kitchen. Alfred was sitting at the table, watching racing on television.

"Not at the pub, then?"

"Nah!" Alfred eyes remained fixed on the screen. "I've cut down on that. Just Friday evening and, when I'm not working on the farm, Sunday lunch-time. And a whisky here in the house before I go to bed."

Well! thought Marigold. What she said was,

"Alfred, I'll come and do your accounts. Three mornings a week should be enough. Let's say every Monday, Wednesday and Friday. I'll come at nine and leave when I've finished. Okay?"

"How about moving back, old girl?"

"Sophie told me you've changed, Alfred. From what I've seen of you today, you may have done. But, I didn't leave in a hurry and I'm not coming back in a hurry. Let's just see how we get on, okay?"

Alfred looked away from the television and at Marigold.

"Thanks, Marigold. I don't deserve that."

"No you don't! So you'd better prove to me that you do. 'Bye, Alfred!"

Marigold left. On the way back in the car she thought, funny how things work out. Well Sophie will be pleased. And, she added, so will that nice Ash.

♦♦♦♦♦♦♦♦♦♦♦♦♦♦♦♦♦♦♦♦♦

Saturday, 22nd August 2015. Afternoon

Raed, Zed, Waahid and Yaaseen were sitting in The Foxes' Den in Leicester. In the King Power Stadium, the second half of a match between Leicester City and Tottenham Hotspur was being played out in heat approaching 30ºC.

"We have a problem!"

Raed, Zed and Waahid looked at Yaaseen.

"As you know, I suggested we bought our Fly Vests from Katch & Kill. I did so because I know the bloke who owns it. Geoff Fletcher. We share an interest in firearms and he's told me he can get them into the UK from abroad anytime I want. He's got a mate who farms on the Lincolnshire fen and owns a light aircraft. His mate smuggles stuff into the UK; drugs; fags; booze; guns; people; you name it. Well, Geoff rang me the other day and he told me the police are interested in us."

"In what way, Yaaseen?" Raed was staring intently at him.

"He told me that a copper had been to the shop the day he rang me wanting to know who had bought Fly Vests between January this year and the twentieth of July."

"When we met in Middlehay Wood."

"Yes, that's right!"

"So, what did this Geoff Fletcher do?"

"He gave the copper the names and credit card details of everyone who had bought Fly Vests in that period."

"Shit!"

"Raed, he told me he had no choice. If he'd refused, the police would have made life impossible for him. He's a legit firearms dealer. He's supposed to co-operate with them."

"So, how in the name of Muhammad, peace be upon him, did the police know about us buying Fly Vests from him?"

The question was rhetorical. None of them knew for certain. But they could guess. Raed articulated their thoughts.

"Someone, one of us, must have told them. So what we now know is that we've got a traitor amongst us; an apostate; a *murtadd*."

"We don't know that whoever it is has abandoned Islam. That he's a *murtadd*," objected Zed.

"Doesn't matter! The person who's betrayed us has denied the teaching of the *Qur'ān* that requires the use of force to ensure that the teachings of Muhammad, peace be upon him, shall prevail. That's enough to make him a *murtadd*, for which the penalty prescribed by the most revered *hadith*, *Sahih al-Bukhari*, is death. So, we have to discover who the *murtadd* is. When we have, we shall then decide how, when and where his punishment is carried out. Agreed?" The others nodded. "We must also assume that our identities are known to the security services and that each of us has been under surveillance; although for how long we don't know. They will know that we are meeting here today. The first precaution we should take is..." he paused, "...do you all speak Arabic? No? Well, Gujerati, then? Yes? Good!" Raed continued in Gujerati, "In future, when we meet, we'll use Gujerati. We don't know if our emails and phones are being intercepted, but, as a precaution, we should assume that they are. Okay? We shall next meet..." Raed consulted his diary, "...four weeks today, the twenty-sixth of September, but not here. There's a risk that even this conversation is being eaves-dropped, although with the level of noise in here, I doubt it. And, anyway, we're using Gujerati."

"They'll have interpreters, Raed," said Zed.

"They will, but it'll make it more difficult for them. Next time, we'll meet in my black cab, okay? Get yourselves to Medborough by eleven o'clock. Park in the station car park. I'll be waiting for you there and we'll drive up and down the A1 in my cab whilst we talk. Even if we're followed, we'll not be overheard electronically."

"Wrong!" objected Waahid. "Conversations in vehicles can be bugged through emergency and tracking security systems."

"I'd forgotten that," admitted Raed.

"The best place," Waahid went on, "would be in the countryside, like a wood, provided no one else is around."

"Middlehay Wood?"

"Makes sense."

"Middlehay Wood it will be then. At eleven o'clock on the twenty-sixth of September. In the meantime, keep your cells meeting. We mustn't let on that we know that one of them is a *murtadd*. The most important thing is to identify who it is. And make sure you're not being followed, yeah!"

"Raed!"

"Yes, Zed?"

"If the security services know about us, does the mission go ahead?"

"At the moment, I have no idea! First of all, we need to discover who the *murtadd* is and, under strong persuasion..." he paused to allow the significance of the word to sink in, "...find out just how much he's told the police. Then we decide whether or not to cancel the mission. Okay?" The others nodded.

Zed said,

"Raed, do you know which Islamist group was responsible for the attempted shooting on the high speed train in France yesterday?"

"Nope! No idea! But it sounds more like ISIL than AQAP. The *šahīd*, Ayoub el-Khazzani, was from Morocco."

"Like Tunisia?"

"Like Tunisia. Okay, let's go! *Allahu Akbar!*"

"*Allahu Akbar!*" they responded and separated.

Although all four were under surveillance and the officer assigned to each was aware of their meeting, no listening device was being used, because, as Raed had surmised, against the din in the restaurant it would have picked nothing up.

As Zed drove back to Medborough, he mentally reviewed every member of his cell and gradually, but with growing conviction, his suspicion fell upon Ash. Of course, he had no proof, but out of the four members of his cell, only Ash had gone undercover to any extent. Ab, Faz and Naz lived in the predominantly South Asian Muslim part of Medborough. To Zed's knowledge, out of school they did not mix with the *kafir* community. But Ash was different;

very different. He was, Zed knew, deeply embedded in Pepynbridge. Apart from his parents and his sister, so far as Zed was aware, Ash was the only Muslim there. He played cricket and had a *kafir* girl friend. Deep cover was all very well, Zed reflected, but with it came a risk of empathising with the community you lived in. During Zed's jihadist training in Yemen, he had learnt about the Stockholm syndrome, where hostages, opposed to a dominant culture, develop close emotional ties with one or more persons within that culture, leading to sympathy with its aims. Whilst Zed acknowledged that Ash's situation did not precisely mirror the criteria of the Stockholm syndrome, nevertheless there were significant parallels. It's what, he told himself, the British imperialists insultingly refer to as 'going native'. In addition, into his analysis Zed factored Ash's demonstrable intelligence. He was brighter than the others in his cell. He decided to keep a very close watch indeed in future on young Aashif Malik. As he drove into Medborough under a threatening sky, there was a flash of lightning and large raindrops splashed against his windscreen.

◆◆◆◆◆◆◆◆◆◆◆◆◆◆◆◆◆◆◆◆◆

Sunday, 23rd August 2015

The thunder storms that overnight had threatened Pepynbridge several miles to the west of Medborough had not materialised. Sunday started cloudless and, despite a stiff easterly breeze, by early afternoon the temperature had risen to the low twenties. In Hall Park, a match was under way between Pepynbridge Cricket Club First XI and

Borthwick Market Cricket Club First XI from Leicestershire. Ash had opened the batting and was facing Borthwick's formidable fast bowler, Angus McArthur, a former Leicestershire County player. A diplomat in his late thirties, he had been stationed abroad for many years, but played for Borthwick Market when he was home on leave.

Ash played himself in cautiously, offering no chances to the slips, the gully and the silly point hovering close to him. The opening over was a maiden. In the next over, Pepynbridge's second batsman scored a single off a medium pace bowler. Ash faced him and stroked a four to leg. Clapping sounded from the pavilion, where Alistair Pemberton-Smith, Richard Maxey and Herbert Onion were sitting together in the line of deckchairs. Nearby were Abi and Sabi Malik and Sophie Wicken.

"Richard! I've got an offer for Ash from Northants in my pocket," Alistair announced.

"Have you!"

"Yes I have! From next season, Northants will pay him a daily rate of fifty pounds plus travel expenses whenever he plays for them. He leaves school next July and Northants will help him financially through university, if he goes."

"He will, Alistair," broke in Herbert. "He's bright and I understand he plans to go to agricultural college."

"And after that?"

"He wants to farm."

"Wants to farm? How's he going to do that? His parents have no land."

"No, Alistair. But he's very thick with Sophie Wicken."

"Ah, I understand. Alfred Wicken's only child."

"Precisely."

"Well, he should be able to combine farming with county cricket. If he plays as well as he is now when he leaves college, Northants will offer him a professional contract."

"Excellent news!" exclaimed Richard Maxey.

"Indeed!" echoed Herbert.

The sunshine yielded to heavy, dark clouds. At half past three it started to rain and the players came off. In the changing room, Alistair Pemberton-Smith broke the news to Ash and handed him the letter. Ash opened it, read it and said,

"Thank you, Sir. My parents will be thrilled."

"And Sophie Wicken? Will she be pleased?" Alistair was smiling. Ash looked at him. So it's got around then, he thought.

"She'll be overjoyed, I should think, Sir. I must go and tell my parents and sister."

"They're in the tea-room, Ash, sheltering from the rain. And be ready to resume batting just in case it stops, although..." Alastair looked out of a window, "...I'm afraid it looks set." A flash of lightning was followed by a rumble of thunder.

"Of course, Sir. And thank you again!"

"Don't thank me! Thank yourself! In my estimation, you have a glittering future ahead of you in the game. Good luck!"

"Thank you, Sir!"

The rain persisted and, just after six o'clock, the match was declared a draw.

◆◆◆◆◆◆◆◆◆◆◆◆◆◆◆◆◆◆◆◆◆

Monday, 24th August 2015

Andrew Hay telephoned the Malik home. Ash was in. Would he please come into Medborough for a chat? "Yes? Good. It'll take about an hour." He gave Ash directions to the child protection unit bungalow in Medborough.

Ash found it and parked outside. There was no sign that it had anything to do with the police but when he rang the bell, Andrew Hay opened the door.

"Hello, Ash. Thanks for coming."

"Not at all, Andrew."

A few moments later, Hay and Ash were sitting in soft chairs in front of a low table.

"Ash, I've been assigned to look after you, okay?" Ash nodded and wondered what was coming. "Now, I need to know as much about you and what you do every day during a typical week as you can tell me. Okay? We're wired for sound and there's a camcorder in here as well, but we'll not be using that. But I shall record our chat for future reference. You don't object?"

"No, not at all."

What followed was an interview so comprehensive that, as it drew to a close, Ash felt that the person opposite him knew almost as much about him as he did himself. Diffident by nature, he always found it difficult to talk about himself, but Hay helped him along with gentle encouragement.

At no point did Hay display any emotion, not even when Ash told him he had been offered a playing contract with Northamptonshire. When Ash spoke about his relationship with Sophie and his hopes to go to agricultural college and, afterwards to marry Sophie and help her father on Pepynbridge Farm, he was relieved that Hay didn't ask him whether they'd had sex. It was over an hour before Hay pronounced himself satisfied. Ash was pleased it was over and was re-assured that the promise of police protection was going to be honoured.

After Ash had left, Hay took the recording of the interview back to his office, converted it into text on his laptop, printed it out and saved it, emailing copies to Paul Evans and Cedric Fane. If anyone else needed a copy, they could forward it on, Hay told them.

◆◆◆◆◆◆◆◆◆◆◆◆◆◆◆◆◆◆◆◆◆◆

Monday, 7th September 2015

The rest of the school holidays passed quietly, with Ash and Sophie spending most of their time together. On Thursday, 27th August, they visited the farm, taking Leela with them after assuring her that, if they met the newly reformed Alfred, he would not be abusive. To Leela's relief, he had not been there. On Sunday, 30th August, Ash played away for Pepynbridge Firsts and, on Bank Holiday Monday, he, Sophie and Leela and others sheltered from heavy rain in the Exhibitors' Marquee in Hall Park at the Pepynbridge Flower and Vegetable Society's Annual Show. On Wednesday, 3rd September, the first day of the autumn term, Ash and Leela caught the bus to Medborough from the bus stop in Station Road from outside the Rectory. After leaving Pepynbridge, as it always did, the bus stopped at the top of the hill by the turning to Summerhay and Sophie got on and the three of them sat together until Medborough.

Usually, they travelled home together on the bus, but today, Monday, 7th September, Ash explained to Sophie, out of Leela's hearing, that he was going to meet Zed at his family's home in Medborough and would catch a later bus to Pepynbridge.

"Be careful, Ash, won't you?"

Ash assured her he would.

Now, together with Zed, Ab, Faz and Naz, he was sitting in the Zahras' sitting room. Zed had produced prayer mats and *salāt* had been performed. Mrs Zahra had placed mugs of coffee on side tables before retreating to the kitchen.

"Dad's a taxi driver." Zed explained. "He won't be home while midnight. And my brothers and sisters are upstairs, doing their homework."

They chatted about what they had done during the summer holidays and Ash said,

"I suppose I'd better tell you. I've been offered a playing contract with Northamptonshire County Cricket Club. Of course, I'll not be around to take it up. But I thought you should know."

"Thank you for telling us, Ash. In one way it's a shame you can't, but, as I'm sure you'll agree, your loyalty to *Allah* and to the Prophet, peace be upon him, must come first. And you know what? Paradise will be whole lot better than playing cricket with *kafirun*."

"Of course it will!" said Ash, struggling to summon enthusiasm, but Zed detected a hint of insincerity. But, he thought, that's not enough; at least not yet. I need more. Not much, but something. Later, Zed said,

"Now we need to discuss how you're going to conduct yourselves at school this term. And I'll tell you why." Zed looked down at a sheet of paper he was holding. "From the first of July this year, all schools have been under a legal duty, and I quote, 'to prevent people being drawn into terrorism'." He looked up. "That means, reporting any suspicious activity to the police, yeah? So, you've all got to be very careful, okay?" They nodded.

"Now," Zed continued, "you're all in your last year, yeah?" Again they nodded. "So all of you saw your personal tutors on the first day of term, yeah?" They said they had. "Okay, I need to know what you told your tutor about what you planned to do when you leave school next July. Ab?"

"My family have a shop in Medborough. I told my tutor I'd be working there."

"Not university?"

"Not bright enough."

"Faz?"

"I said I wanted to become a doctor. My predictions aren't very good, but my tutor told me that entry requirements these days are not that stringent."

"Okay." Zed looked through some papers he was holding. "You'll have to apply to UCAS for a course by sixteenth of October. Don't miss it; otherwise the staff may become suspicious. We don't want that, do we?" Faz shook his head.

"Naz?"

"Like Ab, Zed. My dad, like yours, is a taxi driver. He wants me to do the same. Don't need to go to university for that. That's what I told my tutor."

"And you, Ash?"

"I'm planning on going to agricultural college and my tutor has told me that I won't need to apply to UCAS until January."

Zed looked steadily at Ash, raised his eyebrows and said levelly, "You're planning on going to agricultural college?" He emphasised "planning".

The room went silent and the others looked at Ash. Ash sensed danger. He broke the silence.

"What I meant to say, Zed, is that I told my tutor that. Of course, I won't really be going to agricultural college."

"No, you won't!" said Zed, mentally adding, whether we bomb churches or not. He smiled at Ash with false reassurance, intending that Ash would not think that his mistake had aroused his suspicion. But it had hardened it.

"Still playing cricket, Ash, or has the season finished?"

Relief washed over Ash as he replied,

"I'm playing just one more match for Pepynbridge, Zed. It's the last one of the season."

"And when will that be?"

"Next Sunday."

"At Pepynbridge, Ash?" Ash nodded. "And where's the cricket pitch?"

Ash explained that matches took place in Hall Park behind Pepynbridge Hall.

"How do you get there? I might just come. It'll be my last chance before our *istishhad* to watch you playing."

Ash gave Zed directions.

"When will the match be over?"

"At seven."

"Thanks. Can't promise, you know. I'll see how I'm fixed."

The meeting ended soon afterwards.

Ash's slip of the tongue was sufficient confirmation of Zed's suspicion to justify interrogating Ash under…and he mentally savoured the word…persuasion. He'd contact Raed. The security services are probably intercepting our emails, but since they know who we are, we give nothing away by contacting each other. But, the content will matter.

Zed went up to his bedroom, which, despite the size of the Zhara family, he was fortunate to have to himself. He sat at a tiny desk on which there was a laptop, drew a piece of paper from a drawer and wrote in Gujerati; crossed out; wrote again; crossed out again… After a while, he was satisfied that he had drafted something that would send the right message to Raed without alerting the security services. He typed it into his laptop and pressed "Send". If Raed thought that the content of Zed's message was sufficiently obtuse to mislead the security services, he would reply to it; and if Raed agreed with his suggestion, then Zed would be in Pepynbridge next Sunday, but not to watch Ash playing cricket.

Raed did agree, as Zed discovered when he read his reply an hour or so later.

◆◆◆◆◆◆◆◆◆◆◆◆◆◆◆◆◆◆◆◆◆◆

Tuesday, 8th to Thursday 10th September 2015

Amongst the material from Cheltenham that Cedric Fane read on Tuesday morning in Thames House was a report of an intercept, with copies, of an email in Gujerati from Zaeem Zahra to Raed Gill; and Raed's reply to Zaeem, copied to Waahid and Yaseen with a copy to them of

Zaeem's email to Raed, all of which had been translated by GCHQ from Gujerati into English.

The email from Zaeem to Raed read:

"Lahore selected. Home next Sunday. Stumps at 7. Catch?"

Raed's reply read:

"Sunday nets for 4 at 3 at woodshed."

Fane telephoned Paul Evans. Yes, Paul had read them.

"What is significant," said Fane, "is that the first email comes from Zaeem, who lives in Medborough. If he suspects that someone has betrayed them, and we don't know that, but if he has, then 'Lahore selected' looks like a reference to his suspect. And we know that they have been betrayed by Ash, who is a member of his cell."

"And comes from Lahore and plays cricket. So Zaeem suspects Ash?"

"We have to assume that."

"And the reference by Raed Gill to 'nets'?"

"Nets are where cricketers practise their skills and plan how to improve them. If I'm right, Raed and the other three will want to interrogate Ash to discover if he's the person who's betrayed them and how much he's told us. If they ask him, it's likely that he'll refuse to go with them…"

"…so they'll need to abduct him?"

"Precisely! And they'll need to plan that beforehand. Hence the reference to 'nets'. 'Four' refers to the cell leaders and 'three' to time. My interpretation is that Raed wants the four of them to meet at three o'clock next Sunday to plan when and where to abduct Ash."

"Any clue as to when and where they'll abduct him?"

"Yes, I believe so. If Zaeem has done his homework, and I would expect him to have done, he'll know that next Sunday Ash will be playing cricket in Pepynbridge and leaving Hall Park after the game is over; which will be at about seven o'clock. Hence 'Stumps at seven.' And 'Catch' means kidnap."

"Will Ash?"

"Will Ash what?"

"Be playing at Pepynbridge?"

"Yes, Paul, he will. I've looked at Pepynbridge Cricket Club's website. It's the First Eleven's final match of the season and they're playing at home."

"So, when he comes out...?"

"That's how I read it. Unless I'm very much mistaken, 'woodshed' is a reference to the disused bomb store in Middlehay Wood where they met in July. At three o'clock next Sunday the four of them will meet there to plan how, when and where to abduct Ash; and that's probably where they'll take him when they have done. But we'll discover that for sure on Sunday. All four are under surveillance."

"Do we warn Ash?"

"I've thought about that. If we do, he may refuse to play in the match on Sunday and we couldn't force him to. In that case, not only will nothing happen on Sunday, but Raed and the other three will suspect that we've cracked these emails. They'll then get someone else who may not be on our radar to abduct Ash at a later date and we'll be unable to protect him. In my opinion his life is in danger now. So, No! We don't warn Ash."

"But we could arrest those who will be waiting to abduct him."

"We could, but unless they are armed, and we don't know they will be, the evidential value of arresting them before they actually abduct Ash may not be enough. Apart from this exchange of emails, all we'll have will be any Fly Vests found in their possession and Ash's evidence. We've already agreed that because Ash is, or was an accomplice, less weight will attach to his evidence than otherwise. As for these emails, our interpretation of them is conjectural and of little, if any, evidential value. On the other hand, if we catch the four of them abducting Ash red-handed, we'll have everything we need. And those four are the lead terrorists."

"And the others, Cedric?"

"Well, they're peripheral, Paul, aren't they?"

"They are, I suppose."

"If the four leaders have got wind of the fact that we're onto them, then whether we pull them in or not, they'll never go ahead on Christmas Eve. There's no point in waiting until then. Arrest them now. The lesser fry will go to ground. We know where to find them and can round them up later."

"So, if your interpretation of these emails is correct and we don't warn Ash what's happening, next Sunday will be our best chance of bringing the leaders to justice?"

"Yes! And not just the leaders. We can already prove the association between the leaders and the rest of them. Arresting the cell leaders in the act of abducting Ash will strengthen the case against the others."

"How so?"

"It will prove that the conspiracy in which they are all implicated is more than just talk."

"True." A moment's silence followed. Then, "Putting Ash in the way of danger like that will require the highest possible authorisation. You understand that, Cedric, don't you?"

"Of course I do!"

"I'll see if I can secure that. If I can, we'd better meet in Medborough with Andrew Hay later this week. I don't think the others covering York and Lincoln need be there. Leave it with me."

Following meetings at New Scotland Yard and the Home Office in Marsham Street, during which Paul Evans satisfied those whose permission he needed that he would have sufficient manpower to keep Aashif Malik safe, and a telephone call from Marsham Street to Downing Street, authority was given for an operation that would allow the four jihadists to seize Ash before they were arrested.

Two days later, Paul Evans, Andrew Hay, Cedric Fane and a deputy chief constable from Medborough Police met in Hay's office in Medborough Police Station. Evans had spoken on a secure line to Hay the previous day. After reviewing what they knew or conjectured, Hay said,

"To cover every eventuality, for example if they decide not to take Ash to Middlehay Wood but somewhere else, we'll need a lot of manpower."

"Can you provide it, or will you need help?" asked Evans.

The deputy chief constable said,

"We're stretched. We shall need more."

"How many more?"

"Thirty?"

In London, Evans had already canvassed the availability of reinforcements.

"Okay. We can do that. We'll need to have a briefing here on Sunday. I suggest at noon. Our people will travel up in three unmarked mini-busses and I'll come by car. Do you need any more vehicles?"

"No thanks! With yours, we'll have enough."

There followed a discussion at the end of which, Paul Evans said,

"Okay. That's fine. Andrew, you've been making a note. Please could you prepare an operational briefing paper and email it to me and to Cedric in London? You will? Thanks! Alright, we meet again here next Sunday at twelve noon."

◆◆◆◆◆◆◆◆◆◆◆◆◆◆◆◆◆◆◆◆

Sunday, 13th September 2015, 6am

"Herbie?"

No reply.

"Herbie!" Sharper. More urgent.

Julie and Herbert were in the double bed they had shared in the Rectory since their marriage in February. Herbert stirred from the remnants of slumber.

"Yes?"

"I think it's started."

Instantly Herbert was fully awake.

"You sure?"

"I think so. I can't think what else it could be. And today is the beginning of week forty. Tomorrow is full-term. It could happen any time."

Herbert's mind flew back to the evening of 22nd December the previous year when, after a hugely successful concert in the Abbey, he and Julie had gone back to School House and made love for the first time. Julie broke into his thoughts.

"They're not very strong yet."

"When did they start?"

"About five o'clock. I didn't want to wake you then because it's Sunday. Your busy day."

"Cup of tea?"

"I'm not sure. Make me one, Herbie, and I'll see how I feel."

Herbert put on his dressing gown, went downstairs to the kitchen and switched on the kettle. As it warmed, he planned. At nine o'clock, he was due to celebrate Book of Common Prayer Holy Communion for the Puritan Remnant. Then, at eleven o'clock, there would be a sung High Mass in the Abbey. He glanced at the clock on the kitchen wall. It read five past six. He could take Julie to Medborough General Hospital, half an hour distant, and be back in Pepynbridge in time to lead the nine o'clock service. Pity he had no clergy cover, but he hadn't. He poured boiling water onto tea-bags in two china mugs and took them upstairs. Neither took milk or sugar in tea.

"How soon after it's started did the midwife say you should go to hospital?"

"She didn't."

Herbert took his mug back downstairs, went on-line, discovered the telephone number of the maternity unit and rang it. When it was answered he identified himself, gave Julie's details and asked when she should come in.

"Her first is it, Reverend?"

"Yes!"

"Well, to be on the safe side, I'd bring her in now."

Herbert looked at the clock on the kitchen wall.

"Would half past seven be alright?"

"Fine, Reverend. See you both then." The line went dead.

Just over an hour later, Herbert drove into the Visitors' Car Park at Medborough General Hospital. Ten minutes later, Julie had been admitted to the maternity unit and Herbert was at the nurses' station.

"I'm afraid I can't stay, nurse."

"Work to do, vicar?" she answered brightly, smiling.

"Yes. It's Sunday."

"Busy day?"

"Until twelve noon. I should be able to be back here by one."

"You'll be very welcome. See you then. We'll look after her, no worry! 'Bye!"

"'Bye, nurse!"

♦♦♦♦♦♦♦♦♦♦♦♦♦♦♦♦♦♦♦♦♦♦

Sunday, 13th September 2015, 9.45am

There had been ten people at the nine o'clock service, including Richard Maxey, with whom, at the end of the service, Herbert shared his news.

"It would happen on a Sunday," Herbert observed, despondently. "I told the nurse at the hospital, I'd be back by one. Do you think that'll be too late?"

"Couldn't say, Herbie. These things are unpredictable, especially first time round. If you like, I'll keep in touch with the unit on your behalf. Who's she under?"

"Thank you, Richard. I'd be so grateful if you would. She's under a Mr Brace, but she hasn't seen him. She's just seen midwives."

"That's the way, these days, Herbie. But Nigel Brace will keep a watching brief. I know him well. Good chap. He'll look after her, if she needs looking after."

"What do you mean, 'if she needs looking after'?"

"A consultant is only called in if there's a problem. Perfectly competent midwives do the business otherwise." Richard Maxey's breeziness produced a knot of irritation in Herbert. But then, he told himself, that's doctors! They've seen it all. Still, it is a worry.

"I'd rather it wasn't broadcast at Mass, Richard, in case something goes wrong."

"Of course not, Herbie! I won't say a word."

Sunday, 13th September 2015, 11.00am

Without extra chairs, the Abbey nave accommodated five hundred worshippers. At 11 o'clock that Sunday morning, it was nearly full. Since Herbert had arrived in May 2014, to the irritation of neighbouring parishes, the brilliance of its music, the practised elegance of its liturgy and Herbert's compelling preaching had garnered for the Abbey a rich harvest from surrounding villages as well as from Pepynbridge; and from as far away as Corbury. Burgeoning congregations in English cathedrals had convinced Herbert that what St Aidan's Abbey offered was the path that the Church of England needed to tread if it was to maintain and increase Sunday attendance; and

Herbert was also of the opinion that the best way to evangelise, to spread the Gospel, was through liturgy; but liturgy had to be done, not just competently, but inspirationally. That it was in St Aidan's, the size of this morning's gathering testified.

The Mass being performed by the choir was Haydn's *Paukenmesse* in C Major, with Sophie and Leela singing the solo soprano parts together. As always, the glory of the music filled the sacred space of the Abbey and the hearts and minds of everyone present. Between the five sung parts, *Kyrie, Gloria, Credo, Sanctus* and *Agnus Dei*, Herbert and his acolytes, meticulously drilled by him, lent a beauty, a dignity and a solemnity to the liturgy that, as the Church Fathers had intended nearly two millennia before, evoked in its participants a tantalising glimpse of the numinous.

Since 3rd August, when he had confessed to Herbert his involvement with *IstishhadUK*, Ash had thought deeply about what Herbie had said in their conversations about Islam and Christianity. Not only had Ash not regretted for one moment his abandonment of Islamism; but disillusion with Islam itself had taken root and grown until it too no longer commanded his loyalty, either of heart or of mind. But, to have a faith meant everything to Ash so, he had reflected, if not Islam, then what? Over the six weeks that had followed his disclosure to Herbert, the answer had come to him gradually, in gentle stages. And so it was that, on that September Sunday, when the members of the choir approached the rail to receive communion, Ash joined them and knelt with his head bowed and his hands folded across his chest. When Herbert came to him, he laid his right hand on Ash's head.

"The Lord bless you and keep you; the Lord make his face shine upon you, and be gracious to you…" Herbert removed his hand and placed the tip of his right thumb on Ash's forehead, traced upon it the sign of the cross, and continued, "… the Lord lift up his countenance upon you, and give you peace."

Upon which, Ash was suffused with inner tranquillity and knew what he must do.

From her solitary presence in the choir stalls, Leela watched Ash kneel at the communion rail with disappointment but not surprise. Since 3rd August, without knowing its cause, Leela had discerned a change in her brother. The ambiguity that had so troubled her had been replaced by a relaxed contentment and uncharacteristic self assurance. Significantly, there had been no more mention of Islam. So that's where he wants to go, she thought this morning. Well, good luck to him! But I'm not going there. No way!

When the Mass had ended and Ash had disrobed in the choir vestry in the south transept, he stepped into the nave and saw Herbert in conversation with Richard Maxey. As he approached them, he overheard Maxey saying,

"…probably mid-afternoon."

Ash hovered near them. Herbert turned towards him.

"Hello, Ash! I can guess what you want to talk about. Ash, it wouldn't be convenient just now. Let me explain. Julie is in Medborough Hospital having our baby and I must go and be with her. You understand, don't you?"

"Yes, of course, Herbie! But I should like to come and see you."

"I know you would, Ash. I shall be more than happy to chat to you. I suspect I shall be tied up tomorrow. Why don't you give me a ring on Tuesday afternoon when you get home from school?"

"Of course, Herbie! And I hope all goes well with Mrs Onion."

"Thank you, Ash."

An hour later, Herbert parked his car at Medborough General Hospital and joined Julie in her room in the maternity unit.

"She's doing very well," said a nurse brightly as he entered.

Herbert looked at Julie's face and was shocked at the ageing that the stress and pain of labour had wrought upon her gentle features. Temporarily, he hoped.

◆◆◆◆◆◆◆◆◆◆◆◆◆◆◆◆◆◆◆◆◆◆

Sunday, 13th September 2015, 1pm

At noon, as Mass in St Aidan's Abbey ended, forty police officers and Cedric Fane had assembled in a large conference room at Medborough Police Station. By one o'clock, the briefing session was coming to an end. Chief Inspector Paul Evans was standing behind a rostrum. Sitting on chairs at either side of him were Cedric Fane and Andrew Hay.

"Any questions?" asked Evans. There were none. "Everybody knows what they're doing?" A low "Yes" rumbled around the room. "Okay, we'll break for lunch. It's laid on in the canteen downstairs. Be back here in half an hour, please."

At half past one, they were back in the conference room. Black clothing, bullet proof vests, hand, foot and body restraints, Tasers, Heckler and Koch carbines and G60 stun grenades were laid out on trestle tables.

"Okay," said Evans, "we leave at two. Those wearing black and using special equipment please collect it now."

Some approached the trestle tables, took items and signed receipts for them. When they had finished, Paul Evans said,

"Okay. Assemble downstairs in the vehicle compound and we'll get going."

Unmarked police cars and mini-busses left Medborough Police Station for Pepynbridge. Surveillance officers radioed in that Zed had not yet left Medborough; and that the other three cell leaders were over an hour away from Middlehay Wood.

A mini-bus entered the wood and stopped near the shed where the jihadists had met eight weeks earlier. A technician and ten armed police officers, wearing black overalls, bullet proof vests and baseball caps, got out. The technician concealed a listening device in the roof of the shed. Then, carrying a radio receiver, he and the armed officers retreated some fifty metres into the wood. The mini-bus was driven out of the wood and parked in Middlehay village, half a mile distant. Evans and Fane were confident that the jihadists would approach Middlehay Wood from Pepynbridge and there was no reason for them to drive on into Middlehay. But if they did, the mini-bus bore no markings. Other police officers were placed at strategic points around the perimeter of the wood. Cedric Fane and Paul Evans, together with a Gujerati-speaking police constable, were in an unmarked van fitted with an aerial, parked a hundred metres away on a track parallel to the one that ran past the shed. Everyone was in place by half past two.

Shortly before three o'clock, surveillance officers in unmarked cars discreetly stalked three private cars and a Volkswagen Kudos black cab along the Pepynbridge to Corbury road until they turned right towards Middlehay. Situation reports flew through the ether.

♦♦♦♦♦♦♦♦♦♦♦♦♦♦♦♦♦♦♦♦♦

Sunday, 13th September 2015, 3pm

By three o'clock, the cricket match at Hall Park had been underway for an hour. With the strain of the past months removed and infused with the joy of knowing that he was to become a Christian, for Ash did not doubt that Herbie would allow him to convert, Ash was playing the innings of his life. He was punishing the not immoderate opposition bowling with fours that glided to every part of the boundary and occasional sixes over cover and the bowler's head. At tea, he was not out on 130 and Pepynbridge declared at 243 for 4 wickets. As he walked off the field, the spectators rose to their feet and applauded him up the pavilion steps; applause that, with his customary diffidence, Ash acknowledged with a gentle raising of his bat and a slight smile.

Inside the tea room, Oliver Standard greeted Ash with,

"Well done, Ash. A fine innings. Sadly, the last you'll play for us I suspect."

"Why, Ollie?"

"Well, next season you'll be playing for Northants."

"Not, I think, until I've left school in July."

"You're eighteen this October, aren't you?"

"Yes! On the twenty-fifth."

"I doubt you'll be playing for us next season. We'll have to see."

After tea, Ash opened the bowling for Pepynbridge and, with his third ball, he trapped the opposition's opening batman LBW for a duck.

While Ash had been punishing the bowling in Hall Park, the four jihadists had parked their vehicles in Middlehay Wood in the space under the trees fifty metres beyond where the path led to the shed through the brambles. None had spotted that they had been followed from their respective homes, despite knowing that they were of interest to the security services. They had not been kept under direct surveillance from the turning off the Pepynbridge to Corbury road. If they had driven on into Middlehay village, surveillance would have been resumed there. As they had not been followed from the main road along the lane and into the wood, when surveillance of them might have been more obtrusive, they were confident that the police were unaware of their presence and, therefore, that the rest of their activities that day would be unobserved. Encouraged by that belief, their examination of the shed was cursory and they failed to discover the listening device. Raed had brought a folding canvas chair, which he set up with its back to the open side of the shed. They had brought prayer mats with them and performed *salāt* after which, speaking in English rather than Gujerati, they formulated the plan to abduct Ash.

All four would travel to Pepynbridge in the black cab, driven by Raed, which he would park shortly before seven o'clock in Abbey Way, opposite the gates to the Hall drive. When Ash walked through the gates, the three in the back of the cab would get out, seize Ash and his girl-friend if she were with him, and force them into the cab. Once inside, Ash's wrists would be taped together and, if he started to shout, his mouth would be taped as well. Raed would drive the cab back to Middlehay Wood and they would return to the shed where the interrogation would begin. Raed had brought four handguns with him, one of which he handed to each of the others in case the police intervened.

"And if Ash doesn't talk? Or denies betraying us?" asked Zed.

"I have a packet of cigarettes and a box of matches with me," replied Raed. "Very productive when applied to sensitive parts of the body."

"And if he admits *ridda*? Or we're convinced that he's the one who's betrayed us?"

"We'll bind and gag him here. Then we'll take him in my cab to an isolated bridge I know of over the River Trent in Staffordshire, take him out of the cab, strip him, lean him over the parapet, cut his throat..." Raed pulled a large knife from his belt "...and throw his body in the river. No blood on the bridge or in the cab, but I'll have the cab valeted inside and out anyway by a *mujahid*, a friend of mine in London, who'll not say anything to anyone."

"What if it gets dark?"

Raed held up a Campingas Lumostar Plus portable lamp.

"Thought of that," he remarked.

In the unmarked van Cedric Fane and Paul Evans were listening to this conversation.

"We could arrest them now," said Fane. "There's enough evidence there to put them away for life."

"We could, but that's not the plan. Maybe it should have been, but it isn't. Change it now and we risk a balls-up."

"Plan A it is, then."

◆◆◆◆◆◆◆◆◆◆◆◆◆◆◆◆◆◆◆◆◆

Sunday, 13th September 2015, 6.30pm

At half past six, the Volkswagen black cab turned out of Middlehay Wood and headed towards Pepynbridge. At six forty-five, Raed halted in Abbey Way near the Blue Boar and waited. At five to seven, he drove along Abbey Way, turned the cab around using the entrance to Abbey Gardens and parked opposite the gates to Pepynbridge Hall. The sun was dropping below the tops of the trees that lined the Hall drive. It would not set for another twenty minutes. The sky was clear, so twilight would be long.

By half-past six, Pepynbridge had bowled out their opponents. The bar in the pavilion was crowded with spectators and players. Ash was at the centre of praise for his playing, not just on that day, but throughout the season. The hour hand of the clock above the bar was pointing to 7 when Ash decided to leave for home. He looked for Sophie but she was in the lavatory. He said his farewells and walked down the Hall drive. As he passed through the gates and turned left towards Abbey Gardens, he heard running feet. When he stopped and turned to look, his arms were seized in vice-like grips and another hand caught hold of his collar.

"You're coming with us, Ash!"

Ash recognised Zed's voice.

"Why? What have I done?"

"That's what we're going to find out."

Ash filled his lungs to shout, but before he could, a hand was placed across his mouth and he was forced into the back of the cab. The doors were slammed shut. Someone shouted, "Go!" and the cab started to move swiftly along Abbey Way. At the T junction by the Blue Boar, it turned right and sped uphill out of Pepynbridge. Inside, Ash's hands were forced together and his wrists bound with tape.

Ash recognised the others from the meeting in July. His mind was working fast. *So, somehow they've discovered that someone has betrayed them; and they suspect it's me. And they're right. But they may not know for certain. So, when we get to wherever we're going, they're going to start asking me questions and I shall have to decide what to answer. The thing to do,* he thought, *is to deny that I'm the one who betrayed them. In the face of straight denials, they'll have to reveal how much they know. And since I don't know how much they know, I don't know what I'll do when I do know.* But, he reflected sombrely, with a tightening of his stomach muscles and a contraction of his anal sphincter, *if they decide that I'm the one who's betrayed them, they'll kill me.*

Then he thought, *what about the police? They're meant to be protecting me. Where are they? What are they doing? Are they nearby? They should be! Do they know what's going off?* He remembered the personal alarm in his trouser pocket; but his hands were bound and he could not reach it.

Next he thought of Sophie. *Thank God we didn't leave together, as we'd planned. She would have been kidnapped* too. That would have been more than I could bear; especially if they started to torture her. Inwardly, he shuddered at the thought. As it is they'll probably torture me.

There was no talk in the cab. Zed was thinking, 'Ash is very calm. I wonder if I've got this right? Did I jump to the wrong conclusion? After all, it might just have been an innocent slip of the tongue when Ash had said that he was 'planning' to go agricultural college. Well, if I did get it wrong, this'll do no harm. Ash'll be impressed at the way we're protecting our security. If he's innocent, there'll be no repercussions. And if he's not, he'll disappear and there'll be none either. Raed's clever. He's sorted it either way.'

The cab had reached the turning to Middlehay, which Raed took. Two miles down the lane he turned into the wood. Then the cab turned right and eventually came to a halt in the clearing by the other three cars. Two of them in the back got out of the cab.

"Out!" ordered Zed.

Ash left the vehicle and, as he did so, his upper arms were seized and he was marched into the shed.

◆◆◆◆◆◆◆◆◆◆◆◆◆◆◆◆◆◆◆◆◆

Sunday, 13th September, 7.15pm

In the maternity unit, Herbert was sitting in a room reserved for expectant fathers, reading a copy of New Directions, published monthly for members of Forward in Faith to provide Anglo-Catholics with comfort, support and spiritual sustenance. The door opened and a uniformed nurse put her head round it.

"It's a girl! Mum and baby are both doing well, Reverend. They're back on ward and you can go in and see them now."

"Same room as before?"

"Same room as before."

Herbert went into the single room and was relieved that the strain had left Julie's face and she looked her age again, if somewhat tired. She was smiling broadly and pointed to a plastic crib at the foot of the bed. Herbert looked down in wonderment at a tiny face above a shawl wrapped around a tiny body. Blue eyes stared unseeingly up, operating, to Herbert's alarm, independently of each other. He turned back to Julie and kissed her gently on the lips.

"Is she alright?"

"Alright, Herbie?"

"Yes, alright! Ten fingers and ten toes and all that?"

"Yes, darling! They've done tests. She's fine. Perfectly normal."

"And what about you?"

"I'm perfectly normal too, Herbie!"

They laughed softly together.

"You know I didn't mean that, Julie."

"No! Of course not! Well, I'm a bit sore down below but so would you be if you'd gone through what I've just gone through, but everything's okay now."

"When can you come home?" Herbert paused and added, "Both of you, I mean." Julie smiled.

"Tomorrow, if all is well."

Later, when Herbert arrived back at the Rectory, he emailed the members of the choir to cancel choir practice on

Monday evening; and he rang Julie's parents. They would travel up the next day, aiming to arrive by teatime.

◆◆◆◆◆◆◆◆◆◆◆◆◆◆◆◆◆◆◆◆◆

Sunday, 13th September, 7.30pm

In the shed, Ash's wrists had been unbound and he had been ordered to sit on the canvas chair, facing away from the open side of the shed. The four cell leaders were standing around him, their arms folded. Outside, the light was fading. Inside, it was dusk and Raed had lit the gas lamp. It shed sufficient light to see each other's faces.

"Now," said Raed, moving directly in front of Ash. "We know that someone's betrayed us. And we think it's you."

Ash remained silent.

"I'm not going to tell you how we know that someone's betrayed us, but believe me, we know for sure that we have been. Now we're going to ask you some questions and if your answers convince us that you're not the one, we'll take you back to Pepynbridge. But if we come to the conclusion that it's you who's betrayed *Allah* and the Prophet, peace be upon him..." he left his words hanging in the air, before adding, "...you know the punishment the *hadith* prescribes for *ridda*, don't you, Ash?"

Ash said nothing.

Raed's voice rose menacingly. "Don't you, Ash?"

Still Ash remained silent.

Raed's features suddenly contorted. He uncrossed his arms, clenched his fists and bent down.

"Don't you, Ash?" he screamed, pushing his face so close to Ash's that he felt Raed's spittle strike his forehead. "You fucking well answer me, you bastard!"

There was the faint thud of a stun grenade landing on the earthen floor of the building, followed immediately by a blinding 300,000 candle power flash of light and a deafening 160 decibel explosion.

Bloody hell! thought Ash. A bomb! He felt his hands and feet. Still there! Not a bomb then, but...By the time these thoughts had passed through his consciousness, the shed was full of shouting. Figures in black were holding Raed, Zed, Waahid and Yaaseen, disarming them and snapping handcuffs around their wrists. Other figures, similarly clad, were brandishing what to Ash looked like sub-machine guns.

"Ash!" someone shouted, "Outside!"

As Ash left the shed, muffled by the tinnitus now ringing in his ears, he heard Zed shout,

"Fucking *murtadd*! May *Allah* punish you, you bastard!"

In the dusk a figure approached Ash, which he made out to be Andrew Hay.

"I thought you lot were never coming," said Ash, reproachfully.

"Yes, I'm sorry you had to go through that, but we needed hard evidence against them. Are you alright?"

"Apart from ringing in my ears, I am."

"Don't worry. The ringing will go away. Ash, I want you to come with me to Medborough Police Station. We need to have you medically examined."

"What about Mum and Dad?"

"We're in radio contact with other officers. As soon as we're on our way, I'll ask one of them to visit your parents and re-assure them that you're alright."

"And Sophie?"

"Oh, I hadn't thought of her. Have you got her number?"

"More than that, I've got my mobile phone. They forgot to take it from me."

"Not such smart operators after all, then," said Andrew Hay and they both chuckled, as much from relief as with amusement.

"Can I call her?"

"Of course you can. In the car, Ash."

"Okay."

A car pulled up and Ash and Hay got in the back. After Hay had radioed a colleague to report that Ash was safe and that, as arranged, a PC Phillips should call on Dr and Mrs Malik to re-assure them that their son was unharmed, Ash tapped Sophie's number into his mobile.

"Where the hell have you been? I just went to the loo and when I came out, someone said you'd walked off down the drive."

"Yes, I'm sorry, Sophie! I didn't know where you were. I thought you'd already left."

"And then someone else who'd been walking behind you down the Hall drive said you'd buggered off in a taxi with some of your Pakistani friends. Ash, I thought that was over."

"Sophie, hold on a moment!" Sophie was quiet. Then, "Sophie, it is over. I'm on my way to Medborough Police Station in a police car. Could you ask your mum to collect me from there at..." he turned to Hay enquiringly, who said,

"We can take you home?"

Ash shook his head. He wanted to see Sophie before he went back to Abbey Gardens. Hay looked at his watch.

"Nine o'clock, then?"

"Sophie, are you still there?"

"Yes?"

"At nine o'clock?"

"Ash! Are you alright?"

"Yup! I'm fine, but I nearly wasn't."

"Bloody hell, Ash..."

"I'll tell you all about it when I see you. No secrets. Nine o'clock then? And you come as well. Yes?"

"I'll ask Mum and text you." A few moments later, Ash's mobile pinged. He looked at the screen.

...collect u from med cops at 9...

"Everything alright?" enquired Andrew Hay.

"Yes, thank you, Andrew! Everything's fine! Absolutely fine!"

On the way to Medborough, Andrew Hay explained that he would want to see Ash the next day to de-brief him and take a statement from him covering today's events.

"Will I have to give evidence in court?"

"If they don't plead guilty then, Yes, I'm afraid you will!"

"They won't plead guilty. They'll want to milk their trial for all the publicity they can."

"If it's held in public. Parts of it may well not be."

"Who decides that?"

"We ask. The judge decides."

"Where will it be?"

"Probably at Woolwich Crown Court. It's next to HMP Belmarsh, which is where terrorists are usually held on remand."

"And, if you don't mind me asking, Andrew, what about me?"

"What about you, Ash?"

"Don't you think that I'll be in danger? Not from them, but from others?"

"Possibly. One of the things we'll have to do is to make an assessment of the risks, if any, you face and what action on our part would be appropriate to minimise them."

'Sounds good,' thought Ash, 'but how effective is it likely to be? Ah well, only time will tell.'

"About tomorrow."

"Yes, Ash?"

"I'm supposed to be at school."

"I know, but the Academy head, Mr Metcalf, won't mind if you're not. It was he who put us onto your friend Zed in the first place."

"Not much of a friend, Andrew! Not much of a friend!"

◆◆◆◆◆◆◆◆◆◆◆◆◆◆◆◆◆◆◆◆◆

Sunday, 13th September 2015, 8.15pm

Sophie and Marigold were sitting opposite each other at the kitchen table in Summerhay.

"Well, what's Ash done then that we've got to collect him from Medborough Police Station?"

"Mum, I don't know. I'm not sure how much I can tell you just now."

"What do you mean, Sophie? We've agreed there should be no secrets between us."

"Yes, I know that! But the police have told me to keep it a secret."

"Whatever have you been up to, girl?" Marigold sounded cross.

"Not me, Mum! Not me, I promise you, but Ash. I'll tell you just as soon as I'm allowed to; and because Ash is with the police, that may be quite soon."

Marigold observed her daughter for a moment across the table. Then she said,

"Well, I've got a secret to share with you."

"What's that, Mum?"

"I'm going back to Pepynbridge Farm."

Sophie looked at her mother in mock surprise. She had expected this.

"You're what?"

"I'm going back to live with your dad at Pepynbridge Farm." Sophie decided that if she said nothing her mother would elaborate. "You remember when you told me about you and Ash; and about Ash wanting to farm; and about your father having changed; and that the Shirley woman had left him?"

"Yes?"

"Well, I decided to go round and find out if he really had changed."

"And did you?"

"I did, and he has. He's really quite different. And he asked me to go back to him. I said I'd think about it. Meanwhile, I've been doing his books. I didn't tell you because I wanted to see how it would work out. After a bit,

I came to the conclusion that Alfred is a reformed man. He's like the person I met and married. Believe it or not, Sophie, if you will, but he only goes to the Blue Boar on Friday evenings and Sunday mornings; and, he tells me, he limits himself to one glass of whisky in the evenings before he goes to bed."

"Wow, Mum! What a difference! Why do you think it's happened?"

"It may have a lot to do with you, Sophie."

"With me, Mum? I don't understand."

"He believes that you and Ash are going to get married; and that Ash will come and work on the farm."

"Mum, that's right as you know. That is what's going to happen."

"Well, I hope so, Sophie. I truly hope so. Anyway, I told him I would go back on condition that he'd stop bullying you and me and that he'd keep his drinking down. And he promised he would do both. So I told him, I'd give it a go, but that I wouldn't give up the tenancy of this cottage and that if he reverted to his old ways, back I'd come."

Sophie rose from her seat, stepped around the table, hugged the seated Marigold around her shoulders, kissed her on the forehead and said,

"Oh, Mum. I'm so pleased."

They both burst into tears. Then Sophie said,

"Come on Mum. Let's clean up. It's time we left for Medborough."

◆◆◆◆◆◆◆◆◆◆◆◆◆◆◆◆◆◆◆◆◆

Sunday, 13th September 2015, 8.45pm

The front door bell rang at 4 Abbey Gardens. Inside Abi, Sabi and Leela were becoming increasingly worried about the failure of Ash to arrive back home from cricket. They had watched the match, but when they couldn't find Ash at Hall Park, they had gone home, expecting to find him there. When they hadn't, Abi had rung Richard Maxey who had told him that Julie Onion had been safely delivered of a daughter. But no, he had no idea where Ash was. Abi had rung the pavilion, but everyone had left and there was no reply.

When Abi opened the front door, his heart sank at the sight of a uniformed policeman. He knew what that usually meant.

"Yes, officer? Would you like to come in?"

"Thank you Doctor Malik. I'm Police Constable Phillips of the Medborough Police."

He stepped inside. Sabi and Leela, who had heard his introduction, came into the hall, wearing stricken expressions. Phillips noticed them and said,

"It's alright. Your son's okay. He's had a bit of a fright, that's all. That's what I've come to tell you."

"Well, you'd better come and sit down," said Sabi. "Cup of tea?"

"That would be very kind, Madam. Thank you."

PC Phillips explained that Ash had been abducted from the Hall gates and taken to Middlehay Wood, where police officers had been waiting for them. When the abductors had arrived, Ash had been rescued unharmed.

"So, how did they know that's where Ash would be taken?"

"Intelligence," remarked Phillips, adopting an air of mystery to discourage further enquiry; which it did.

"And where is he now?"

"At Medborough Police Station."

"And how's he getting back here, constable?"

Phillips drew a notebook from a top pocket in his blouson, flipped over some pages and said,

"A Mrs Wicken will be collecting him shortly."

'I wonder why Marigold Wicken is fetching Ash rather than one of us?' thought Abi but he did not voice it. Ash is safe and that's all that matters. Phillips finished his tea and left.

Leela said, "I'm going for a walk."

"But, Leela, it's dark!"

"Yes, Dad, I know! But I just need to think about what's happened. I won't be long."

She put on a jacket and left by the front door.

"Abi, don't worry. Leela's alright. She's a good girl."

"Yes! I know Sabi. And she's a good Muslim as well. Better than me."

"And me."

◆◆◆◆◆◆◆◆◆◆◆◆◆◆◆◆◆◆◆◆◆

Sunday, 13th September 2015, 9.00pm

The medical examination of Ash had been oral and perfunctory. Yes, he was fine. A bit shaken, that was all. And his ears were still ringing. He agreed to return to Medborough Police Station the next morning at nine o'clock, when he would normally attend the Academy. He would drive himself in, if his mother did not need her car. Otherwise, he would catch the bus.

"No! No! Ash! We'll collect you," said Andrew Hay.

The telephone rang and Hay answered. Then he said,

"Mrs Wicken and Sophie are waiting for you in the reception area downstairs."

"How much am I allowed to tell them?"

"Well, you've told us that Sophie knows most of it anyway. One moment!"

He left the room. A few minutes later he returned.

"Ash, Chief Inspector Evans says that you may discuss what has happened with members of your immediate family and with Sophie and Mrs Wicken; and of course with Mr Driver, Dr Maxey and Reverend Onion. But please do not discuss it with anyone else; especially not the Press. We shall be issuing a press release this evening and if the Press gets wind that you were the hostage, they'll want to interview you. Please don't let them! Careless talk at this stage can prejudice legal proceedings later, okay?"

"Yes, Andrew! I understand."

Ash left the room and made for the stairs. When Sophie saw Ash come into the lobby, she ran to meet him and they hugged and kissed. Holding hands, they went with Marigold to her car.

As Marigold was driving Ash and Sophie out of Medborough Police Station Visitors' Car Park, Guy Richards, Paul Evans, Andrew Hay and Cedric Fane were exchanging emails. They agreed that it would be impracticable to suppress news of the rescue of a hostage from Middlehay Wood; or to conceal the identities of the four men in custody, who would be produced in

Medborough Magistrates' Court the next day. Putting all that into the public domain would alert the other sixteen jihadists, who might go underground, making it more difficult to arrest them, but that was a risk that would have to be run. Ports and airports would be alerted that night. A Press Release was drafted and agreed, which Andrew Hay then emailed to the Press Association and the BBC.

On the way to Pepynbridge, Ash told Marigold and Sophie what had happened; and that he would not be going to the Academy the next day, "...but helping the police with their enquiries."

Marigold dropped Ash in Abbey Gardens. Leela had returned from her walk and Ash told Abi, Sabi and Leela everything that happened to him since he had met Zed and had started attending the meetings in the prayer room the previous January.

"I hope you're not going to be cross with me?"

"Why should we be?"

"Well, Mum, you're Muslims and I've betrayed Islam."

"No you haven't!" said Sabi sternly. "You've rightly rejected Islamism, which is a curse on all decent Muslims, whether observant or not, the world over."

"I agree," said Abi.

Ash turned to his sister.

"And what about you, Leela?"

"Ash, you knew that I suspected something from word go, didn't you?"

"Yes, I did!"

"Well, I think that what's happened to you is dreadful and a stain on Islam. But I'm not abandoning it, Ash. It means a lot to me and I don't believe that Islam's all about violent *jihad*. It can and should be a peaceful religion and I'm not giving it up. But you are, aren't you, Ash?"

"I'm what, Leela?"

"Giving up being a Muslim."

"How do you know?"

"Because this morning, you went up to the rail to be blessed by Herbie, didn't you?"

This morning! thought Ash. Heavens! It was as if what had happened in the Abbey that morning had been on another day and another planet. Was it only this morning that he had been singing in the Abbey, had gone to the communion rail for a blessing, and had decided to become a Christian? But he hesitated.

"I don't know at the moment," he said. "I wanted to talk to Herbie about it this morning but..."

"Mrs Onion has been safely delivered of a daughter," interrupted Abi. "Dr Maxey rang and told me."

"Great!" said Ash. He went on, "Leela, I don't know if Herbie will allow me to convert, but if he does, then I may do. Would that upset you?"

"Oh, I expect I'll get over it, Ash."

Leela smiled at him. She would not go down the same path, but, she acknowledged privately, I'm very fond indeed of this brilliant and brave brother of mine. And very proud of him as well. And this challenge to my faith, unsettling though it's proving to be, is one I'm confident I can meet and overcome.

"Speaking for myself," broke in Abi, "I wouldn't mind at all, so long as you don't try and convert me, Ash. I may be non-observant but I'm too long in the tooth; too culturally set to change."

"Me, too!" said Sabi.

'Very Islamic!' thought Ash. He smiled at them and they smiled back.

"Have you eaten, Ash?"

"No, Mum! Been busy."

"It's ready and waiting for you."

◆◆◆◆◆◆◆◆◆◆◆◆◆◆◆◆◆◆◆◆◆

Monday, 14th September 2015

At 6 o'clock the following morning, as it was set to do, the Greenwich time signal on Radio 4 pierced the torpor of Richard and Mary Maxey in their cottage; of Herbert Onion in the Rectory; and of Jack Driver and Francis Metcalf in their respective homes in Medborough.

"It's six o'clock on Monday, the fifteenth of September. Good morning. This is Today with..." The presenter introduced himself and his co-presenter, who announced,

"The headlines this morning. Yesterday evening, anti-terrorist officers foiled a serious terrorist plot near Medborough." She continued with the other headlines, briefly previewed up-coming items and concluded: "The BBC News is read by..." with the name of the newsreader, who started,

"Yesterday evening, officers from Medborough Police and the Metropolitan Police Service, assisted by other security service personnel, foiled a terrorist plot to explode suicide bombs in four cathedrals and sixteen other churches later this year. Four men were arrested after a struggle in woods near Medborough. No one was hurt. A hostage the suspects were holding was released unharmed. All four suspects are due to appear at Medborough Magistrates' Court this morning. They have been named as..." and the full names of the four jihadists followed.

Richard Maxey said,

"Mary, did you hear that?"

"I did."

"Herbie was right to be worried."

"Who do you think it was that was rescued? Ash?"

"Bound to be. Thank goodness he's safe!"

Jack Driver thought, Good for young Ash! I'll persuade my partners not to charge the Maliks for my time.

Francis Metcalf thought, I never trusted Zaeem Zhara. Thank goodness he's left the Academy! I wonder who the hostage was? None of the other pupils who attended those Friday meetings were named as having been arrested. With luck, I may be able to keep the name of the Academy out of the Press.

In the Rectory, Herbert guessed that Ash was the freed hostage and privately thanked God for keeping him safe. He got up, showered, dressed, said his Morning Office and made coffee and toast. At eight o'clock, the telephone rang.

"Yes?"

"Reverend Onion?"

"Yes?"

"Medborough Hospital Maternity Unit here, Reverend. Mrs Onion and your daughter are ready to go home today. Will you collect them?"

"Of course I shall. What time?"

"Any time after ten o'clock."

"I'll be there at ten."

A few minutes after 10 o'clock as Herbert, carrying their daughter with Julie alongside him, made his way from the maternity unit to the hospital car park, half a mile away.

Amidst the tightest security that any of the sitting magistrates could remember, Raed, Zed, Waahid and Yaseen were in the dock at Medborough Magistrates' Court, each charged with kidnapping, contrary to Common Law, terrorism contrary to Section 5 of the Terrorism Act 2006; and firearms offences in respect of the handguns found in their possession the previous evening contrary to Section 5 of the Firearms Act 1968, as amended by Section 1 of the Firearms (Amendment) Act 1997. The public gallery was packed and the Press Box overflowing. The accused were committed for trial at Woolwich Crown Court, to appear there on 30th September 2015. They were remanded in custody. Later on Monday, they were transferred under high security to Belmarsh Prison.

That same Monday, a police car collected Ash from Abbey Gardens and took him to Medborough Police Station, where he spent several hours being interviewed and making a witness statement about the events of the previous day. At the trial of the terrorists, he would be the principal witness for the Crown.

The security services concluded correctly that, outside their number, the jihadists had maintained secrecy over the existence and plans of *IstishhadUK* within the United Kingdom. Accordingly, the decision was taken that, provided the fifteen still at large were traced, arrested and remanded in custody, it would not be necessary to remove Ash into the Witness Protection Scheme, in which, at considerable public expense, he would be given a new identity and isolated utterly from his existing community ties, including Sophie and the members of his family. A full risk assessment would be carried out after he had given evidence at the trial. In the meantime he was assigned a personal protection officer by Medborough Police. As well as the personal alarm that Ash already had, another alarm linked directly to Medborough Police Station was installed in 4 Abbey Gardens. For the time being, a marked and manned police car would be parked outside 4 Abbey Gardens at night; and an armed police officer would accompany Ash wherever he went and be close by him within the Academy whenever Ash was there. This level of protection would be kept under review and, dependent upon current intelligence, it was hoped it could be reduced in due course.

When Julie and Herbert arrived home with their daughter, they decided that, for the rest of Monday, they would allow no calls except from Julie's parents to disturb their precious first hours together as a family. Like their mobiles, their landline telephone was equipped with caller ID display.

◆◆◆◆◆◆◆◆◆◆◆◆◆◆◆◆◆◆◆◆

Tuesday, 15th September 2015
On Monday, Francis Metcalf had been informed that Ash had been the hostage who had been rescued. On Tuesday morning, Leela and Sophie travelled to Medborough on the bus, followed by Ash in a marked police car. When Ash, Sophie and Leela walked through the Academy Gates on Tuesday, the caretaker told them that

the head teacher wanted to see them in his study. Metcalf told them that, until it was in the public domain, he did not want any information about what had happened to Ash to be discussed within the Academy; an instruction with which all three were happy to comply.

On Monday Richard Maxey had been trying unsuccessfully to reach Herbert on the telephone. Eventually, just after nine on Tuesday morning, Richard heard the ring tone stop.

"Herbie?"

"Yes?"

"Richard here."

"Hello Richard. It's a girl!"

"Oh..." momentarily, Richard was knocked mentally off balance. Then he recovered. "Herbie, I know. Nigel Brace rang and told me on Sunday evening. Needless to say, I'm simply delighted. How's Julie?"

"Julie's fine. And so is Alice."

"Alice Burton?" Richard sounded puzzled.

"No, Richard," replied Herbert patiently. "Alice Aida Onion. Alice after Alice Burton. And Aida, the feminine of Aidan."

"And what about Ash?"

"Hadn't considered it. It's a boy's name, anyway."

"No! Ash Malik, Herbie! You've heard the news?"

"Yes! That's wonderful news too. Sunday was a good day for Pepynbridge."

"It certainly was, Herbie! It certainly was!"

Late on Tuesday morning, another Press Release was issued by Scotland Yard with more details of the operation the previous Sunday, including, after a heated debate within SO15 and MI5, Ash's identity as the freed hostage. Whilst potentially it placed him at greater risk of harm, too many people knew that he had been the person rescued. It was a piece of news that would have to be carefully managed.

It did not take journalists long to confound Francis Metcalf's expectations and a crowd awaited Ash at five o'clock on Tuesday afternoon when, accompanied by Sophie, Leela and an armed and uniformed police officer, he walked out through the gates of the Academy.

"Holy Cow!" exclaimed Ash.

"Don't worry, lad. Just walk straight through them."

"Ash! How are you feeling?"

"Ash! Were you scared?"

"Ash! How was it for you?"

On and on went the questions and flashes from cameras. Later, when photographs appeared in newspapers and on television, Sophie, Leela and their parents were relieved that, unlike Ash, their faces had been pixelated.

Ash and the policeman got into a police car parked by the gates. When Sophie and Leela tried to follow,

"Sorry, girls! Only Ash. Official business."

As the car drove away, to Sophie and Leela's relief the journalists displayed no interest in them. But, with mounting irritation, Francis Metcalf had observed the scene from his study window. He would make arrangements to smuggle Ash in and out of the Academy by another entrance in future.

◆◆◆◆◆◆◆◆◆◆◆◆◆◆◆◆◆◆◆◆◆

Sunday, 20th September 2015

On the following Sunday, when High Mass in Pepynbridge Abbey was over, so many people crowded around Ash that Herbert went up into the pulpit and called for silence.

"I know" he began, his voice amplified by the sound system, "that all of you will share my relief that Ash has been with us this morning." Applause. Herbert raised his hands to still it. "The full story will emerge at the trial of the terrorists, which will probably take place some time next year, but what I can tell you is that, firstly, St Aidan's was one of the places of worship on the terrorists' list of targets."

This was greeted by a collective sharp intake of breath and some soft cries of dismay.

"And secondly," Herbert went on, "the foiling of this horrific plot is largely down to the courage of Ash in going to the police a few weeks ago and telling them about it." The applause that followed this unexpected revelation persisted for several minutes and Herbert let it run. Then, as it subsided, he added, "And let it not be forgotten that Ash is a Muslim." Not for much longer, thought Ash. Herbert continued, "Ash is a shining example of how Muslims should react to the terrible things that Islamists do. If there were more Muslims like Ash, there would be no Islamists."

That's so true! thought Leela. More Muslims, but not like Ash, because I believe he'll convert; but rather like me. But I'll not say so. Not now, anyway. And, whatever I said to Ash last Sunday when he came back from the police station, I don't know how I'm going to cope with him being a

Christian. But then, she thought, perhaps Mum and Dad are right; that being a good Muslim in Pepynbridge means I should integrate, so I'll stay in the choir.

Leela wondered whether the move to Pepynbridge had been good for the Maliks. Ruefully she concluded it had been. If they hadn't moved to Pepynbridge and if Ash hadn't fallen in love with Sophie and Sophie with him, would Ash have gone to the police and betrayed *IstishhadUK*? Because if he hadn't, he would have died on Christmas Eve in St Aidan's Abbey, or some other church, and brought shame on Dad and Mum and me. Sophie had said that love solves all problems. Well, maybe not all problems, but it seems to have solved this one. It's all very confusing. But of one thing I am sure,' Leela told herself firmly. I'm going to look after my friendship with Sophie. After all, she's going to be my sister-in-law; a member of our family; another Mrs Malik. That's integration for you!

As the Abbey emptied, Ash approached Herbert and said,

"Herbie, I'm sorry I didn't phone you last Tuesday…"
Herbert shook his head and waved away the apology, but Ash persisted, "…but I would like to come and see you."

"Made up your mind, have you?"

"Yes, I have!"

"Playing cricket this afternoon?"

"No! Season finished last weekend."

"Not all that finished last weekend, then?" They both smiled. "Well, you'd better come and see me at…let's say five o'clock?"

"Sure!"

At five o'clock, when the bell rang Herbert answered the Rectory door and he and Ash went into his study, where, as Herbert had anticipated, Ash asked him if he would baptise him.

"Have you discussed this with your parents?"

"Yes, Herbie, I have!"

"And their reaction?"

"Was that as long as I had a faith and as long as it was peaceful, they had no objection."

"Very liberal of them. But, knowing them, I'm not surprised. And Leela?"

"It will come as quite a shock to her. She looks up to me but, as you know Herbie, she's a more committed Muslim than Mum and Dad."

They talked on and Herbert agreed to instruct Ash over the next four Sunday afternoons. "Then, if we're both happy that you're ready, I shall baptise you, together with my daughter, Alice, and anyone else who wishes to be baptised, in the Abbey during Mass on Sunday, the twenty-fifth of October."

"My eighteenth birthday, Herbie."

"Well, what a lucky co-incidence!" Herbert paused before adding, "Bishop Julian is confirming candidates in Medborough Cathedral on Sunday 22nd November, the Feast of Christ the King. If you and I think it's right, I'll present you to him for confirmation."

And so it was left.

◆◆◆◆◆◆◆◆◆◆◆◆◆◆◆◆◆◆◆◆◆◆

Monday, 21st September 2015

At nine o'clock on the following Monday morning, Marigold walked into the kitchen at Pepynbridge Farm. Alfred was eating breakfast.

"'Morning, Marigold!"

"'Morning, Alfred!"

"What's all this I see on television about young Ash, then? Has our Sophie made a mistake?"

"Far from it, Alfred! Ash is a very brave young man. He's served this country proud." Marigold went on to give Alfred an outline of what, eight days earlier, she had been told had happened; and what had led up to it. "If you ask me, Alfred," she concluded, "I think Sophie's a lucky girl."

"Sounds like it," responded Alfred cautiously.

"Alfred, when you've finished your breakfast, would you mind helping me in with my suitcases?"

Alfred looked at Marigold and smiled broadly.

"It would be a pleasure, Marigold! And what about Sophie?"

"She's at school right now, but I've got her things in the car as well. She'll be coming back here this evening."

"More convenient then for Ash! Her living here rather than at Summerhay, I mean."

"Indeed, Alfred!

◆◆◆◆◆◆◆◆◆◆◆◆◆◆◆◆◆◆◆◆◆

EPILOGUE

By 25th September the other fifteen *IstishhadUK* members had been arrested, some of them at the point of leaving the country, produced before magistrates' courts and remanded in custody. The CPS discovered from Francis Metcalf that Ash would be sitting his final A Level paper, Economics, on 6th June 2016. On 30th September, all nineteen appeared at Woolwich Crown Court, where their trial was provisionally fixed for 6th June 2016, with a time estimate of eight weeks. Ash would not be required to give evidence until the second day of the trial at the earliest.

Herbert baptised Ash and Alice Aida Onion in St Aidan's Abbey during High Mass on Sunday, 25th October. Abi and Sabi were present. Leela was in the choir.

Alfred Wicken continued to visit the Blue Boar only on Friday evenings and Sunday mornings and was home in time for dinner and lunch; and he limited himself to one, albeit generous, glass of whisky each evening before bed.

On Thursday, 5th November, a removal van drove through the gates leading to Pepynbridge Hall, followed a few minutes later by a Range Rover, with a large African man at the wheel and a small, dapper figure beside him. Both vehicles came to a halt outside a double-fronted cottage, beyond and to the left of the Hall, where Alistair Pemberton-Smith was waiting to greet them. The arrival of Ralph Waters QC, MP, and Pascal Legrand in Pepynbridge was unobtrusive and unannounced. A short while later, while Legrand was supervising the unloading and placing of furniture in Coronation Cottage, Waters drove alone in the Range Rover to the Conservative Constituency Office in Corbury to conduct a surgery.

At the feast of Christ the King on Sunday the 22nd November, Bishop Julian Ross confirmed Ash in Medborough Cathedral, accompanied at Ash's request by Mozart's Mass in C Major, the *Coronation*. The solo parts in the sublime *Agnus Dei* were sung by Sophie and Leela together, which moved Abi and Sabi, sitting at the front of the nave, to tears.

The recording that had been made in July proved to be as successful as the one the year before. After the ticketed concert in the Abbey on 19th December, only sixty-five thousand of the million pounds needed to repair the roof remained to be raised, all of which was then donated by Alistair and Augusta Pemberton-Smith and Alice Burton.

At half past eleven on Christmas Eve, in a packed St Aidan's Abbey, Herbert began to celebrate Midnight Mass. The world had long since learnt of the targets of the Christmas Eve plot, which lent poignancy to the masses being celebrated that night in all twenty of them. In St Aidan's Abbey, the poignancy was made the more acute by the knowledge that the recently converted and confirmed Aashif Malik had been one of the jihadists; and that it had been he who had foiled the plot and averted the most terrible catastrophe.

Ralph Waters and Pascal Legrand were sitting unobtrusively at the back of the nave, but when they joined the queue to take communion, a gentle ripple of whispered surprise spread through the nave.

The BBC had decided to broadcast the service from St Aiden's Abbey on Radio 3. In consultation with its

Controller, Herbert had chosen *Missa Santi Nicolai* by Haydn to accompany the liturgy, which the choir performed to perfection. The Mass ended with *"O Come all ye Faithful..."* including the final verse, *'"Yeah Lord we greet thee, born this happy morning..."*

And as Herbert, resplendent in a white cope, heavily embroidered with gold thread, faced the congregation in front of the high altar and intoned the closing Christmas Blessing, from across the chancel Sophie caught Ash's eye, smiled and mouthed,

"Happy Christmas!"

And Ash, with a wider smile, did likewise.